W9-BUY-595

THE
SACRED
LIES
OF
MINNOW
BLY

STEPHANIE OAKES

Dial Books
An imprint of Penguin Group (USA) LLC

DIAL BOOKS
Published by the Penguin Group
Penguin Group (USA) LLC
375 Hudson Street
New York, New York 10014

USA/Canada/UK/Ireland/Australia/New Zealand/India/South Africa/China
penguin.com
A Penguin Random House Company

Library of Congress Cataloging-in-Publication Data
Oakes, Stephanie (Young adult author)
The sacred lies of Minnow Bly / by Stephanie Oakes.
pages   cm
Summary: "A handless teen escapes from a cult, only to find herself in juvenile detention
and suspected of knowing who murdered her cult leader"— Provided by publisher.
ISBN 978-0-8037-4070-9 (hardcover)
[1. Cults—Fiction. 2. Juvenile detention homes—Fiction.
3. African Americans—Fiction. 4. Amputees—Fiction.
5. People with disabilities—Fiction. 6. Murder—Fiction.] I. Title.
PZ7.1.O19Sac 2015   [Fic]—dc23   2014033187

Printed in the United States of America
3 5 7 9 10 8 6 4

Designed by Nancy R. Leo-Kelly
Text set in Janson MT

To Mom,
who taught me to be powerful.

And to the handless girls
who are teaching themselves.

· · ·

Chapter 1

I am a blood-soaked girl.

Before me, a body. Pulped. My boots drenched with his blood. I search out his eyes, but they're gone, hidden away behind pale lids.

My breath comes hard and white in the freezing air. Inside each breath is the understanding that this is how it feels, controlling someone, bending their body to your will.

I wonder if this is how the Prophet felt the moment he ordered my hands ripped from me.

Above, a car races across the bridge with a metal shudder. Fingernail-sized flakes of snow fall through the yellow haze of streetlights, and a few cold stars blink in a dark sky. I want to hold my hand flat to catch the snowflakes like I used to when I was little. But, I remind myself, my hands are gone, and I'm not five anymore. The girl I used to be could almost be dead.

I hunker beside a snowbank, watching the red on the ground slowly ice over. I feel suddenly cold. Colder than even the outside air. Colder than I've ever been in my life.

Chapter 2

When the police arrive they are blurry white shapes, like ghosts, stuffed inside tight blue uniforms. My eyes can't follow their features. One moment, I grasp an eye, a nose, but it slips away just as quickly and all I sense are their voices, scribbling over the light of the new morning. The ruined mess of the boy's body is shoved inside an ambulance, and it screams down the street.

The cops try handcuffing me around my stumps, but the metal slides off. I bite my lip against the cold steel grating over my newborn pink skin.

"Do we even need to cuff her?" one cop mutters.

"Look at what she did," the other insists. "You saw the kid, looked like he'd been run over."

"But, just look at her."

Look at me. My arms are crossed over my stomach and, at the end of the arms, an absence of hands, of fingers, of fists, of nails. Of any way to fight back. I feel the cops' eyes inch over the homespun trousers and the disgusting rag of a shirt Jude gave me, the fabric blazoned with blood.

In the end, they squeeze the cuffs around my elbows, the pressure nearly popping my shoulders from the sockets, but I don't scream. I don't say anything. I feel like I have said enough for my entire life.

Chapter 3

My first view of the city is from a police car. I stare out the thumbprinted window as the sun peels back over buildings locked in by snowfall.

"You better hope he lives," one of the cops says, and suddenly the boy is all I can see again—the broken face, teeth chucked in the snow. My veins are still tight from adrenaline.

• • •

At the police station, it's wood walls and stained ceiling tiles. The smell of charred coffee.

They are discussing the best way to fingerprint me.

"It must be done," they say. "How will we identify her without fingers?" Just like that, they've said something I've felt for months but never said aloud. One of them leafs through a police manual, searching for the proper procedure, while the other pushes each stump into a pad of ink and presses them onto paper. Two warped black ovals in a field of white.

"Looks like we only need a DNA sample," the first one says, glancing up from the manual. He rummages in a drawer and pulls out a small square of cotton, unwraps it, and holds it before me. "Spit."

"You want my spit?"

"Just do it."

I gather up all the moisture I can in my mouth and let it fall to the cotton square. He closes it in a small plastic box with a sliding lid and places it on his desk.

The mug shot they take burns half circles into my vision, worse than any firelight. I clamp my arm to my eyes, and they have to lead me with their hands to a sterile examination room. When I crack my eyes open, I see they've faced me toward a tight-sheeted bed with stir-rups, pushed against a tile wall. Beside the bed, a tray with tongs and a flat white depressor. A dark blond woman takes me by the shoulder and walks me toward the bed. I balk.

"It's okay," she says. "It's procedure in abuse cases."

She's got her head turned to the side, and I see myself as she must see me, skinny, filthy, and handless, wearing clothes that smell of blood.

"I—I don't need that," I say, avoiding looking at the bed. "Nothing like that happened."

"Are you sure?" she asks, and the feeling of her eyes

skating over my body makes me itch. I want to get angry, but I just give her a sharp nod.

She needs to take pictures to document my injuries, so she leads me to a plastic bin of clothes the color of dish-water and lets me choose underwear. I lever up a beige pair of underpants and, though I can tell they've been laundered, somehow they hold the shape of other girls still, the ones who came through here before me.

Behind a blue paper curtain, she tugs away my trousers and shirt till there's nothing left but skin, naked feet on tile, my body a sliver of white. I've never seen it like this before, so bare, blotches of blood still stuck to my skin. She doesn't know it, but the blood isn't mine.

They haven't told me yet if the boy from the bridge is dead.

The woman eases the underpants up my legs, fits a bra over my chest. I roll my shoulders beneath the tight elastic as she lifts my trousers from the floor. With a soft clatter, an object falls from the pocket. We stare at it, a skeletal hand held together at the joints with golden wire.

"What's that?" she asks.

I hold up a stump to show her.

Her mouth drops so low, the bags under her eyes go taut. After a tick, she fixes her features back to normal, just the same way I remember people in the Community doing after witnessing some everyday atrocity. We didn't linger on those things. The cows needed milking, and the daylight was wasting, and somewhere there was always a baby wailing for one of its mothers.

The policewoman reaches in my other trouser pocket, lifts out the second hand, and places both on a silver tray.

"Will I get them back?"

Her head tilts to the side again. "That won't be possible."

"Why not?"

"They're human remains. There are laws about things like that." She clears her throat. "They'll be held as evidence, and when they're no longer needed, they'll be incinerated."

"Burned?" I choke. Not burned. Anything but burned. "You can't do that. They're *my* hands," I shout, trying to shove past her. "Give them back!"

She rolls her fingers into a fist and blocks me with an arm across my chest. "If you force me, I will subdue you."

The skin around her mouth is bunched with lines deep and thin as needles. When I don't move, she picks up the tray and leaves the room. She returns a minute later, the tray empty.

And it's then that I realize the Prophet's not the only one capable of taking a girl's hands away.

Chapter 4

When I'm marched to the police car, the two cops from earlier are already inside, eyes tight and sleepy. They're eating from bags in the front seat, some food I don't recognize, bright colored and crunchy between their molars. They hold the food in their meaty hands like fragile things they're afraid to break.

When they're done, they shrivel up the bags with a *scritch* sound and throw them to the floor. We drive through the snow-clotted streets to a huge white building that they tell me is a hospital.

In an exam room, the doctor waves for me to show my stumps, but I hold them behind my back, and one of the cops has to wrestle my arms into the artificial light.

The doctor's face turns grim. My stumps are smudged black with fingerprinting ink.

They open up my stumps when I'm sleeping, with small knives and needles, and pack them with bright white cotton until they can steal a patch of skin from my leg. Days later, they cut them again, putting me to sleep with chemicals in suspended plastic bags. It's a while before I figure out they're not making me new hands. They can't do that, the doctor says like I'm slow, and I turn away to glare at the wall, eyes burning.

Growing up, I believed in miracles. I guess I don't anymore.

• • •

In the morning, a woman dressed in a mauve suit drops her briefcase on the linoleum in my hospital room and introduces herself as my public defender. She sits heavily on the side of my bed, glancing down at my stumps wrapped in layers of bandages. Beneath the blankets, I shift my feet over a few inches.

"My name's Juanita," she says. "And you must be the famous Minnow Bly, yes?"

I watch her out of the sides of my eyes.

"I'm here to provide you with defense counsel during your trial. I'll also be making sure you get everything you need until you're transitioned to the next stage."

"What's the next stage?" I ask. "Jail?" I've heard of jail. The Prophet told us it's full of people so bad, even the Gentiles don't want them. They're angel murderers and God deniers, and some of them can kill with a single touch.

Juanita smiles in a way that isn't cheerful. "We don't need to worry about things like that right now."

She takes me for a walk around the hospital hallways. I can barely get traction in the lambswool slippers they gave me after they stole my boots, and my chest burns when we go more than ten steps. I wonder what's in my lungs that's making this so hard. Blood? Smoke? Or something heavier?

Juanita asks if I want her to hold my elbow, but I shake my head. I slide my shoulder down the wall, holding the balls of bandages gingerly before me.

We pause beside a big plastic-paned window, my breath heavy and my arms shaking. Outside in the distance, ash hovers in the air like a dirty cloud. It looks like a heaven nobody'd ever want to go to.

"That's all that's left of the Community now," Juanita says. "They put the fire out, but the air is so stagnant in winter, the smoke is still locked overhead. It burned everything for miles. They say it'll take a month for the smoke to completely clear."

"Did—did you hear if anybody died?" I ask.

She turns toward me. "They found two bodies so far, but everything's snowed in. They're still looking."

"Let's go," I say. I shuffle away from the window, though my lungs still burn.

. . .

The nurses give me morphine and the days start to bleed together. I glimpse the shadow of a policeman standing guard outside my room. He's almost comforting, the bulk of him, and when pictures of the Prophet enter my head, and the hatchet, and the fists of those men, all I have to do is stare at the blue shoulder of the policeman to calm down.

I know he's meant to keep me in, but I figure he'd also keep anybody else out.

Every other day, a physical therapist visits to teach me about living without hands.

"It will be difficult at first," she says, and I nod as if the thought hadn't occurred to me. "You may need to rely on others until you can get routines down yourself."

She places a pair of sweatpants on the floor and teaches me how to slowly inch the waist up my legs with my stumps. My stumps are round with Ace bandages and every movement shoots an ache through the bone, but eventually I pull the waistband over my angled hips.

She tells me once my stumps are healed, the muscle will thin and they will taper to points, smaller than wrists. They will work like large fingers. I will hardly miss my hands at all.

Chapter 5

Juanita comes to my room just as I'm finishing breakfast, a mush of porridge and some slivered strawberries. She tells me it's been three weeks since my arrest, and it's time to start getting serious. I ask her what she means when she upturns a sack stuffed with formal clothes onto the bed. They are machine-made, dyed colors that shouldn't exist. I shake my head no.

"You have to let someone wash that. You've been wearing the same thing since you arrived," she says, pointing to my shirt. It's Jude's. He gave it to me when I stayed at his cabin, right after I lost my hands. It smells, I know, but I won't let them take it away. It's the only thing I have left of him.

I wrap my arms around my middle and poke a toe at the pile of clothes. "What for?"

"Court."

There are a couple of well-worn suits, the seams all limp from multiple uses, and several lank dresses, some ivory, some gray, all dead-looking. She pulls out each dress and presses the hanger into my collarbone, watching the way it falls over my front.

"I don't want to wear a dress," I say.

"That's what everyone says."

All the dresses are too big. Juanita settles on a blouse opaque enough for me to wear Jude's shirt beneath, along with a knee-length skirt. She cinches it with a belt above my belly button.

• • •

On the day of my trial, the outside air is bright and dry, and I get a nosebleed as we pull out of the parking lot. The blood tumbles over my chin before I can call out. Juanita clamps a napkin over my face. I don't know why, but I'm crying. Warm, slow tears that get absorbed by the napkin and hardly make any noise. That's how I always cried in the Community, never loud enough for anybody to notice.

The prosecutor uses phrases like "brutal beating" and "left for dead" and "no remorse." He gestures wildly at the evidence tacked on a corkboard, X-rays illuminating the hairline fracture running along the boy's mandible, the splash of navy where his spleen ripped open like a broken tangerine.

I glance over my shoulder to where Philip Lancaster sits with his father in a suit too big at the shoulders. His eyes are clear today, lacking the frenzied, shifting look they had that night near the bridge, though I can hear the squeak of his rubber shoes as he jiggles his knees and drums against his legs with flattened palms.

"Members of the jury," Juanita says when it's her turn to speak, "the facts of this case are undeniable. A mentally disturbed young man made threats to a girl who had, within the previous twelve hours, survived the destruction of her home. This is a girl who endured years of traumatizing fear. My client's actions were entirely in self-defense, and the testimony and evidence you hear during this trial will prove her innocence."

When I look behind me at the watchers gathered on the polished wooden benches, I see Philip resting his fingers inside the opening of his jacket, over the place where I kicked enough times to burst organs. His front teeth bow outward where his mouth was wired shut.

He stares down at me when he passes to take the stand, and I gaze straight into his green eyes. In the fluorescent light of the courtroom, they look unremarkable. Celery-colored and plain. There is nothing there but a boy. A human boy.

Tears pool in my eyes, and after a moment, I start crying loudly, doubled over, my nose almost touching the thickly waxed table. Juanita glances around the courtroom. "That won't help you, Minnow," she whispers.

"This judge doesn't have any sympathy for crying."

I shake my head because everything has become very clear now. How wrong I was, wrong about myself, wrong about everything because there, in front of me, stands the hard evidence of my wrongness, limping in glossy shoes and bruised bones and regular eyes that shouldn't have made me lose my mind.

Chapter 6

After weeks of court dates and interviews and the incessant droning silences that intersperse moments of terror, the judge says it's time for the jury to deliberate. Juanita marches me to a small room to await the ruling.

I sit on a leather-upholstered chair. Juanita gives one of her cheerless smiles. I know she doesn't want to tell me everything will be okay because that would be a lie.

After ten minutes, she takes a phone call, and I'm alone.

My eyes scan the room, and everything becomes suddenly important. A ceiling fan thick with dust. A small, glass-topped vending machine where color-wrapped foods are lined up, trapped. A little pot of brown-edged violets. I can smell the varnish they used on the floor, the powdery cleaner in a can beside the sink, but I can't smell the violets.

My head jerks when the door opens and a man strolls in. He's a policeman; I can tell, I've been around enough of them now, though he looks different from the others:

glasses, herringbone suit, and in his eyes a kind of soft-
ness, like he's winking with both eyes open.

He nods at me and shuffles in his leather shoes to the
vending machine. He surveys the contents for several
long moments as though this is the most important decision he's made in years. Slowly, he inserts three coins,
turns a knob, and pulls out a yellow-wrapped rectangle.
As he tears the wrapper open, I glimpse multicolored
candies lined up in a row, toothlike. He unwraps one,
chews it, and leans against the machine like he's totally
alone in the room.

I should look away, but I don't. Every stranger is still a
thrill, having gone so many years never knowing anyone
but the same hundred wind-burned souls. I read every
part of this man, the mechanical motion of his jaw, the
gold wedding ring, the fan of lines across his forehead, like
I imagine people read books. At least he's a distraction
from the idea of the jury in some room nearby discussing
how evil I am.

He turns toward me. "Want a Starburst?" He holds a
pink-wrapped square between his thumb and forefinger.

I do want it, but I shrug, holding up my stumps. "Can't
unwrap it, can I?"

And then he does something strange. He smiles. The
kind of smile that pushes every feature upward by an inch.

"Don't be so sure," he says, placing the candy on the coffee table in front of me. "You might be more capable than you think."

He puts the remaining candies in his pocket and walks toward the door. "See you later," he says, like a promise.

I glare at the square of pink on the brown table. I know there's no way I can unwrap it. I'd need fingernails, a thumb.

I swallow the saliva that's filled my mouth and lean forward. I pick up the candy in my teeth. I run my bottom teeth over the wrapper until it lifts away, and my tongue nudges the other edges. The wrapper falls to the tabletop, and I press the candy to the roof of my mouth. Instantly, my jaw aches and my eyes prickle. I haven't tasted anything so vibrant since I was five. It is wonderful.

There's still a sliver of candy on my tongue when Juanita leads me back to the courtroom. I see the man with the candy sitting in the back, chewing. The judge reads the verdict. Guilty. Six years with the possibility of parole on my eighteenth birthday. The judge informs me that, unless I maintain a spotless record in juvenile detention and receive a character recommendation from a staff member, my chances of earning parole are slim.

I take another ride in a cop car. This time to the Missoula County Juvenile Detention Center.

Chapter 7

How do you handcuff a handless girl?

The answer is remarkable. There is a man. His name is Early. He's the first person to introduce himself after I arrive at the white cinder-block building that houses every underage female criminal for five hundred miles. He enters the blank-walled processing room with a measuring tape and a mouth full of crooked smiling teeth.

Early's job, he tells me, is to make all the custom restraints for the Missoula County Correctional Department. You wouldn't think a man could possibly make a full-time job out of this; after all, how many handless people could possibly be imprisoned at one time? Early says he makes ends meet in all manner of ways—making fox traps for hunters, altering the stretchers where they do lethal injections for obese prisoners. He tells me that he even tinkered together a silver necklace for the warden's daughter's sweet sixteen.

He's a strange-looking man, like I imagine an old

gnome might look, a hooked nose and black brooms of hair coming out of his ears and a circular hole in his left front tooth. Early chatters at me the entire time, and I don't ask how the hole got there, but I wonder.

He unsheathes the orange measuring tape and hooks it around my elbow. I flinch.

"It's okay," he says in the quiet way you talk to skittish animals. "No one's gonna hurt you. No need to be afraid."

I want to tell him that I have more reasons to be afraid than he could even count. I keep my teeth pressed together in silence.

• • •

Juvie is just a shaky, tin-walled place, a repurposed alternative high school the county purchased for juvenile delinquents. All the windows in the big gymnasium were bricked up years ago and scaffolded into three stories of light metal cells.

I can hear the girls—voices, movement, metal clanging on metal—the minute I enter the cell house. It smells of bodies in here, just like the Community.

A guard named Benny leads me to a white-tiled room. She snips the zip-tied restraints around my elbows and I shake out my arms. Benny is big and her skin is a lovely shade of brown, almost exactly like Jude's, and I trust her, even when she tells me this strange room is for undressing.

"We'll make two piles," she says. "A keep pile and a trash pile. Things like jewelry and keepsakes usually go in the keep pile."

In the corner, there is a black camera that watches Benny yank the belt efficiently through the loops of my skirt, unbutton the pearls of my blouse until I'm standing in only Jude's shirt. It's fraying badly, hardly even a shirt anymore.

"Trash?" she asks.

I shake my head. "Keep."

She raises an eyebrow but puts it in the pile with the rest of my clothes.

With a flap she shakes out a stiff orange jumpsuit. She helps me into it, slips the buttons into the holes, and straightens the shoulders. She finds me a pair of Velcro shoes and watches while I fumblingly fit my feet inside.

Benny picks at the knot on the ribbon that ties the tail of my braid, and my hair slowly unwinds. "You ought to get a haircut," she says. "Could be a liability here."

"We hardly ever cut our hair in the Community," I say.

"Doesn't look like you're in the Community anymore."

We walk out of the room, down a hallway that ends in a heavy door, thick with coats of white paint.

"This is the last free ground you'll walk on for quite a while," Benny says. "Are you ready for it in there?"

I shrug.

"Ours is the only mixed-offender facility in the state," she says. "All the girls are under eighteen, but some were tried as juveniles and some as adults, like you. When you turn eighteen, you'll be paroled or transferred to an adult facility. Do you understand what that means?"

I shake my head.

"There're girls here who've killed, who would kill again. Just . . ." she glances at my stumps. "Watch yourself. I don't want to be scraping you offa any floors, you hear?"

• • •

Benny leads me down a grated pathway on the third floor. Hazy ovals of faces press against the bars of cells as I walk past, the occasional hoot or shout from an inmate following me down the skyway.

"You'll be in what we call Angeltown," Benny says.

"What's that?"

Benny stops and walkie-talkies to another guard. The cell door before us buzzes loudly and swings open.

Benny looks down at me. "If I were you, I'd try to get on her good side."

With a flat hand, she pushes me into the cell. The door swings shut behind me and the whole complex of interwoven metal shakes. I look over my shoulder. Benny's gone.

On the top bunk reclines a girl in the same violent

orange as me. She ignores me, reading a book perched on her lap, something with a view of the stars on the cover.

"What's your name?" I ask.

She looks at me with sharp, pale blue eyes. "Angel."

Angeltown, I think. I know about angels. Sometimes they speak to Kevinians, whisper in our ears and make terrible things happen. They are hairless and androgynous and the height of small buildings.

I wrap my arms around my middle, lean against the concrete wall, and slide to the ground across from her. She picks at the edges of her book with fingernails stained yellow.

"So, let me guess," she says, casting her eyes over the bunk. "Petty theft?"

I glance at her face. "What?"

"Stealing. Food probably, by the look of you. You got all your teeth, so I doubt it's drugs."

I shake my head. "Aggravated assault."

She lets out a small chuckle. "Right," she says.

"You don't think I could?" I ask.

"You don't look it. My leg weighs more than you."

"Anyone can hurt someone."

"What about your hands or whatever?" she says, her eyes avoiding the empty spaces below my wrists. Where the bandages and sutures were removed, my stumps look purple and thin.

"What about 'em?" I asked.

"Alls I'm saying is, you don't look like a murderer. Sheesh, take it as a compliment."

My father once told me that all you needed to hurt someone is a single word, said just wrong enough. Anybody is capable of enormous harm, anyone with a mouth or a hand to write with.

"So who was the guy?" Angel asks. "The one you beat up."

"How do you know it was a guy?"

"You got that look, like you been messed around by men."

I swallow hard. I want to tell her it was me who messed up Philip Lancaster, but that would require saying his name. "I don't want to talk about him."

She shrugs and turns toward her book again.

"What'd you do?" I ask.

"Same as you, I expect. Tried to kill a guy. Except, unlike you, I succeeded."

"Really?"

Though her face is relaxed, it forms a natural scowl, a cord of muscle tight over her eyebrows, and though her cheeks and nose are dotted with freckles, she doesn't look dainty or young or delicate. On her scalp, bands of pale skin are visible between tight cornrows of dirty blond hair.

"They wouldn't stick a murderer in with another prisoner," I reason.

"Who said it was murder?"

"Well, what was it then?"

"Self-defense," she says. "Only, they might not've believed me one hundred percent. My uncle was a real upstanding citizen, and I don't exactly look all innocence and peaches and cream. In any case, these jails are so overcrowded, they'd put a murderer in with a shoplifter just to save money."

"How do you know that?"

"Everyone knows. It's common knowledge on the outs. Half my class has ended up here, one time or another. Shoot, coming here's practically a school reunion." She squints at me. "What school do you go to?"

"I don't."

"Homeschooled?"

"No. Just . . . not schooled. I was raised out in the national forest. Past Alberton. South of Cinderella Rock." In the hospital, one of the nurses found me a map and I figured out where we'd been living.

Angel looks at me sidelong. "Nobody lives out there. That's, like, real wilderness. Grizzlies and shit."

"Grizzlies didn't bother us. They stay away from noise."

"But the only people who live out that far are, like, religious freaks who hate the government and sell their daughters to creepy old men."

My eyes flick to the metal floor.

"That was you? That cult?" Angel says, sitting up. "Dang, I saw that on the news. Heard you lived in holes and ran around naked."

"You heard that?"

"Something like that. Did you really not have running water?"

"Or electricity."

"Why?"

"It was my parents' decision, not mine. I was five when we moved to the Community."

"Why'd they do it?"

"The Prophet," I say vaguely, and find I can't finish the sentence. It takes effort to push through the tangled memories of the past twelve years living in the forest, to when the Prophet arrived, holding prayer rallies in our run-down trailer, his big black-robed presence shoving meaning into every corner of our lives. He made us believe we were saints. That we were being lied to never crossed our minds.

"Hey, I get it," Angel says, softening. "Your dad probably spouted some bullshit about God, probably sold out his family to follow this guy. Seen it a million times."

"You have?" I ask.

"Sure. My whole family's religious. I've been around this stuff my entire life."

A pleasant, electronic tone pulses from the intercom. Angel jumps down. From the front of the block, I can hear the buzz of doors unlocking and feet traversing the skyway.

"What's going on?" I ask.

"Dinner."

Our door is the last to buzz open, and for the first time, I see the whole population of criminals this place holds. Before us, spaced by five-foot gaps, are girls in orange jumpsuits walking two-by-two.

The jail has opened up its metal body and shoved out these girls, these prisoners, this pilgrimage.

Chapter 8

In the morning, after the lights snap on and I lurch up from my bunk, after I stumble behind Angel to the cafeteria for a breakfast of mushy oatmeal in a blue plastic cup that I have to tilt into my mouth, after the other girls noisily gather their books and binders for school, I walk back to my cell alone. A guard stands down the hall monitoring my progress, but I risk a moment to tilt my head toward a small, wired window in the cinder-block wall. The glass is reflective and I only see my own face: my sunken eyes, my hair tumbling down my shoulders like a frayed brown shawl.

I arrive back to find a man sitting in my cell. I can tell by the silence on every side of me that there isn't another soul on this level but me and the man sitting on a low stool beside my bed, like he belongs there. One hand holds a pen racing across a yellow pad of paper in his lap.

With a buzz, my door opens.

The man stands up. Immediately, the taste of artificial

fruit fills my mouth, and into my head comes the memory of the trial day when I met him.

"Morning," he says, gesturing toward the bunk. "Take a seat."

I walk slowly forward and sit cross-legged on my mattress. He sits back down, sandwiched between the toilet and my bunk, with his knees pushed high from the lowness of the stool. I stare at the ink-covered notebook he holds on his knees. I can't read a thing.

"I know you," I say.

"Starburst," he says.

I nod.

"That was a hell of a day," he says. I grimace at the word, remembering all the Prophet taught us about Hell, the hollowed-out middle of the planet where bad people are tortured in darkness forever, hearing but not seeing the droves of others shrieking in every direction.

"A hell of one," I agree.

"My name's Doctor Wilson." He holds out a plastic-coated ID card. His picture makes him look stuffy, necktie cinched high, his mouth an unsmiling line. In the corner, even with my level of illiteracy, I can distinguish three letters: FBI.

I'm about to question why the FBI cares about what I did to Philip Lancaster when I recall that there's another crime, a bigger one. Even with the Prophet lying in a frozen drawer in some state morgue or whatever it is that happened to him after the fire, he isn't gone. Maybe he'll never be. Maybe he'll hover behind my ear forever, speaking his bile and clinking his chains until he's succeeded in killing me like he wanted.

I look from the card to the man's face. His brow is folded in an accordion of wrinkles. I can't tell how old he is. People look so different here than in the Community, where hard winters and blasting sun made the young look old and the old look dead. "You're, what, a detective?"

"Forensic psychologist."

I squint. "What's that?"

"Whatever I want it to be. Usually I talk to people."

"Like a counselor."

"Kind of."

"I don't need a counselor."

He smiles. "Good thing I'm not here to be your counselor."

"Because I don't like talking about feelings."

"God, me neither," he says. "Anything but feelings."

It sounds like a joke and for moment I draw in a breath and concentrate on the feeling of that. Jude used to try to make me laugh, and when I'd crack a smile he'd keep the joke going, like breath on an ember, making it grow into a fit of giggles that'd echo around the whole forest and make all the birds in the trees quiet. I'd go back to the Community at night afraid they'd somehow detect the smile hidden in the muscles of my face.

I shake Jude out of my mind. The man in my cell is looking at me. "What's the FBI want with me?"

"The local police are no longer handling the investigation into the events at the Community. That's been passed off to the FBI."

"So . . . this," I say, waving between him and me with a stump, "is about the Community? The Prophet?"

"It's about what's right for you. We're most familiar with your case at the FBI. The warden and my bosses discussed it and they decided you warrant special attention. I've been appointed as your mental health coordinator while you're in juvenile detention."

"Is that really why you're here?" I ask. "My mental health? Or are you here to collect evidence about me? I've been through a trial; I know what people like you do for a living. You want to figure me out."

He laughs. "Oh, I already have. I knew everything about you the minute you walked into the courtroom with that candy in your mouth."

• • •

My father taught me how to tell when you're being swindled, and I think about that now, in my cell with this doctor.

My father used to gamble at the greyhound races. He said he would never set foot in a casino because the other players cheated and the dealers dealt dirty. He liked the races because it was just him and the dogs, nobody to cheat him out of his hard-earned pay. He'd take me sometimes, always at night when the smell of yellow beer could grow right inside my skull, the aluminum seat freezing my rear. Lacy flocks of white moths clustered around the gargantuan lightbulbs along the track, beating one another to get closer to the bulb.

"Why are they trying so hard to get to the light?" I asked my father once.

"They think it's the sun," he replied. "They can't tell the difference."

It was here that he taught me how to detect when a person's lying. They got eyes too needy, like they're desperate for you to believe the lie, and their stories are always too good to be true. Later, I remembered the signs, though I never mentioned them. They all sounded too much like the Prophet.

"So, what's your goal in all this?" I ask Dr. Wilson.

"Helping you," he says. "Just helping you. You don't have to believe me, though."

"Good," I say. "I don't believe you. The FBI's goal isn't helping me."

"What's our goal then?"

"Figuring out who killed the Prophet."

His eyebrows rise. "What makes you think there was a killer?" he asks. "What makes you think the Prophet is even dead?"

I make my face go still, but even so, I can tell that he sees it within me now, the lies unwinding like smoke.

"You were nowhere near the Community when the fire started," he continues. "That's what you said in your statement to the police after you were booked."

"Well, if that's what my statement said, it must be the truth," I say, leaning my head to the side. The muscles in my neck hurt from propping up a mouth so full of lies.

I cross my arms and wince.

He points his pen at me. "Do those hurt you? Your arms?"

"Sometimes," I say.

"Maybe someday you'll get a pair of those bionic hands they're developing," he says. "The technology for prosthetics is getting better every day."

"Oh, yeah, that'd be great," I say.

"Yeah?"

"Yeah, that would fix everything."

He frowns and tucks his chin, scribbling something on his yellow paper. I try to read it, but I can't shift the letters into words. I shut my eyes and wonder how I will ever beat people like this man, with his pen and his badge and his words. All I've got is a mouth and nothing to say.

When I open my eyes, he's still writing.

"Where are you from?" I ask.

"Washington, DC." The name means next to nothing to me, beyond the sense that it's far away from here.

"You came up here just for me?"

He nods.

"You must've been thrilled to get that call. Middle of winter, travel for miles to interrogate some criminal girl."

"Firstly, I won't be interrogating you. My assignment is what I said already, to get to know you. And, actually, I volunteered."

"Really?"

"I believed I could help you. I wanted to try."

"Please," I say, holding up an arm. "Don't say that again."

There's a long pause. He sighs.

"Do you know what I do every day?" he asks. "For my job? I spend most of my time sitting this close to the vilest people on the surface of this planet. I sort out whether they're lying, what questions I can ask that'll produce a confession, what part of their minds can be turned against them. I do puzzles all day. That's what my job has become.

Turning these reprehensible people into puzzles because I can't stand to think of them as human."

"Why do you keep doing it?"

"I still love it, in a way, breaking someone down to their most basic building blocks, combing through it all and finding that one shining lie that puts them away. It's a thrill. But, I don't know, it's nothing a really good computer couldn't do. I never get to talk to people anymore. I never help anyone."

"So, what, I'm your vacation?"

He smiles. "You might say that."

"Huh," I say.

"What?"

"Nothing. It's just, you might be sitting across from someone a lot worse than any of those people."

"I don't believe that."

"That's all right," I say, leaning back. "No one ever believes me."

He surveys me for a moment, weighing something behind his eyes. "You were right earlier," he says. "The Prophet is dead. How's that make you feel?"

My eyebrows flatten. "I thought you said no feelings."

"Yes, of course." He rummages in his bag, pulls out a sheaf of paper. "The autopsy came back the other day, and it's basically not worth the paper it's printed on." He reads from the paper in his hand. "'The deceased was badly burned. Most of the trunk, neck, and face were totally compromised. Inadequate lung tissue remains to confirm smoke inhalation. As a result, it is unknown whether the deceased died before or after the fire.' And the arson investigators haven't done much better. They found traces of accelerant, though they say that may have been the weatherproofing on the thatch roofs, which won't stand up in court."

My muscles grow light listening to this. "So, you're not even sure a crime was committed."

"I am sure," he insists.

"How?"

He extracts a small manila envelope from his bag and starts pulling out photos.

"Part of my job is to analyze crime scenes," he says. "I haven't made it up to the Community yet—the snow is so deep, the investigators have had to snowshoe in—but I've seen the pictures they brought back."

The photos show the Community as it must've looked after the fire was extinguished, empty black husks on a backdrop of snow, a gauze of smoke graying the air. I remember the smell, burnt-off grain alcohol and sagebrush, the bugs and beetles that lived inside the dung-and-mud walls squirming to escape the heat.

The doctor places the photos in a circle on my mattress.

"Twelve structures encircling a courtyard," he says. "After the fire started, everyone escaped their houses before they collapsed. Every single person—old men, infants. *Everyone*," he repeats. "Everyone, it seems, but the Prophet. There was plenty of warning, so why didn't he?"

I try to arrange my features normally, as though I don't know the answer to his question.

"I think he was already dead when the fire started," the doctor continues. "The Prophet's body was found lying on the floor next to his bed, facedown. The soft tissue was largely destroyed, but murder usually leaves its thumbprint and the medical examiner found no evidence of knife wounds, no gunshots, no blunt force trauma. They examined the contents of his stomach and found no poison. So how did he come to be lying on the ground?" He throws his hands in the air. "The question you always ask after someone dies under suspicious circumstances is 'Did they have enemies?' We don't even need to bother with that question because of course he did."

"Why do you say that?" I ask. "Nobody in the Community ever disagreed with him." No one but me.

"He systematically brutalized an entire population," the doctor says. "Even if they didn't advertise it, it's very possible someone out there wanted him dead."

"You didn't know them."

"Maybe it's possible you didn't really know them, either."

I set my jaw. I want to tell him that these are the people who lashed their children with switches thick as forearms when the Prophet commanded, married their daughters off at sixteen to men generations older. These are the people who beat Jude until there was nothing left but a mess of blood and bone. They had to cover him in a sheet because it made the women sick to look at.

I lean back so my spine presses against the concrete wall behind my bunk. "Why do you want to know the truth so badly?"

"Because I believe nobody benefits when the truth is buried. Lies have a way of turning poisonous over time. I want justice. And for purely selfish reasons, I want to solve this. But I also want to help you. I wasn't lying about that."

I rest my chin on my breastbone, staring abstractedly at the floor. "What would you do in exchange for the truth?"

He cocks his head to the side. "What are you offering?"

"My parole meeting comes up in August, when I turn eighteen. I need someone to recommend my release."

"And you want me to be that person?"

"Maybe we could work out an arrangement," I say.

His eyes narrow. "And what happens if no one speaks up for you?"

"Maybe they consider good behavior and let me go free anyway. But maybe I get transferred to the adult facility to serve the rest of my sentence."

"Sounds like you have a lot to lose."

"Sounds like you really want answers."

"Your information in exchange for my recommendation?"

I nod. He watches me a moment, and I wonder if he can read in my expression that I will never tell him the truth. I'll give him a version of events, a half-truth, but I haven't told anyone what happened in those smoke-filled moments in January when I stood over the Prophet's body and watched him breathe his last ungodly breath. And I never will.

"All right, then," Dr. Wilson says. "It's a deal."

I sit up straighter. "I'd shake your hand, but . . ."

He smiles.

"So," I say. "Where do we begin?"

Chapter 9

The lunch bell tolls, and the jail wakes up with the sound of doors buzzing unlocked and feet traversing metal walkways.

"Why don't we pick this up another day?" The doctor closes his notebook.

"You just got here," I say.

"I'll be back later in the week." He lifts his stool up from the ground and tucks it awkwardly beneath his arm.

I walk the opposite direction down the skyway, glancing behind me at Wilson's back. He's about to walk right out of here, to freedom. He can do that and I can't. The moment I realize this, I hate him for it, just a little.

In the cafeteria, I look around for Angel through the throng of girls with grizzled faces and big fists who make the blood jerk in my chest. Without hands, everyone else's are a threat. Angel told me how these girls can fashion a weapon out of anything, an elbow, a bolt loosened from a classroom chair, a sharpened shard of plastic broken off a laundry basket. When someone gets you with one, they don't just stab you once. They have a partner hold you down while they stick you in any soft places they can.

Angel strolls in through the cafeteria doors, and the orange sea of bodies parts around her. She is one of the only first-degree murderers here and even the big girls with eyes like caged bulls' steer wide of her. There are so many people here that it seems like every mealtime someone is glimpsing me for the first time, gaping as though they've never seen anything as bizarre. As though we're not all missing some pieces.

I stand behind Angel in line. She's reading a book with a red cover. When I ask her what it's about she doesn't even look up. "Too complicated to explain," she says.

"Try," I say.

She pauses. "Do you know what Mars is?"

I shrug.

"Well, some people think we ought to go there. Leave Earth behind."

"It's supposed to be better there?" I ask.

"Supposed to be."

We wind toward the counter where the girls hold their trays out to the lunch ladies behind a plastic partition. A tray will be waiting there for me specially, everything on it items I can either suck through a straw or carry to my mouth with my stumps without much trouble.

Nearly to the counter, a tall girl pushes in front of me in line and I lose sight of Angel. The back of my neck prickles. I glance behind me at the pulsing wall of thirty or so girls, pinched eyes and bulbous knuckles and shifting weight. I put an arm on the girl's shoulder to push in front of her. "Get outta my way," I say.

Without looking, the girl jerks her elbow back and connects with the side of my face. I blink sudden tears and scan the room for a guard. None are looking this way.

I dodge to the side so I can make sure Angel is still there in front of the girl.

"Back in line!" comes the voice of Officer Prosser, one of the few guards who makes us refer to her by her official title. She has a pile of wiry red hair clutched to the top of her head with a large plastic clip.

I step back. The line moves achingly slow, and when it's my turn, I lever my tray up with my forearms and nearly run to where Angel's sitting.

"Calm down, crazy," she hisses. "You weren't gonna get shanked with that many guards around."

I shake my head. I touch my forearm to my cheek, which still stings from the sharp plane of the girl's elbow.

"God, you are greener than green," she says. "Stop

looking around at everyone. Keep your eyes down."

"It's hard," I say.

"They're not that scary," she says. "See that one over there?" She nods at a brown-haired girl hunched over her tray, placing peas on her tongue and swallowing, one by one, like pills. "Her name's Wendy. She's going to Billings after this, that's the adult prison. She confessed to assaulting her eight-year-old neighbor with a baseball bat. I read about it—they didn't have hardly enough evidence to convict. Lots of girls confess just to feel like they're doing the right thing. Sometimes the cops'll make them think they can go home if they just say they did it, though you'd have to be a total idiot to believe that." She swallows a huge mouthful of mashed potatoes. "These girls, naw, they're pancakes. Most are pumped so full of Adderall they can hardly walk, let alone shank you. The real crazies aren't allowed in gen pop. They live up in the hospital most of the time."

"It's different for you," I say. "You make them scared."

"Then give them something to be afraid of," she says. "You're a badass bitch. You've done way worse than half these girls." She rummages with her fork into a small pot-pie and chews for a moment. "Is there some other reason you don't like them?"

"What do you mean?" I ask.

She gives me a hard look from the corner of her eye. "You just see it a lot, is all. Little country girls get thrown in here." She waves to the other girls, and I know in that gesture she's acknowledging their differences, their different-shaped eyes, some ringed in charcoal-like lines, their different lips with shades of sparkle and shine adhered to them. "Let's just say it wouldn't be the first time I got a roommate who had a problem with it."

"I'm not looking at them because I'm scared," I say. "It's just . . . for all those years, I never saw anybody different from me. The Prophet didn't believe it was possible, all these people living side by side. He told us people who didn't look like us were evil."

She nods her head knowingly. "Yeah. There are plenty of people out there who think the same thing."

"There was a boy I knew," I say tentatively, and I know I'm speaking almost too quiet to be heard above the din of the cafeteria, but I can't speak louder because it feels wrong bringing him to life in this place. "His name was Jude. He lived in the forest. I met him when I was fourteen."

Angel puts down her plastic fork. "He was your boyfriend?"

I nod, though I never called him that.

"And he was a different color?" she asks, wariness palpable in her voice.

I nod again.

"And what happened to him?" The way she asks it, I know she already knows the answer.

I look straight into the miniature blue discs inside each of her eyes, inside the angry folds of her face, and tell her. "They killed him," I whisper. "I think they really killed him."

Chapter 10

The night we met was warm, stars hot in a black sky. I sprinted through the trees with tears tumbling down my face. I was fourteen, and I had decided I was going to run away.

I knew I must've been one of the first to ever leave the Community. The Prophet taught us that our little clearing was protected by God, that if we ever left, the Gentiles would hunt us down with their bullets and heat-seeking missiles and poison gas, that on every telephone pole in every city hung wanted posters with our faces. He said that every Gentile knew the name Minnow Bly, and they cursed it.

Earlier that night, I'd fought with Vivienne, my father's third wife. I'd dropped a dish during washing, and she stuck out her rigid finger and gave me that tired old lecture about how it was almost time for me to marry and no man would want me if I didn't arrange myself into the shape of a good woman. "Fine, then I won't marry!" I said, and she reminded me that the job of a Kevinian woman was to marry. If a woman doesn't marry, what's the purpose of her? I threw down my dishrag right then, because I knew everybody else agreed with her.

I was out of breath from running. A stitch in my side made me gutter to a stop at the edge of a clearing.

My footfalls were almost silent over the scattered, dead pine needles, but he noticed. The boy, sitting on the front porch of his family's handmade cabin. I had never seen someone like him for so many reasons, for the way his shoulders fell back easy as he stripped pine needles from a twig, for the way his feet sat bare and dusty inside the rolled hems of homespun trousers, for the way his skin was a brown color I hadn't seen since we moved to the Community. I could feel the window through which I viewed the world—no larger than a pinhole back then— broadening somewhere at the back of my mind just by looking at him. I couldn't open my eyes wide enough. I wanted to stare at him for lifetimes, the perfect pores of him, his high eyebrows serene, like he'd never seen how angry God could be.

His eyes found me where I stood, sheltered in the shadows. There was a quiet moment when neither of us spoke, each of us standing with a new tension in our backbones, his shocked forehead, my parted lips and fingers splayed to my sides.

"Are you one of those cult people?" he asked after a moment.

My lips snapped shut. "We're not a cult."

"That's not what my daddy says."

"Well, I'd know, wouldn't I?"

He squinted at me. "You sure look like a cult person."

I glanced down at my long navy dress, belled at the elbows and waist. I touched my little white bonnet self-consciously.

"And you look like a ragamuffin," I responded. "Don't you have shoes?"

"I got 'em. I just don't wear 'em unless I need to." He buried his toes in the fallen pine needles. "You're not supposed to be here. There're signs all along our land. 'Keep Out,' 'Private Property,' 'No Trespassing.' Didn't you see 'em?"

I remembered the livid black and red signs speared to tree trunks with railroad spikes. "I saw."

"Then why didn't you keep out? Cain't you read?"

I pulled my bottom lip into my mouth and pressed my teeth together.

"You cain't read?" he asked, quieter.

"And you can?" I asked.

"Sure, my momma taught me."

"You got books?" I asked, taking a step closer.

"We got two Bibles."

"What's a Bible?"

"You don't know what the Bible is?" His mouth opened so I could see a minuscule chip in his front tooth.

"No," I said. "Else I wouldn't ask, would I?"

"It's, like, a big book with stories that God wrote," he said.

"We got one of those. The Book of Prophecies."

"But the Bible don't just have prophecies; it has stories."

"The Book of Prophecies has stories, too," I said. "Like Chad and the Golden Bear, and Eric turning blood to gold, and Victor stealing a demon's pheasant-green slippers that held all its power. And—and Marcus, the first man, who married the first three women, who were born out of three chestnuts in the same lime-colored pod—"

But Jude was shaking his head. "Those sound made up."

"They're not. Marcus made all the wheat fields out of the hair of his blond wife, and the trees out of the hair of his brown-haired wife, and fire out of the hair of his redheaded wife. We wouldn't have fire and trees and wheat if it weren't for those first wives."

"That ain't in the Bible."

"So?"

"So they ain't real. They sound like bedtime stories."

I fell backward a step. Nobody had ever talked like that. If the stories were wrong, the Prophet was wrong, and even thinking that could poison the blood in a person's veins. God had claimed the Prophet years ago, had cured his astigmatism and taken away his asthma so he no longer needed to puff from his inhaler as he walked across the factory floor. I was there when he took his thick, yellowed glasses in his fists and bent them until they broke. The Prophet was a miracle.

"You—you don't know what you're talking about," I sputtered. "Your Bible's probably just lies."

"No, it ain't! It's all true and if you think that, you're not a real Christian."

"You're right, I'm not a Christian! I'm a Kevinian."

"A what?" he asked.

"That's our religion. Our prophet's named Kevin."

"A prophet named *Kevin*?" Jude scoffed. "Now it's definitely all made up."

"How do you know, huh? You're probably telling tales just so you can be right."

"No, I ain't. My daddy taught me everything I know, and he's not wrong about nothing."

One of the little twists of his dreadlocks fell onto his

55

forehead and he brushed it aside angrily. All at once, I had to purse my lips to keep down a breathy, giddy laugh. Here I was talking to someone. Fighting with someone. What a novelty. What a prize.

"You didn't even choose it yourself, then?" I asked. "You just go along with what your *daddy* says? Some of us make our own decisions. Some of us don't just think whatever our parents tell us to." I didn't mention the fact that everything I believed, I believed because of my parents, too.

Jude's face fell. "I have to do what my daddy says." His voice came quiet.

The sorrow that pounded out of Jude's eyes made me stagger backward a step. It was hard sorrow, hot sorrow, the kind that's had a long time to ferment. I couldn't have known that, in that moment, Jude wasn't thinking of me but of the empty cavern of his mother's skull, the aftersmell of a gunshot.

"I better go," I said softly. "I'll get in trouble if they know I left."

"Okay," Jude said. "Maybe . . . maybe we'll see each other again sometime."

The wind whipped past my ear, and I imagined it was the Prophet's cold breath.

I wasn't supposed to talk to people like Jude. He was

a Gentile, an outsider, and that meant he was wrong and wicked and wanted us dead.

Worst of all, he was a Rymanite, people the Prophet had warned us about, people God had abandoned centuries ago, and they were the worst kind of evil.

Except, I thought, and after that nothing was really the same again. Except Jude didn't seem evil at all.

I clenched and unclenched my fingers.

"Yes," I said, holding my hand up in a wave. "I know we will."

Chapter 11

"You're remembering," Angel says.

I look up at her. "What are you talking about?"

"They don't prepare you for the remembering," she says. "You'll be staring at the ceiling, at some pattern of light on the metal, and without realizing it you're back in the house you grew up in. And it's like you've walked right back into that place, the feelings, the smells. All that from some pattern of light your brain recognized. Funny, eh?"

She's lying on her bunk with her head propped on the wall, feet crossed at the ankles so I can see the dirty soles of her white socks.

"The key is choosing what you remember," she says. "Choose the happy things, 'cause the bad things are waiting at the corners of your mind for the moment you're not ready."

I nod. Almost every day, I'll be lying on my bunk and, without thinking, hop up because I have the impulse to walk to the tree house to meet Jude. Angel watches me, her eyes peeking over the top of a book, because by now she knows everything that's flicking through my mind in those moments: The tree house is burned. The larch tree with it. I'll never see Jude again.

• • •

Jude used to talk about the way his father could quote any line from the Bible. He hated that when he got older, but when we first met, he mentioned it with something like pride. He must've believed his father was as holy as I once thought my parents were.

After the night we met, I went out looking for him almost every day, but the forest looked different in the daylight, the shadows rearranged and the trees smaller somehow. It took about a week to find him, and the day I did, I'd already been wandering the woods hopelessly for hours, wondering if I'd imagined the cabin and the strange boy in the night. I leaned against a tree to get my breath. The woods ticked with the noise of insect bodies, the trills surging from inside sparrows' throats as though celebrating something greater than feathers and hollow bones. I closed my eyes and listened.

Music. I could have sworn I heard music. I hadn't heard anything like it in years. It was forbidden. I followed the sound, my neck craned till I found a mossy western larch. Above, high on a branch, Jude sat hunched over a guitar.

One shoeless foot was hanging down, tapping. He was playing this little concert for nobody but himself and the birds
and the trees and whatever else lived that deep in the forest.

It's that idea that hurts worse than anything, because
it's all a pile of ash now, so burned maybe nobody will
ever go there to play a song again. That's the real tragedy,
even worse than the idea of Jude being dead.

"Hi ho!" he called.

My eyes shot open. "Hi."

He hopped out of the tree, clutching the guitar's neck.
I could see that his fingers were calloused from picking at
the strings. I was very conscious of his fingers after that,
followed them as they rubbed an eye or scratched his hair,
which he hadn't yet shorn off. His fingers took on an air of
importance I'd never attributed to anything. If his fingers
could do that, what was the rest of him like? What was
inside this boy?

"You can make music," I said.

He nodded.

"How'd you learn that?"

"My mama taught me," he said.

"And your mother . . . you only got the one mother?"

"One mother? Yeah. You got more than that?"

"Four."

He made a face. "That's too many."

"Says who?"

"Says nobody. It's just a common fact."

"But, if you lose one mother, you have three others to take her place."

"Nobody could take the place of my mother," he said seriously.

I felt nervous, like I was walking very closely to some precipice.

"You all alone out here?" I asked.

"Just my daddy and me."

"No brothers and sisters?"

"Nope," he said. "I bet you got a lot of siblings over there."

I nodded.

"Bet you're never lonely."

I shook my head. "There are a bunch of little kids, and some older ones who are married off or getting close. I guess—I guess you're the first person my age I've met in a long time."

He scratched the underside of his chin with the head of his guitar. I knew he was thinking about how he'd never met someone his age, either.

"Why do you live out here in the forest?" I asked.

"I was born here. My momma and daddy settled here before I was born. My daddy told me once about the people down there, in the city, how the smoke and chemicals cover everything. That isn't how man was meant to live. But this is." He lifted a finger toward the blooming wilderness. "This is what God wanted for us all along."

"The Prophet said the same thing."

"You think it's true?"

"Well, sure," I said, tossing my shoulders up in a shrug. "It's gotta be. I mean, the Prophet says God's in the stars, and you can hardly see any stars in the city. If you look real hard, you can see angels playing in the forest at night. They don't got angels in the city."

"You've seen an angel?"

"'Course," I said.

I don't know why I lied. Every night, I'd stare into the dark canopy, even for the seconds I snatched walking from the house to the Prophet Hall, but never saw the flash of wings or blinding pixels of skin. Never. No matter how hard I looked, there was only ever just darkness between those trees.

Chapter 12

"Constance, Jedediah, Regent, Patience, Hershel, Amos, Leah, Eliezer, Prudence, Tobin, Silence, Ephraim, Solomon, Halla, Eustace, Gideon, Martha, Liberty."

"You missed one."

"What?"

"That was only eighteen," Angel says. "You said you have nineteen siblings."

"Oh," I say. I lean back against the cinder-block wall, and in my mind sort my siblings by their mothers. Donna Jo with stocky limbs and wide fingers, Vivienne who gave her black eyes and hair to her children, Mabel who was only seventeen when she married my father. And my mother. We weren't supposed to know our true mothers, but all of her children could easily be picked out by their pale hair and cornflower eyes. I was the only one who looked like I didn't belong to her.

"Virtue," I say finally. "I forgot Virtue. She has the strangest eyes I'd ever seen, such a pale blue they are almost white. We thought she was dead when she was born. There were a lot of babies like that. She took a minute to pull in any breath, and when she finally did, she didn't cry or make a sound. Just stared straight ahead." I recall the image of my mother, leaned over Virtue's blue-red body lying between my mother's feet on the packed earth floor, her knees up and shrouded in the cloth of birthing.

"She never did learn to talk," I say.

"They didn't take her to a doctor?" Angel asks.

"My mother asked, but..." I trail off. "My father wouldn't hear of it. He said we made that choice, long ago."

My eyes stray to the spot where the doctor sat a couple days ago. A square foot of grated metal flooring. Whenever I think about him, about the truth that he came here for, I can't arrange my thoughts properly. Everybody's better off without the Prophet around. Why can't he see that?

"What's wrong?" Angel asks, looking down at me.

"That FBI agent," I say. "I'm just wondering when he'll come back."

"Maybe you'll get lucky and he won't," she says. "Those guys, they're great at intimidation, not great with the follow-through."

"No, he'll come back. He's looking for who killed the Prophet. There's an investigation. They think he was murdered."

Angel props herself up on her elbow. "And what's this guy think you're gonna tell him?"

"Who killed him."

Her eerie pale eyes, like the petals of a flax flower, regard me. "Will you?"

I shake my head. All at once, bile rises in my throat. I run to the toilet and throw up a couple heaves of acidy amber liquid. I press my forehead against the cold steel of the toilet rim and sense Angel crouching beside me, though she doesn't touch me.

"I remember the moment he died," I whisper.

Angel crouches still, a black shadow on my periphery. "Did you kill him?" she asks flatly.

I grip my eyes closed. Something soft and delicate inside me tears at her question. Because I wonder the same thing. *Did I really? Is he dead because of me?*

"Hey," Angel says. "Don't you *dare*."

I turn toward her, my forehead wrinkling.

"Don't you dare feel guilty," she says. "That guy deserved everything he got."

"No one deserves to die."

"Are you kidding me? Of course people deserve to die. When you make life unbearable for other people, you deserve to be taken out. That's all there is to it."

"I'm afraid," I say.

"Do they have a confession? Have you admitted anything?"

"No."

"Good," she says. "Don't say a word to him. There ain't no reasoning with cops. Not with detectives, or lawyers, or judges neither. They see what they want. And what they want's an easy target. The crazy girl who's been messed up her whole life's the easiest target of them all. Why do you think I'm here? Why do you think any of us is here? He'll send you away for life if you give him the chance."

I nod slowly, feeling like I'm getting my bearings again.

"You fought back. There ain't no shame in that," she says, quiet. And, even quieter, "Don't let them do to you what they've done to me."

Chapter 13

Dr. Wilson returns a few days later, his notebook wedged beneath his elbow, his square teeth smiling like he's actually happy to be sitting inside my metal cell.

"Tell me about Jude Leland."

I grip my tongue between my molars. "How do you know about Jude?"

"You gave a statement to the police, remember? After your surgery."

I frown, trying to recall my days in the hospital. "There was a detective."

"He wrote of a boy you mentioned, Jude, and I did a little digging, interviewed some of the wives who are in protective care. They told me how you came to the Community with a boy the night of the fire. He's totally off the grid. No birth certificate, no social security number, not even any medical records."

"He was born in the woods."

He nods. "So, the last time you saw Jude was the night of the fire?"

"The night they killed him, you mean."

"You're certain he's dead?" he asks. "They've found a few sets of human remains at the Community, but other than the Prophet, they haven't confirmed identities yet. From what I gather they could've been natural deaths— we know through interviews that people died out there in incidents unconnected to the fire—an old man, a teenage girl mauled by an animal, stillborn babies. We don't *know* Jude is dead."

"You weren't there." I choke out the words. "You didn't see it."

"You know," he says uncertainly, "there was talk among some of the wives, even some of the children, that you'd been killed in the fire, Minnow."

I flinch. "Well, you're sitting here talking to me."

"Your little brother Hershel couldn't believe it when I told him you were alive. He says he saw you die in the fire. He knew it was you because you had no hands."

My stomach begins to squirm. "Hershel's six years old," I say. "And I doubt he could tell you what I even look like."

Wilson gives me a meaningful look, then presses his hands together efficiently. "I'm curious. How much of your relationship with Jude was an act of defiance? To be with someone who was supposedly so evil."

I narrow my eyes at him. "You've been learning about Rymanites."

He nods. "Interesting stuff. The Kevinians I've talked to seem pretty impressed by it, even now. How Ryman rebelled by marrying a Gentile woman and ignored his father's order to kill her. And how as punishment, the spirit of God fled Ryman's body while he writhed on the ground, turning his skin black."

"And so it shall be that the descendants of Ryman bear till eternity the mark on their earthly skins and the evil in their celestial hearts," I finish.

"So you were aware that your family wouldn't approve of Jude."

"I wasn't with Jude to rebel, if that's what you're saying. I was with Jude because of who he was."

"Still, I think this is important. Did you notice the color of his skin?"

"Of course I noticed it. That's a stupid thing to ask."

"Why?"

"Because . . . because if I didn't notice his skin, how would I be seeing him? If I missed that, what else would I have missed?"

"But, you were raised to hate people like Jude."

I shrug off the suggestion. "It's a good thing I hated the people who taught me to hate, then."

"When was the first time you realized that? That something wasn't right about the Community?"

"I don't think you can trace it to a single event," I say. "You don't change everything you believe all at once."

"What was one of the moments, then? When you disagreed?"

I press my dry lips together. "That girl you mentioned, the one they said was mauled by an animal."

He nods. "Roberta Hallowell? Her mother gave a statement that it was probably a grizzly bear."

I chuckle darkly. "No, not a bear." I reach over and tap his notebook with my stump. "Get your pen ready. You'll probably want to take notes."

• • •

That first summer in the Community was the best I remember, when I was five and tiny and completely in awe of the Prophet, when the men were large and the women efficient and our very bodies shone with holy light. That summer, we watched a thousand ears of corn waggle out of the earth. We watched the men tear a pond of silty brown water into the ground. We broke in our stiff new clothes.

We saw the first of us killed.

Bertie was sixteen with ash blond hair and a top lip broken by a pink fold she'd had since birth. She was what the wives called "uncouth." She showed a little too much of the skin around her neck, talked a little too loudly. She left a boyfriend back in the city, and had to be dragged to the Community by her parents.

Donna Jo, the second of my father's wives, already bow-backed from the weight of my first half sibling, Jedediah, told me to walk to the pond to gather water. As I tottered beneath the weight of the bucket, I spotted Bertie's blue-clothed back beneath the willow, hunched over something open in her crossed legs. I walked forward, mouth agape at the way her fingers rested on the pages delicately, as though on the skin of someone she loved.

"It's a sin," I gasped.

Bertie's head turned. "Minnow, go away."

"Where'd you get that?"

"I found it."

"But there aren't any books here," I protested.

She sighed. "All right, fine. I snuck it in with me."

"It—it's from outside?" I asked.

"Where else would it come from? 'Course it's from outside. And you have to promise not to tell."

"But, it's forbidden. God'll hate you for it."

"God doesn't give a toot."

"Girls aren't supposta read."

"I been able to read since I was three years old and nobody's going to take that away from me. Not the Prophet. Not God."

Bertie's face was set hard. When I remember her, I picture that expression, like behind her eyes she had entire rooms that she didn't let anyone see. And I realize now it was the book in her hands that'd made them.

"What's in it?" I asked, taking a tentative step forward.

"If I say, you have to promise never to tell. Not anyone, even your parents."

I dragged in a deep breath. "I promise."

"Come here then."

I sat down beside her on a thick mound of moss that crept all the way to the pond's edge. All around, the air rang with birds trilling and insects vibrating.

"They're called fairy tales. Do you remember those?"

"Kind of," I said.

"Here, let me read you one."

Bertie opened up the book and leafed through the pages expertly. The edges were stained tea-colored from all the fingers that had touched them over the years.

"Godseyes," I breathed. The text was so cramped, it made my mind swim. Attached to each story was a black-and-white woodcut of kings or dwarfs or maidens. Some of the

maidens were being held at the jaw by some knight, which meant they were kissing, which meant they were in love. I couldn't remember ever seeing a love like that.

Bertie read me the story, and when I begged for another she indulged me, until an hour of stories had passed.

"Are they real?" I asked.

"No, they're just stories for children."

"Why are they evil?"

"They're not," she said, her face settling into a scowl. "Only the Prophet says they are. He doesn't want us to know how to read. He doesn't want us to figure him out."

That summer, Bertie taught me about letters and how to sound them together, and that's why I can patch a semblance of meaning from words sometimes, if they're not too difficult. I might've learned to read proper if Bertie's mother hadn't found the book under Bertie's pallet and taken it straight to the Prophet.

The Prophet had been saving a pair of metal slippers. They were crude, two rectangles of steel with straps soldered to the sides. A deacon put the slippers in the fire pit at the center of the courtyard and let them burn to a blistered red. They sent up sparks when he lifted them out with tongs. Everyone crowded around to watch.

The deacons wrestled Bertie's feet into the slippers. She danced around the courtyard, screaming in pain, the skin on her feet popping, the smell of burning flesh warming the air, dead and smoky. When she fell to the dirt, the Prophet gestured and someone put her on her feet again and forced her to keep dancing, her braid rising and falling with each leap.

The others looked on, their faces like puzzles I couldn't solve.

A few days later, the Prophet received a revelation to marry Bertie. He mostly married girls who had transgressed in some way, and he always managed to tame them. On her wedding day, Bertie couldn't stand. Flies swam through the air around the dressings on her feet. The Prophet wore a smile that was slim and sharp.

"The time hath come," he chanted.

"Thy deeds be done," Bertie replied quietly.

Bertie's feet eventually healed but she walked crooked. Her entire body wilted. Weeks later, when the Prophet was conducting a sermon in the open air of the courtyard, Bertie stood, surveyed the sea of us, bonneted and buttoned, and hobbled away. I was the only one to notice her pass through the tree line and into the shadows there. I said nothing, even knowing she might be killed at any moment by the Gentiles' heat-seeking missiles. I knew, somehow, that she would be safer out there than in the Community.

When he noticed she had disappeared, the Prophet's eyes were like clenched fists. He told the men to secure Bertie with any force necessary.

They brought her body back. I caught a glimpse through the throng of blue-clad bodies. Her face. It looked almost normal at first. Then I saw the other side, kicked in at the eyeball so the whole side of her face sloped inward.

What I remember most was that nobody screamed.

• • •

We knew to expect punishment for sin, but Bertie got the worst. It was hard in the beginning. With every kick, it's like they were trying to quash everybody's doubts. Because everyone had doubts back then, when we were just getting used to the mud and cold and realizing what it meant to be holy all the time.

When I first told Jude this story, his face crumpled. "What will they do if they catch you out here?"

"They don't think I'd ever run away," I said. My family knew I took walks in the forest, but I always came back, and as long as I did my chores, nobody bothered about it. That's what happens in a household with twenty children. You get a little forgotten about.

"What if they knew you were with me?" he asked.

"They'd . . . they'd kill me," I answered.

He shook his head. "Ain't you scared?"

If I'd answered honestly, I'd've said no. Fear floated around like constant pollen, but none of us were allergic. But there's a moment when it all becomes too much. And it was coming like a wildfire bent on burning the whole place to the ground.

Chapter 14

I walk down to the cafeteria for lunch. Benny stands inside the doors and nods at me when I enter, her mouth hitched up in a slight smile. She's been helping me since I arrived here. I gather she was more or less assigned to me, or maybe she took the job herself because she saw how wobbly I still was on my feet. She's usually got a book rolled up in her back pocket, and when I asked her about it she explained that she always carries a book in case she's stuck somewhere with nothing to do.

"What do you read?" I asked, still gobsmacked to hear a woman talk about books out in the open, where anybody could hear.

"Nonfiction," she said. "I've got a good one right now about the Haitian Revolution."

"Benny studied history in school," Angel explained, "before she sold her soul to the state government."

When I grab my tray of food and find our normal table,

Angel's already seated, sneering at an Asian girl with a thick band of dull black bangs.

"Minnow, it's so nice to meet you," the girl says brightly when I walk over. I don't recognize her. Normally, Angel and I eat alone. "I'm Tracy. I just wanted to make sure I introduced myself. I know how scary this place is the first week. The girls can be a little ruthless." Her eyes dart quickly to Angel.

"What did I miss?" A girl so skinny that her limbs remind me of a deer's slides her tray down the table and sits beside Tracy.

"Minnow, this is Rashida," Tracy says.

"Nice to make your acquaintance," Rashida says. "What happened to your hands?"

"Rashida, don't ask things like that," Tracy exclaims.

"Why not? Something happened to 'em. It's not like they fell off by accident. They's saying you got chopped by a serial killer, but I told 'em naw, she definitely a farm girl, probably got sliced by a combine."

"My father cut them off with a hatchet," I say, just to see how the words sit in the air.

Tracy's breath catches in her throat, and Angel cocks an eyebrow from her fried chicken, but Rashida's head falls back and she laughs a booming laugh that echoes across the cafeteria. "For real? I'd be telling that to everyone if that happened to me. With a hatchet? That's way better than a combine any day."

I smile, too, because it's impossible not to when she says it like that.

"Rashida and I are in the youth group here," Tracy says. "You should come sometime. We talk through things that are bothering us."

"And you think Minnow wants to talk through the fact that her dad chopped off her hands with *you and Rashida?*" Angel asks. "Now that's funny."

"Someday, Angel—" Tracy seethes, "someday you're gonna do something you can't talk your way out of. And then you'll be sorry."

"I think I already did," Angel says, putting her fork down. "And do I feel sorry? Did I repent like a good little girl?" She holds her hands together as though in prayer. "Did I cry in front of the judge and say I made a big boo-boo and I'll be good from now on? Fuck no. I don't need forgiveness from some six-thousand-year-old pervert who sticks it to virgins when they're not looking."

There isn't another word out of either of them for the rest of lunch.

• • •

"Why don't you believe in God?" I ask Angel after lights-out. We're both in our beds, though I can tell Angel's up reading by the line of yellow light visible between her bunk and the wall.

She doesn't answer right away. She's quiet for so long, I wonder if she's fallen asleep.

"Because I don't need to," she says finally.

"What's that mean?" I ask.

"Some people need cancer medication. I don't, so I don't take it."

When I don't reply, she sighs. "I understand why people used to believe in God. Maybe I would've, too. They wanted to understand the world better. To explain why things happen the way they do. And God was pretty good at that. But we don't need him anymore."

I know she's talking about those books she reads, the ones that tell her what the earth is made of and why the sun burns and what happens when lightning strikes, but I can't read those books. The Prophet never allowed girls to read, and I think it's probably that fact more than my hands that makes me feel like I never stood a chance.

"You don't still believe in that stuff, do you?" Angel asks. "God and everything?"

My mouth forms a frown. The silence stretches up through the dark lines of the jail.

We were still in trailers when the Prophet taught us about God. We weren't saints yet, just a bunch of fleshy forklift drivers and foremen beside their children and meek wives in old dresses. Everyone sat on couches inside our metal-walled house while the Prophet spoke, me on the carpet playing with alphabet blocks. I remember the look of my fingers, inflated with fat, bent around letters and spelling gibberish.

The Prophet stood before us in my living room. "What you are about to hear is strange and wonderful. It is a story nobody has ever heard until now." He drew a large breath. "It is the story of God."

God's real name is Charlie, he told us. He was born in York, Pennsylvania, in 1776, in the summer of the signing, when temperatures were high as rockets and humid as seas.

Charlie was the son of a poor miller, a mean man with a gammy leg and a spray of powder burns over his right temple from the war. When Charlie was just becoming something more than a boy, he went out into the creaking, old-growth forest to collect firewood. He came upon a stream that fell away, suddenly, into the earth. Charlie wanted to see where the water went. He leaned down and peered in.

A spark. An alien pulse of light.

He stared, transfixed, as every star, every galaxy in the universe flicked across his vision. The rings of Jupiter.

The broken, sunburned back of Mars. Sights no human had ever captured with their eyes. And, just as suddenly, the feeling of every cell of every living organism hovering just beneath his fingertips, like piano keys. He could touch each one, if he wanted. He could control them.

There are some who insist Charlie was simply lucky. That anyone who happened to walk by that stream on that morning, curious enough to lean over the odd water gushing into the ground, would be made God. They are wrong. Charlie was God before he was even born. It was only a matter of him finding out.

Charlie lives in every generation. When he dies, he is reborn nine months later, a baby God. At any moment, you might meet him. He has been a Confederate soldier. He has been a bank teller. He has sat behind an oak desk in wire-rimmed glasses and a day's growth of beard graying his cheeks. He has cooked dinner for his mother. He has driven to the ocean. He has fallen in love.

The Prophet met Charlie once. Only once, but it was enough to transform his life forever, to transform all our lives.

That incarnation of Charlie was a seventy-five-year-old janitor at the only mall in Ogden, Utah. The Prophet was seventeen, needed to pee, and ran into the mall to find a restroom. Charlie was mopping the floor when the

Prophet entered the bathroom, sprinting toward a urinal. Charlie whipped out a bony hand and clutched his bare wrist.

"Be careful, you," Charlie said in a low croak. "Floor's slippery."

The Prophet looked into Charlie's face, taking in the name tag pinned to his uniform and his eyes, a startling, bottle-glass green. The teenage Prophet couldn't know that the touch had transferred something so powerful into his body that, in the coming years, he'd possess the ability to hear the ministrations of God. He relieved himself, jiggled himself dry, and left.

It wasn't until years later, when the Prophet found a glyph-printed foil in the mountains, that he realized he'd been touched by God. When he heard God speak through the earth, it was in the old croak of Charlie the janitor from all those years before.

We never knew when Charlie would die. This was the precarious thing about believing in a human God. At any moment, he could pass on and the world would be without a God until he was born again.

A day before we left for the wilderness, the Prophet called for a final meeting, each of us wearing our newly constructed blue garments that sat up around our bodies rigidly. I could sense the significance of this day, so I sat quietly with my hands folded in my lap. The Prophet swept through our front door, tears streaming down his face.

"Why are you crying, Prophet?" my father asked.

"I am crying, Deacon Samuel," he breathed, "because God is dead."

The room gasped.

"Oh, yes! He has died a dozen times. You have felt it. When He dies, the earth mourns. Catastrophe reigns until He can be reborn. Five years ago, the great wildfires overtook Montana. The flames of hell pushed through the crust of the earth while God gestated. When he was birthed, the heavens opened up, and the fires were doused with sacred water. All became right with the world again."

"So, God isn't really dead?" asked Deacon Timothy.

"God is always both alive and dead. His great sorrow is dying, always dying."

"Who is God's mother?" asked Deacon Sean.

"Her identity is inconsequential. Her only purpose is the duty her womb performs in growing the body of God. That is truly the highest calling of womankind. Any of you should be lucky enough to birth God."

He looked down into the near audience, where the children sat on the curled carpet, boys and girls separated. His eyes caught on mine.

"Maybe you, Sister Minnow, will someday have the honor of giving birth to God. How would that be?"

"That would be . . . glorious," I breathed. "Glory be to God our savior."

The Prophet's approving gaze filled my stomach with burbling pride. I looked back at where my parents sat. A smile had crept through my father's new beard. My eyes flicked to my mother. She was heavily pregnant with Constance and doubled over her stomach, drawing designs on the stretched fabric of her dress. She hadn't heard a word.

"Does He live in our country?" asked Deacon Karl.

"Of course. God is American."

"How did He come by the name God, if His real name was Charlie?" asked Deacon Martin.

"There has always been a name for God. He just wasn't there to use it yet."

None of the children asked questions, even the older ones. I was the youngest child by far, but I still felt bolstered by the Prophet's suggestion that I could birth God, so I raised my hand.

"What happens when Charlie dies?" I asked.

"You shouldn't call Him by that name, Minnow," the Prophet said. "It's a special name. One reserved for special times."

"What happens when God dies?" I asked.

The Prophet smiled, his eyes crinkling. "He is reborn."

"But what if He decides not to come back?"

"He always comes back. It's His great sacrifice, to live among us and concern Himself with human problems instead of dwelling in the Great Infinity."

"Will Char—I mean, will God always come back?" I asked.

"Always," he said. "God is the one person you can always count on."

Though the Prophet discouraged it, I never stopped thinking of God as Charlie. A human God. How preferable to an invisible God, I thought, one you're not even sure exists. I was never taught basic math, but by the time I figured out how to finger count, I deduced that Charlie was around my age.

Sometimes I could barely remember what came before the Community. I had to remind myself forcefully, create faces of people I might know if I ever found a way off the mountain. Somewhere, there was a girl by a train. Somewhere, there was an old man swinging loaves of bread into a shopping cart. There was a woman selecting the clothes she'd wear to work, the coral-colored blouse that would touch her skin all day while she typed at a computer and commuted on a bus that smelled of the seconds after lightning.

And somewhere was a teenage God. A boy with vibrant green eyes. A boy named Charlie. I could meet Him, if I left here. So why didn't I? And why didn't they?

It was years before I asked. The Prophet stood before the congregation again, but now at the front of the massive wooden structure of the Prophet Hall, nestled inside an unending sea of evergreens. Stretched between his two hands was the Scroll of Salvation, the sheath of silver foil he found on the mountain the day he discovered he was a prophet, covered in glyphs that contained the language of God.

I still sat on the ground with the children, but now I was the oldest, my half sisters Prudence and Leah sitting to my left and right. Constance sat behind me, and every once in a while I could feel her stroke the tail of my braid with her tiny fingers.

"Why don't we live in the lowlands?" I asked. "If that's where God lives, why don't we live where God lives?"

"We will, Sister Minnow," the Prophet replied. "He will let us know when the time is right."

"How?"

"That's for Him to decide."

"So, we have no way of knowing when we can go back?" I asked. "I could be eighty by the time He decides. I could be dead."

"Don't be impertinent," my father's third wife, Vivienne, hissed. In that moment, I became aware of the creaking of dry wooden pews as the dozens of adults behind me shifted in their seats.

"You're not a prisoner here, Minnow," the Prophet said in a measured tone. "You are free to go whenever you want."

I swallowed. This wasn't true. I knew the consequences of running away. I recalled Bertie's dead-eyed face, indented like a thumbprint in a peach. "No, I wasn't saying . . . I'm just excited to meet God."

The Prophet smiled and extended his hands gracefully toward the congregation. "Aren't we all?" The room nodded as one.

The Prophet focused his eyes on me once more. "I hope you decide to wait for God's call, Minnow. We are the chosen. The Sanctified Prophets of Heaven. We will be rewarded grandly if we do God's will. You won't just meet Him. You will dine at His table every night. He will bathe you and heal you. He will touch you with His unknowable green eyes, and you will be saved."

Chapter 15

In the Community, I woke up early each morning to milk goats and punish the earth with a trowel to fill it with seeds or dig grown things out. I'm used to waking up before dawn, so every day, without thought, my eyes open at exactly the same time, when the air is the bruised color of winter mornings and everyone in the jail is still sleeping. Sometimes, the echoed weeping of a girl winds through the scaffolding, but most mornings the place is quiet and still, and it's possible to imagine the bars and the guards and the razor wire away, imagine there's nothing surrounding you but your own soul.

Until six, when every fluorescent bulb in the place spasms to life, the light like a punch to the face. The noise starts a moment later, talking and shouting and girls using the toilet and trudging down to the showers.

During showers, I have no choice but to strip down in front of the others, their eyes taking in the parts of me I was taught to keep hidden.

Here, the scars usually shielded beneath yards of orange cotton are on display, the whip marks scoring my back from countless childhood punishments, the thick bands of red scar tissue cuffing both ankles. But, when I cast my eyes at the other bodies, I see skin tarnished with small holes of cigarette burns and pink puckered knife wounds and white lines like hash marks on forearms. Here, my scars are the only part of me that could be called normal. It seems like every girl here has had their own personal Prophet.

And then it's breakfast, and runny oatmeal and juice with a straw, and after that, the pill line.

There's a long corridor beside the cafeteria by the nurse's office. From a small window in the door, white paper cups are passed to each girl. Every ten seconds or so a new girl approaches the window, picks up her cup, and slams the tiny white and blue and red circles down her throat.

Angel sidles up to the window. Her cup is heavy with pills. She upturns it over her mouth and chews.

"Why don't you just swallow them?" I ask.

"Makes them work faster," she says. "Plus, the Adderall tastes like Skittles."

They give me only one pill, a giant speckled one shaped like a bird's egg.

Angel's asked me a hundred times what it is. "It's not Ritalin. It's not Xanax. It might be Thorazine, but why'd they be giving you that?"

I never respond. I don't want her to know. The woman doctor who saw me when I was locked up only said it was very important I take it every day.

"Don't let anyone try to buy this pill from you," she said firmly.

She explained that my growth had been severely stunted, probably from malnutrition. She instructed me to eat everything that's put in front of me and take the high-dose multivitamin every morning, even though it rakes my throat on the way down.

We arrive back at the cell and I can tell the pills are starting to work because Angel's talking to me, her voice higher and faster than when she's unmedicated.

"I think it's time I educated you," Angel says.

"In what?"

"Prison life." She flops down opposite me on the floor. "First thing you gotta know, there's cliques here worse than on the outs. Girls stick together and the alliances mean something. The Mexicans are okay. If you ever got nail polish to trade, they'll be your best friend. Don't mess with the meth girls. Most of them had their brains turned mushy from it, still talk about finding more meth, like they can just buy it at the commissary. And when you remind them nicely that they're in jail, they scratch. Crazy bitches."

"Which one are you in?"

"Don't really got one. The lezzes can be all right. Mostly just stick to themselves, and sometimes I talk to the smart girls, the ones who always go to class and study and stuff. Really trying to make their lives better. But they can be so damn serious. I don't know. Ain't no one here really just to talk to."

"What about me?"

She shakes her head. "You're a trial run. I'm still feeling you out."

"Not like you could get rid of me if you decide you don't like me."

"I can. You be here as long as me, you start calling the shots."

"How long's your sentence?"

"Nunyo."

"What?"

"Nunyo business. That's personal."

"Ha, real personal," I snort.

"What's that sposta mean?"

"*Godseyes*, I can hear you pee at night," I say. "Not like we got much personal stuff, anyway."

"That's why I like to keep private what I can. Not all of us are little blab mouths like you."

"Have your secrets, then, Splashy," I say. "That's my nickname for you. Because of the pee."

Angel's eyes narrow and she looks like she's thinking about smiling, but the muscles in her face tighten just as quickly. "Couple things you should know," she continues. "You gotta lose the way you talk."

"What way?"

"Like you're in church all the time. You don't talk like the girls here. '*Godseyes!*'" she mocks. "You sound like they dug you out of a time capsule."

"But I don't know any swears."

"Jesus, I'll make you a list then."

She stands and rips a square of paper from a spiral notebook on her bed and scribbles out five or six words with a small pencil. She hands it to me.

"I can't read," I say.

"You can't even sound the letters out?"

"Only a little."

Her mouth shifts to the side. "Here." She places her finger next to each penciled word and pronounces it, then makes me repeat after her. My heart beats hard, and not only because I'm holding the Devil's words in my mouth. This is the first time anyone has taught me to read since Bertie.

"Get these ones down and you should be all right."

"Why are you helping me?" I ask.

"It saves me a headache later on. If you get in trouble, you'll look over at me with those pathetic eyes and expect me to help you. Well, it ain't happening."

She leans heavily against the wall again. "And second, if you don't understand what someone's saying to you, don't respond. Don't say a word. You'll get yourself trapped."

"Like what?"

"Like, if anyone ever holds up their hand like this," she makes a circle with her fingers, "that means they're asking if you're gay."

"What?"

"They're asking if you like girls. And if they wanna know if you have a friend on the outs named Britney, they're trying to claim you, 'cause a Britney's the name for someone's bitch, someone to have sex with. A Candy is a coward and a Tricia is someone with something to trade."

"Gawl," I say, my head teeming.

Angel scowls at me.

"I mean . . ." I clench my eyes, thinking. "Shit."

"Better."

"I guess I can't ever ask someone if they like girls," I say.

"Huh?"

"No fingers."

Angel squints.

"That was a joke," I say. "Don't you ever laugh? Even I laugh sometimes and I got a lot more reasons than you to be depressed. About..." I hold up my arms and look down to where my fingers had been. "...ten reasons."

Angel carries on, ignoring me. "You'll be deciding soon what gang to join," she says. "I 'spect you'll be with the Christian girls."

"I'm not Christian," I say.

"No, but you're leaning in that direction, I can tell. You got religion in your blood. Trust me, by next week you'll be quoting Job to me, telling me what Jesus said about this and that. I heard it all before."

"You were raised religious, right?"

She nods. "Everyone around me was. My uncle ... he was real religious."

I don't ask if this is the same uncle she's locked up for killing.

"What're the Christian girls like?"

"Like Tracy," she says. "You know, fake."

"Like how?"

"The dumb ones really think they mean it 'cause they're scared, and they think they can actually turn their lives around. But the smarter ones are only pretending 'cause they wanna look good in front of the parole board. That's all religion is. Strategy."

"How are you so sure?"

"I'm good at spotting liars. And that's all they are. They're just real good at lying to themselves," she says, her voice low. "Real good at it."

Chapter 16

I've been wondering if jail does anything it's supposed to. It's not true justice, not really. Philip's organs aren't knitting themselves together any faster because I'm locked in here, and it's not fixing me, either. It's punishment, and for now I probably need a little time sitting under the weight of everything I've done. I deserve to feel the blackening caverns of my heart pull inward every time I remember Philip's blood sketched across the fallen snow. To look my guilt about Jude and Constance straight in the eyes. To sink down in the pain and let myself feel exactly as bad as I should.

"You did nothing wrong," is what Angel says on the occasions I talk like this, but I know it wasn't natural or right what I did, and I question how it all could have happened. Not just for me, but everyone in the Community. How each of our hands went from farming and praying to hurting and killing.

It was never supposed to be like that. From the beginning, things were supposed to be better than they'd been.

Before we came to the Community, nobody could've mistaken us for saints. With my parents, there was always something unspoken and static-charged beneath the surface, but I was too preoccupied with childhood to notice. My days were simple and divided up into clear segments: the time of eating cereal, the time of watching my mother fold laundry, the time of my father arriving home. My mother would pull the zipper on his yellow jumpsuit, and he'd step out of it like a discarded shell, his undershirt salty with drying sweat.

The world was small where we lived, on a dirt lot that all the trailers on our street backed crookedly on to, where the neighborhood children ran on chubby legs in raggedy, stained clothes and diapers that dragged on the ground. We'd congregate at the rusty swing set and dented slide that sounded like sheet metal shaking every time someone went down. The lot wasn't much to look at, covered with trampled brown snow in the winter, and in the summer a weed clawing out of the earth every few feet. The only spectacular things in that place were the view of the mountains, so big they could stun you every day with your own smallness, and an apple tree that grew from the very center.

The day my father brought the Prophet home for the first time, the leaves of the apple tree shone almost silver in the sunlight, and the apples were unripened green buds the size of my fist.

I stretched my hand high in the air, trying to reach the lowest hanging apple, just to see if I could.

A hand darted out and wrenched the apple from the branch. The stem was green and unbreakable still. The hand had to pull so hard that, when the apple came free, the tree shook its boughs like arms waving in anger.

Above me hung the face of a man with pebbled eyes, peering through a pair of thick, yellowed glasses, a heavy beard patched over his cheeks. He looked normal, like any of the paunchy dads in the neighborhood who drove beat-up trucks and tuned their TVs too loud.

"Here you go," he said, holding the apple by the stem.

I reached for it and he placed it on my palm. My fingers closed around it.

"Aren't you going to eat it?" he asked.

"It's not ripe. They don't taste good yet."

He plucked the apple from my hand, stuffing it into his mouth whole. He watched me as he chewed and swallowed.

The screen door opened with a screech. My father was standing on the back porch. He said something odd then. He told me this man was holy beyond understanding. That I was to do whatever he asked. That I was to believe everything he said.

Because he spoke to God.

Chapter 17

I walk down to lunch with Angel and Rashida. It's become easier since I discovered that, even without Angel around, the girls don't mess with me. In fact, they avoid me. It's my shoes.

They gave me Velcro shoes because of my hands, but Angel told me most of the girls who wear them aren't allowed real shoes. She says they're the ones who will kill you if you look at them wrong. The ones who can't be given shoelaces for fear they'd hang themselves or strangle someone else.

"Why do you never eat the chicken nuggets, Rashida?" Angel asks. I've been staring down into my watery red trough of tomato soup. I glance over at Rashida's tray which contains only mounds of coleslaw and fruit cocktail.

"Why do you care, Angel?" Rashida asks.

"'Cause you eat more'n anybody here, and everyone knows the chicken nuggets is the closest thing to appetizing we got."

Rashida's smile drops a couple notches. "I been in the prison when they electrocuted somebody. Visiting my uncle in Deer Lodge. After they cooked the guy, you could smell it in the whole place, and it smelled just like it does here on chicken nugget day."

Angel's face is serious for a moment then splits open in a laugh. "You're lying. You've never been to Deer Lodge in your life."

"I have too! And I could smell the guy's brains being cooked inside his skull, bitch."

"I think your brains got cooked a long time ago, Rashida."

"I'll have you know I'm passing all my classes," she says. "Miss Bailey says I have a unique intelligence that can't be defined by normal standards."

"You're abnormal, she means," Angel says.

"Who's Miss Bailey?" I ask.

"My reading teacher," Rashida says. I nod. I've seen the guards watch me sidelong, trying to decide if I'm ready for school. During the day, there's not much to do except stare out the bars. Angel's brought me a couple of comic books from the library, and I make my way through those pretty quickly, even if I don't know half the words. Sometimes, from her cell next to mine, Rashida describes what the weather was like outside the classroom window that day, and I can usually persuade Benny to tell me about the book she's reading, always some time and place I've never heard of, but mostly I'm alone with my thoughts and my rememberings.

The closest I've gotten to school, besides those weeks with Bertie, were the mild, green-smelling days in the Community when the Prophet taught the children beside the pond. He read aloud from the Book of Prophecies, tales of sage believers garbed in golden feathers fighting the hell demons of the Gentiles with swords made only of God's light.

One afternoon, when I was eight or nine, the Prophet called the children for a lesson. Constance walked, hand in mine, in that jerky way of almost-babies, and we arranged ourselves around the pond. In the distance, men thunked axes into wood, and nearby my mother breathed through her nose as she stared into the murky surface of the pond. She couldn't do much else, so she was put in charge of the children while the Prophet gave his lessons.

From his billowing cloak, the Prophet extracted the Book of Prophecies.

"'Do not stray into the land of the Gentiles, for they humiliate God with their arts that pay Him no homage, with dances that contort the body in evil motions that defile purity, with the wicked writings that question Him and criticize Him and say He doesn't exist and never has.'"

I had heard this passage a thousand times. It formed the rule book for our behavior—the Gentiles do these things, so we do not.

"Why can't we write, Prophet?" I interrupted.

He let the book fall a few inches as his sharp eyes took me in. "Because it is an abomination in the eyes of God."

"You write," I noted.

"The only people who need to write are those who record God's deeds."

"Then why can't we read? So we can know the deeds of God."

"If you could read, you would be able to read the wicked writings, too, and God does not approve the risk. You have a Prophet to read to you, and that is just as good as reading for yourself."

"Why can't we do painting?" I asked. "Surely that can't be an abomination to God."

He crossed his arms. A darkness darted across his face, a storm growing in his gray-shot eyes. "I'm not sure I can explain it in a way you will understand. You are merely a girl child."

"I'll try to understand, Prophet," I replied.

Maybe he knew that the question wouldn't die without

an answer. His eyes roamed upward. "Do you know what the sky is?"

He raised his hand as though to touch the clear blue expanse above. "It is a great piece of canvas stretched all the way across the world. And on it, God paints. We do not paint because there is no need. The greatest painting of all already exists."

"The sky is a canvas?" I asked, turning my eyes to the bright blue that, to me, appeared endless. It looked like a clear pond that went on forever.

The Prophet nodded, his hand shadowed darkly against the brilliant blue. "God made the sky for us to know Him. When it's sunny, can't you feel His joy beaming down? When it storms, you can't mistake His anger. And rain— what do you think rain is?"

"Tears," I said, catching on. "But what about at night? What does the darkness mean?"

"It means He's sleeping. It means His eyes are closed."

"But what about lightning and—"

"God's bad dreams," he cut in, already one step ahead. "Now, does that answer your questions, Minnow?"

I chewed on my lip and nodded.

I barely heard the rest of the lesson because, over my head, the universe was receding, the world growing smaller and smaller, and the Prophet growing larger and larger.

Somewhere, far off, I sensed a sound like pressure rising in the air, the feeling that a hinge was squeaking. The next time I looked, the sky didn't seem so endless anymore.

I shot a glance at my mother. She didn't appear to even see us, the way she swirled her toes in the water.

"But what are the stars?" I demanded too loudly.

The Prophet turned to me, his lower lip twisted. "Why do you want to know, Sister Minnow?" he asked pointedly. Constance, her body a warm presence at my side, grew tense. "Your questions could lead one to believe that you are doubting God. There are consequences for disbelief."

My heart began to thump loudly. "I just . . . just want to know . . . about the world He created."

He considered this. "The stars . . . they are a way for God to see us even when He is asleep. They are His eyes. And when you see the stars flickering, that's how you know He is watching you."

My heart squirmed in my chest, my hands pink and tightly fisted in my lap. Whenever I pictured God, I didn't imagine an omnipotent force that could observe us from on high. I imagined a boy my age, going to school, living in the world. A boy named Charlie.

"But—" I sputtered, "but how are His eyes up in the sky if He's really Charlie? I thought He was walking the earth right now."

"Do you think God can't do two things at once?" the Prophet asked, his voice rising so my mother's head finally flicked up. "God can do anything. God can watch every person alive at the same time, and even the dead, and He can walk the earth, because He is God, and He is almighty."

Suddenly, he snatched Constance up from where she sat beside me. He propped her up on her tiny legs facing me, her expression bundled up in fear. "I said there are consequences for disbelief, Minnow," the Prophet said, shaking Constance by the shoulders. "But consequences sometimes have a way of missing their target."

He shook Constance again, a whimper escaping her mouth. "If you ever have a question, Minnow, the answer is always God. Anything you wonder about the earth or the sky, the answer is always God. *Always God*," he repeated. "If you doubt, the cure is God. And if you continue to doubt, the fault is yours, not His."

A heat had crept into my face. I nodded because I knew enough to do that. He turned Constance's body toward him, smiled broadly, and let her slump back down near me. I could feel her body shaking.

"Remember, God created you and that means you owe Him a life. *Yours*," the Prophet pronounced firmly. "You will be in debt to God for the rest of your days."

Chapter 18

Valentine's Day just passed. We never celebrated in the Community, but I remembered what it was supposed to look like. Some girls got cards in the mail and some smuggled little candies inside and passed them around beneath the cafeteria tables, and the guards pretended not to notice the wadded-up red foils littering the floor. A few boyfriends visited and passed over fistfuls of carnations wrapped in wet paper towels and, even if they weren't allowed to touch, the girls looked buoyed for days afterward. They wore the flowers in their buttonholes till they turned brown.

In the Community, holidays frightened me. The one I liked least—Saint Jared's Day, which celebrated the killing of the last giant in America—called itself a festival. It was always in winter, with a bitter wind that flung the eerie chanting of our voices up into the frozen air. "Killed the giant, yes indeed. Cut his throat, oh yes indeed. Fell to Earth, oh yes it did. Died in agony, oh yes it did." My feet frozen as a glacier, I carried an icicle in my open palm while the little children made to stab the air like they were killing monsters. My stomach fumbled watching them. It was always entirely too easy for us to imagine killing.

• • •

"Do those things hurt you?" Angel asks around a mouthful of corn muffin.

She's staring at my stumps, lying next to my tray of watery soup and shrunken bread. "Not as much as they used to. Why?"

"Because you got a look on your face," she says. "Sorta pained."

"It's just . . ." I stretch my toes out the side of the cafeteria table. "My bones hurt. My leg bones. They feel like they're being stretched."

"You're growing," she says. "You're not the first girl to put on a few pounds in juvie. Most of us aren't used to three square meals."

I've already grown out of my first jumpsuit. The new one is roomier and has a zipper down the front with a cord that I can grab with my teeth. Going to the bathroom takes less time now that I don't need to ask Angel or a guard to fumble buttons back into holes.

"That's the problem with this whole thing," Angel says,

waving her arm. "They want you to be contrite for getting thrown in here, but this place makes a fuck ton more sense than the outside, if you really think about it."

"Like how?" I ask.

"Like," Angel searches. "Like this." She lifts something yellow from her tray.

"Is that a banana?" I say. "I haven't seen one of these in years."

"Outside, everything gets so distorted. In here, a banana's just something they give you because the government says we inmates gotta eat less junk. But, you know what the pastor at my uncle's church used to say about bananas? They prove the existence of God."

"How?"

"He said they must've been designed by a creator because they're easy to open and are shaped perfectly for the human hand. But you know what else is shaped perfectly for the human hand? A dick, but don't try telling them that means God intended people to masturbate because that will get you kicked out of Sunday school. I can vouch from experience."

A shadow crosses our table. Officer Prosser surveys us, her face beet-colored at the cheeks, tiny orange hairs escaping the knot of her bun.

In her hand, she holds small squares of paper.

"Notices," she says simply. She flicks one at Angel who catches it in the air. With a serious look, she lets a notice fall to the plastic tray in front of me.

"What's it say?" I ask Angel.

"It's your notice of rec time. The better you act, the more you get."

"What do we get to do?"

"Hardly nothing. The options are lame. You can choose from exercise time in the yard, the library, the TV room, or the visitors' lounge if anyone comes to visit you, fat chance of that happening. Oh, and youth group."

"Where do you go?" I ask.

"Library most days, but I've read all those books practically. They have to bring books in for me from the county library, but my newest ones aren't here yet. So today, I guess it'll have to be the TV room."

When the bell rings, we walk together to a small concrete-walled room with stains on the carpet and a television sitting on a low wooden stand covered in peeling wood-printed plastic. The couch in front of the TV is already full of girls, but they scoot off when Angel comes in. "You know," I say, sitting beside her, "everyone here is so scared of you. But you don't seem that tough to me. Bet you're all talk."

She snorts. "You're funny."

Angel takes the TV remote and presses some numbers until the picture changes. In the center of the screen, a blue ball hangs suspended on an ink-black background. The black is impossibly black, and the ball is laced with wisps of white.

"What's that?" I ask.

Angel turns to look at me, her forehead bunched up. "Earth."

"Our world?" I shake my head. "It looks like that? How'd they get a picture of it?"

"A spaceship or satellite or something."

The camera zooms in to the surface and I shut my eyes. When I open them, the camera is beneath the ocean, a dark wilderness of shadows and pockets of blue light. It is vast, much vaster than I ever imagined. My brain is stunned watching it, taking in all the endless blue.

"All right, Angel. Enough science shit." Rashida snatches the remote from Angel's hand. "I'm switching it to my show."

"Don't even try, Rashida," Angel says lazily.

Rashida stands with her fists on her hips. "You ain't gonna beat me up, Angel. You like me too much."

"Oh, really?"

"Yeah, really," Rashida says. "I see you admiring my fine body day after day." She does a quick twirl and slaps her butt. "Too bad I got a boy on the outs. Else, you and me'd make a cute couple."

Angel cocks her head. "Please, Rashida, you look like a bunch of chopsticks got tied together with a rubber band."

Rashida gasps, her hand flying to her hair, tied back into a puffy bun. "Angel, someday you gonna come asking for me and I'm gonna say, 'Bitch, I don't think so, you had your chance.'"

Angel laughs.

Rashida falls heavily into one of the ragged, duct-taped armchairs and punches a number into the remote. The image of the ocean is replaced by a picture of tanned girls shouting at each other.

"Give that back," Angel says, tackling Rashida in the armchair and grappling for the remote.

The screen starts flicking through channels and the pictures fire past so quickly, my brain can barely keep up. An advertisement with a car driving through a forest. And an impossibly perfect-looking family eating dinner. A woman in a doctor's coat talking to the camera. And—a man with a graying beard in a khaki prison jumpsuit.

"Stop!" I shout.

Rashida and Angel freeze where they've been shouldering for the remote and look at me sideways. It's the loudest I've spoken since I got here. Most of these girls haven't heard me say a single word.

"Go back."

Rashida clicks back a few channels. "There," I say.

My father's face peers up from the screen. I slide off of the couch and sit on my knees, so close to the television I can see the tiny squares that make up the screen. My father shuffles slowly into a courtroom, his hands and ankles fastened to a chain around his waist. His beard has grown. Photographers and news people line the back of the courtroom, flashbulbs firing every few seconds.

"Samuel Bly will be the first of the leaders of the Kevinian cult to stand trial," a woman's voice narrates. "The DA is assembling a case against him that includes charges of statutory rape, accessory to statutory rape, endangering a minor, assault, and manslaughter. Bly was reportedly second in command to church leader Kevin Bilson, a self-described prophet who led the group into the woods twelve years ago."

The image changes to a picture of the Community, perfectly preserved in a layer of snow and encircled in yellow police tape bright enough to shock the senses. The snow is so unbroken and white, it hardly seems anything unusual happened there, until strange shapes begin to reveal themselves beneath the snow. A large triangle betrays what was once a roof and, just as suddenly, the shapes of fallen-down houses start to materialize, a dozen of them, in a ring.

At the corner of the shot hangs a noose, drifting lazily in the wind. My throat closes at the sight of it.

"Bly is one of twelve men charged in connection with the events that took place in this clearing, where a religious group existed in total isolation and self-sufficiency for more than a decade. The world only came to know of the cult when a fire started here two months ago, killing the group's leader. The group's total population is estimated at over one hundred. The remaining women and children are being housed in undisclosed locations."

The image switches to a slick-lipped woman talking too fast about an upcoming snowstorm. I stay kneeling in front of the TV, my head falling forward on my shoulders.

"You all right?" comes a voice behind me.

I turn and see a girl I vaguely recognize standing with a hand on her hip. She's tall and big-chested with thin eyebrows. I don't know much about her, but she wears Velcro shoes.

"Fine," I say, standing.

"Your name Britney?"

My eyes pinch in confusion. "My name's Minnow."

She laughs like I just made a joke. "My name's Krystal," she says, placing a hand on my breastbone so I can't turn. "I think you and I should get to know each other."

I glance away. Angel's eyes stare firmly at the TV screen. Rashida sits cross-legged on the duct-taped chair, her bottom lip between her teeth and a wrinkle between her eyes. Nobody in the room moves.

"You got real pretty hair," Krystal says. She pulls a lock of my long, crooked hair out of the wild mop that cascades down my back. I shiver at the feeling of her fingers. In the Community, our hair hid inside bonnets and braids, never touched by anyone.

Slowly, she slides her hand across my chest until it reaches my arm. She squeezes.

"Don't touch me," I say, the words coming out mild and strange. Krystal's smile stretches even broader.

I'm shuddering. This girl could be the Prophet. The fingers gripping my arm could be his rough and wire-haired fingers. The feeling in my chest is the same wasted, powerless feeling he always put inside me. I can't break free, and I'm about to start dragging frantic breaths into my lungs when the girl's head snaps back. I stumble backward, free of her grip.

Angel's fist hangs in the air.

Krystal has miraculously managed to stay on her

feet, but her cheek is crimson where Angel's fist connected.

"Krystal, we've missed you in gen pop," Angel says. "What a shame your latest attempt to off yourself was unsuccessful. Next time I suggest drinking the *whole* bottle of bleach."

Krystal chuckles darkly. "I like your new toy, Angel," she says, raking her eyes over me. "I didn't think pink-bellied newbies were your type. I thought you went for older men."

Angel slugs Krystal in the stomach before she can react. When Krystal is doubled over, Angel forces her to the floor, her knee pressing hard into her gut. One hand leans against Krystal's forehead and the other is suspended in the air, ready to strike.

Angel's next words come in a muttered breath. "You don't get to hurt people," she says. "Not here."

Krystal twists her head to the side and screams, but is silenced when Angel lands one punch into her temple, then another, then too many to count. The room is quiet but for Krystal's grunts. I glance around the room for a moment and everyone's faces are still. Krystal's arms flail against Angel's face, but Angel doesn't slow. Her jaw is set but otherwise her face is relaxed.

For a moment, I can imagine her killing her uncle, strangling him or stabbing him or shooting him with that look painted on her face, and it doesn't seem so impossible anymore.

Finally, Angel stands, shaking out her wrist. Krystal is still on the floor, dazed, the side of her face blown up and purple.

Angel walks to the window in the metal door and knocks twice. Benny's large face fills the meshed glass. At the sight of Angel, she opens the door.

Benny looks over to Krystal, who's moaning on the carpet.

"She tripped," says Angel.

Benny nods and grips Krystal by the armpits. "Get up, Krystal."

Krystal shakily rises to her feet, darting an evil look at Angel with quickly swelling eyes. She and Benny shuffle out of the TV room as Angel falls back down onto the couch.

"Now, I'm changing it back to the science channel," she says. "Anybody going to disagree?" The remaining girls exchange big-eyed, terrified looks.

Angel laughs.

Chapter 19

I don't hear anyone talking about what Angel did to Krystal, but by dinner, it's clear that everyone knows. They always avoided her; now they retract into themselves when she comes near, make themselves unnoticeable, turning their eyes to study the floor.

I wonder, at the back of my mind, how they would react if they knew what I did to Philip. A little pang jabs just beneath the breast pocket of my jumpsuit, somewhere near my heart, like it does whenever I think about that night beneath the bridge.

"I can tell you're dying to ask something," Angel says after we get our dinner. "Just get it out. I can't stand looking at your face all folded up in concentration like that."

I turn my head to the side. "Why does everybody do what you say?"

"You're really asking that?"

"I mean the guards and everything."

She shrugs. "I practically run this place. Been here longer than anybody. I've seen three wardens, a couple dozen guards, hundreds of girls come and gone, and here I am, rock steady through it all."

Angel's bashed-up fingers rest on the table, the hard skin on her knuckles split open like grapes.

"What about Benny?" I ask.

"I got here when I was twelve. Benny was the first person I met. If anybody raised me, you could make a pretty good case for Benny."

• • •

Dr. Wilson visits the next day after breakfast. Immediately, he eyes the new additions to my cell: two stuffed animals and a paper crane. I have recently been inducted into the complex trading system in juvie. Angel gave me a pack of gum Benny gave her for helping clean up puke in the cafeteria, and at lunch I traded the gum with a red-headed girl with a neck tattoo for a powder-blue stuffed bear. Later, I got a red turtle whose stomach had been removed to smuggle something inside, and an elaborate origami crane an albino girl hands out to everyone as part of her counseling.

"I love what you've done with the place," he says.

"Decorated it myself."

"And might I compliment you on your choice of stainless steel." He nods toward the toilet. "Timeless yet functional."

I almost laugh but in the next moment he's opening up my file and scanning his notes.

"I heard the guards talking about your roommate. Said she got into a fight."

"She was defending me," I say.

He nods. "You should be careful with lifers like Angel. They have less to lose."

"Lifers?" I ask.

"Angel's here on murder charges, and she's not getting out anytime soon. Inmates with longer sentences sometimes like to groom other girls. Get them to do things for them on the outside."

"She's not like that."

"Maybe not. Just be careful. You're out of the Community, and that's a good thing. That's the best thing, but it doesn't mean there aren't people here who'd take advantage of you."

"No," I mutter, and I feel my brain tip sideways. His words smack me as something obvious, something basic that I should've come to on my own. Since I've learned all the wrong the Community held, I'd begun to think of the cities as peace-realms, places I might really be safe.

It's not true. No place is ever safe.

"When do you want to talk about what happened with Philip?" Dr. Wilson asks.

I look up quickly. "How about never?"

"You'll have to at some point. He's part of this, too."

I shake my head. "I don't want to talk about him ever again. Ask another question."

"All right," he says, leaning back. "Tell me about losing your hands."

"That?" I shrug. "I barely remember it."

He lifts his eyebrows.

"Fine," I say. "But I want to tell it my way."

"Of course."

"No interrupting," I warn.

"I'll do my best."

• • •

When I woke up that morning, my bedroom was humid with the breath of my ten sisters. The plastic sheeting stapled over our only window was beaded with moisture.

I smelled the smoke before I opened my eyes. Everyone knew what it meant when the purple smoke unfurled from the Prophet's chimney and smudged the sky. It meant that, at that moment, the Prophet was in his house, talking with God, hearing the whisper of it inside his ears, and writing everything down into the Book of Prophecies.

Everyone was a little on edge, waiting for the prophecy. We tried to go about our daily chores—the women milking, the men carving new tools out of fallen pines—

but it was difficult with the smell of that smoke filling our nostrils. Prophecies could be meaningless—"And lo it is Commanded that thee plant wild onion in ampler supply." But prophecies could also change everything. It was a prophecy that brought us to the wild. It was a prophecy that named each deacon, and it was prophecies that punished us.

In the courtyard, I did laundry with my younger sisters Martha and Regent, both raven-haired like their mother Vivienne, until the Prophet rang the little silver bell on his porch that meant he was ready to speak the message that God had told him. He waited for us to congregate, his long black robes shaking in the cold breeze, arms stretched in the air.

"God has sent me a message," he called. "I am to take another wife."

The crowd exhaled. The Prophet had received this message many times since we moved to the Community. He already had eight wives. They were huddled close to the porch railing, looking lost. No children jostled into their calves like the other women. None of them, not a single one, had managed to bring a baby to term. They'd produced some crooked little skeletal things that might've been babies in some daydream of God's, but that's all.

"And the woman who will be my new wife," the Prophet

continued, "who will serve God through me, who will bear beautiful children of light, is our own dear Minnow." A smile bloomed under his big, gray beard.

I didn't understand at first. I was too conscious of other things, like my hands chapped from scrubbing clothes on a washboard, the purple smoke burying into my sinuses, and the image of Jude's face that I couldn't shake out of my eyes no matter how hard I tried.

The Prophet approached me.

"What do you say to this, Minnow?" he asked. "Do you not rejoice?"

"No," I said, my voice traveling.

He placed his hand on my shoulder, his thumb tracing the strap of my undergarments.

"Does it not please you, Minnow, to know you will be servant to God's chosen messenger? That you will bear the children of God's chosen messenger?"

I searched the crowd but no one would catch my eye. No one but my mother. She stood at the other end of the courtyard. From beneath her bonnet, I could see a strand of the simple blond hair I didn't inherit and the dead eyes I'd grown used to, not registering any of the unfolding events. Silent, impassive.

"I don't want to marry you," I whispered.

The Prophet smiled as though I'd made a joke. And it

was a joke. There was no choice. I'd be forced to marry him whether I wanted to or not.

"I am sure you will feel differently when your belly is round with a child of God."

I breathed a sharp breath and, without thinking, slapped him hard across his bearded cheek. Everyone gasped, including me. I held my hands together over my open mouth and took a quick step back.

His fingers found his reddening face. I could practically see the plans forming inside his head, the tortures, the punishments marching into formation like soldiers, hot pokers and stocks and cleverly tied rope.

He took one step toward me, then another, until all he had to do was lean forward to place his lips near my ear.

"You *will* be my wife," he whispered.

He straightened and looked for my father. "Take her to the maidenhood room where she shall be sequestered until our wedding day, praise God."

Chapter 20

Dr. Wilson holds his hands on either side of his face. He hasn't written any of this down, just listened. It occurs to me that he may have heard this story before.

"What did your father do?" he asks.

"I told you not to interrupt."

He dips his head. "Sorry."

I exhale and stare at the black paint peeling away from the frame of my bunk. "What do you think he did? He followed the Prophet's orders."

"Yes, but how did he appear?"

"Just . . . the same as always. Like he'd had his insides ripped out and the Prophet's hand thrust up in his body cavity, like a puppet."

"Stunning visual," he says. "How do you feel about your father now?"

"I hate him," I say without pausing.

His head tips to the side.

"What?" I demand. "You think I shouldn't?"

"No," he says. "I think you should be angry if you're angry. But it's also true that hate has a way of hurting you more than the person you're hating."

He pulls a pad of Post-its from his bag and writes something down. He reaches over and sticks it to the wall behind my bunk.

"What are you doing?" I ask.

"Starting your affirmation wall."

I stare at the letters on the Post-it. I can make out a general sense of words, but can't understand the entire sentence. "What's it say?"

"Anger is a kind of murder you commit in your heart."

If this is true, I'm a daily murderer. My heart is more full of blood than I ever imagined.

"Have you talked to your father since the fire?" he asks.

I shake my head. "I saw him on the news at his trial."

"He will almost certainly be convicted on all charges. He'll be in prison for a long time."

"Is that supposed to mean something to me? I don't care what happens to him."

"I don't blame you. He'd be a difficult person to have as a father. I interviewed him a couple of weeks ago."

I blink.

"Did he say anything interesting?" I ask. "A revelation that the Lord is reborn in a chicken nugget, maybe?"

He smiles. "He mostly wanted to quote the Book of Prophecies at me. I got a lesson in the rather interesting Kevinian theory of astronomy, and he showed me dozens of journals filled with scrawl he says was written by the angel Zachari. He thinks his prison food is poisoned. And two days ago he was thrown out the courtroom for disruption."

"What'd he do?"

"While the judge was reading the charges, he started shouting in tongues and writhing on the floor."

"What an act."

"It won't help his case."

I want to ask, Can you get the death penalty for killing because you're told to? How does the legal system prosecute someone under the influence of faith, someone who kills because God wants a little death sometimes?

"He did say one thing I found interesting," Dr. Wilson says. "He had a message for you."

"I don't want to hear it."

"Are you sure? It might help."

I shake my head, my face contorting as though it doesn't know whether to laugh or burst into tears. There is nothing, I am confident, nothing my father could say to fix anything.

"Go on then," I say.

"He asked me to tell you how sorry he is. How terribly sorry. For everything that happened."

I freeze where I'm sitting, like the moment after a bone is broken when you know the pain is coming but you foolishly hope it won't. And the full force of the words slams into me. My head begins to shake back and forth, my hair whipping the orange canvas of my jumpsuit. I want so badly to scrub my fingers against my face, to take great fistfuls of my hair and pull until I have a real reason to scream.

This is what thinking about my father does. Into my head comes the picture of him swinging the hatchet, the picture of the Prophet's dry lips speaking into his ear. But there's also the memory of those aluminum benches at the greyhound park, him smiling, leaning forward so his belly thrust out, eyes following the dog wearing the bib labeled lucky number seven. And how he'd rise up off the stands when the dogs neared the finish, dirt flying beneath paws, and my father's fingers clenched in fists that weren't for punching but for thrusting into the air when he won.

More often, he lost. I guess that's what it comes down to.

I never knew my father like I knew my mother, hadn't memorized the curve of his hip with my body, but he meant something to me, down deep. Before the Community, when he railed about his boss, and his face turned florid against his black mustache, I'd sit in my place in the plushest part of the carpet and feel my small world teeter. His voice could do that.

And then my father stopped gambling and started attending rallies with other men from work. Just drinking with the boys, he called it, though he'd stopped drinking by then. And shaving. He came home with new ideas and the word "Prophet" on his tongue. And soon it was like my father had stepped into a new identity. He wasn't Sam anymore. He was Deacon Samuel, suddenly sober, suddenly bearded, suddenly righteous.

My mother became pregnant with Constance, and the house grew quiet with my father's praying and my mother's sitting in silent rooms not moving. I thought she was praying, too, but now I wonder if it was something else. The Prophet told us soon after that we were to take the bus to a rest stop, walk into the trees and never return.

By the time we got to the Community, my mother was round and immovable. While the men raged against the trees and the earth, the wives gathered in a circle in front of the A-frame structures of the first versions of our houses to sew simple baby garments for her.

One of the wives handed me a tiny muslin dress to

bring to my mother where she sat on a felled log. I held it to her ballooned stomach. "My baby," I said.

"No, Minnow, your sister," my mother corrected in a voice like a croak.

"My baby," I said again. Nothing belonged to me, not really. My mother belonged to my father and my father belonged to the Prophet. This baby, I knew, was supposed to be mine. She was the closest thing to mine I'd ever had.

The day she was born, her hot body made steam in the frigid morning air. My mother passed out on the dirt floor of the new-hewn house so I was the first to hold her, all scum-covered and wailing with her flat livid gums, tongue waving like an angry fist. Holding her felt like cradling a part of myself, my liver or kidney, outside my body.

When my father ran outside to shout, "Another saint is delivered to the righteous establishment of the Lord," I held Constance tighter. I decided, right then, that I would protect her like the vulnerable, screaming thing she was.

Chapter 21

The next day, after showering and stuffing myself, half damp, back inside my jumpsuit, I sit on my bed and try to pick through my hair with a large yellow comb held between my stumps. Benny offered again to cut it for me. Easier to manage, she says, and I know she's thinking a handless girl ought to have priorities above vanity. But it's more than that, something muddied that I can't sift out. Jude never knew me without hair like this.

"Bly!" Officer Prosser calls from the skyway. She's holding a thin piece of paper. I throw down the comb and catch the paper as she drops it inside the cell.

I turn to Angel. "Can you read it?"

"It's a class schedule," she says. "Looks like they're finally making you go to school."

I'm only signed up for one class, which meets on Mondays, Tuesdays, and Fridays. It's called Reading Is Power. I didn't know classes could have names like that, in complete sentences, but all the classes here do, things like "Cooking Is Cool" and "Math Is Fun." Angel told me about a group therapy session she'd had once called "Coping Mechanisms Are for Rock Stars!"

After breakfast, I walk in line toward the bay of old classrooms in the west wing of the detention center, the only area of the repurposed school that's actually used for its original purpose. A youngish teacher in a violet cardigan stands at the doorway of the classroom. She shakes the hand of each student and looks them in the eyes, pronouncing their names easily. When she sees me, she puts her hand behind her back.

"Minnow?" she asks. "I'm Miss Bailey."

"How do you know my name?"

She nods. "Your file showed up in my mailbox today."

"You've read my file?"

She shakes her head. "I choose not to read students' files."

"Why?"

"I find it helps with the idea that detention is the start of a new life, not the continuation of an old one."

"But wouldn't you rather know if you're teaching someone who's killed before? Who might knife you in the back?" I ask.

"You aren't your crime. I don't look at the files because I refuse to treat you like you are." She clasps her hands together. "You'll be at computer number one today. Everyone takes a reading assessment when they arrive. For goal-setting."

She gestures to the back of the room. I walk to a gray cube of a computer with a piece of masking tape on top labeling it #1. From the back of the room, I observe my ten classmates, all around my age, dressed in the same bright jumpsuits. I spot Rashida sitting on an overturned orange bucket in a half circle around Miss Bailey's rocking chair. "Where did we leave off?" Miss Bailey asks, opening a blue book.

"Bud was going to the library," a girl with freckles says.

Miss Bailey nods and begins reading. My eyes move to the gray screen in front of me. A passage from a text perches at the top of the screen above four possible answers and their corresponding bubbles. I recognize the letters, but they are assembled in words and sentences that mean nothing. I blink, the strange light from the computer making my eyes blurry.

I turn toward the window. Cellophane hearts in purple and pink are stuck to the windows with tape, rippled from sunlight and dust-covered. The classroom windows face a residential street, the first view I've gotten of the outside. Beyond the window, there's a slash of short brown suburban homes, snow-covered lawns, and a twenty-foot fence fringed with double loops of barbed wire—the only thing separating *us* from *them*.

I raise my arm in the air. Miss Bailey looks up from the book.

"Okay, ladies. Stop and jot down what you think the Amoses' motivation was for adopting Bud."

"They wanted the money," shouts Rashida.

"Write it down for me," Miss Bailey says. Rashida makes a clumsy fist around her pencil and begins eagerly printing block letters into her notebook that even I can see from the back of the room.

Miss Bailey approaches the computer.

"Yes?" she asks.

"I don't know what to do," I say.

"You click the answer you think is correct."

"Click?"

"With the mouse."

I shake my head.

"Here," she says, crouching down beside me so her knees pin her calico skirt to the ground. "You tell me the answer you want and I'll click it for you. The question is 'Which word best describes the tone of Mercutio's speech?' What do you think the answer is—a, b, c, or d?"

I stare at the text and look back at her, a prickling heat creeping into my cheeks. "I don't know."

"Have you read the passage?"

"No."

"But you've been sitting here for ten minutes."

"I don't know how," I say.

"To read?"

I shake my head.

Her hands fall to her lap. "Well, you've come to the right place. This classroom is full of emergent readers. Why don't you join us in the lesson space and listen to the story. And later we'll get you started on some phonics exercises."

I sit with the other girls and Miss Bailey continues reading. It reminds me of the days beside the pond with Bertie, the stories she'd bring alive with just her voice. I listen to the story and I don't do any remembering for a long time afterward.

Chapter 22

The next day, during the strange lull that happens after classes and between lunch when everyone sits in their cells and keeps house the way they know how—organizing the photos tacked to their walls, chatting through the bars of cells like neighbors—a sudden cheer goes up farther down the cell block. Angel throws down her book and presses her face to the bars.

"Oh, no," she says. "Not again."

"What?" I ask, standing. Just then, Rashida and Tracy approach our cell, each carrying a battered cardboard box. Tracy looks away from our cell, absently touching the tiny metal cross hanging from a length of dental floss at her neck.

"What do you want?" Angel asks. "I didn't think door-to-door evangelism was allowed in jail."

"We're here on official business," Rashida says, smiling so that I can see all of her teeth which today are stained an otherworldly blue. She reaches into the cardboard box and pulls out two long cylinders, one vivid green and the other purple. "Mrs. New chose us to distribute popsicles that the food bank donated."

"How'd you two get chosen?" Angel asks.

"Tidiest cell," Tracy says, twitching her thick bangs from her eyes. "Something you'd obviously never win." She glances at the balls of wadded-up notebook paper along Angel's bed, sloppy worksheets pushing out of her binder.

"I wouldn't take it anyway," Angel says. "I'm immune to Mrs. New's bribes. Minnow can have my popsicle."

Rashida passes them through the bars and I cradle the plastic coated frozen things against my chest. Tracy and Rashida walk down the skyway, finishing their popsicle rounds.

"This should be illegal," Angel says, arms crossed, surveying the jail.

"Why?" I ask, tearing open the top of one popsicle with my teeth.

"Every springtime this happens," she says. "It's either popsicles, or a makeshift water park in the yard, or picnics in the cafeteria."

"Sounds fun," I say, and when Angel darts me an incredulous look, ask, "Why springtime?"

"It's statistically proven that prison riots occur more often when the weather gets warmer. The pills, the bars, and the bribes. Their proven cocktail for keeping us numbed and behaving. Bet you I can get one of the guards to cop to seeing Mrs. New bring those things in, not some food bank people."

"Is it really springtime?" I ask.

Angel looks at me. "I think you're missing the point."

"I loved springtime," I say, lying down on my bunk and chewing on the end of the lime-flavored frozen stick. "We got to change out of our blue dresses for gray ones. I could always trick myself into thinking things would be different this year."

Angel climbs back up to her bunk, mumbling about my brain being turned like bad roast beef.

At this time of year in the mountains, there would still be snow on the ground, but there'd be a smell in the air of the world beginning to experiment with spring. I'd be marching through the snow-clogged forest to meet Jude and would be struck by the green scent of wild onion or fiddleheads. Out there, you could smell it even with three feet of snow on the ground, like the plants were asking us to wait for them—they were still there, just buried deep, just smaller than the best versions of themselves. In jail, I don't smell anything but cleaning products and cafeteria food, but the missing Jude washes over me anyway, and I have to bite down hard to stop the tears. It's like Angel said. The remembering never stops.

There was a time before Jude and I loved each other. A time when we were just figuring out what friendship looked like, each for the first time. It was about then that the tree house bloomed out of Jude's mind. It was our first spring together. We met by the larch tree most afternoons, and on days I couldn't slip away from the Community, Jude would write little notes and stick them to the bark with a tack. When I told him I couldn't read, he drew pictures instead.

He stopped the drawings the older we got. Instead, he only wrote two words, words that I learned to sight-read even in the pitch darkness: *Miss you.*

On one of those early days, he walked out of the woods and pulled from the pocket of his rough, homespun trousers a yellow oblong of cake, smashed against the cellophane wrapper.

"What is it?" I asked.

"A Twinkie," he said, a sparkle in his eyes.

"Where'd it come from?"

"Down there." He nodded in the general direction of civilization.

"You go there?" I asked. Nobody but the Prophet was allowed to leave the Community for basic provisions. Only he was pure enough to resist the Gentiles' temptations.

"My daddy goes sometimes in his truck to buy stuff," Jude replied. "Tools and supplies mostly. But sometimes food."

He thrust the Twinkie at me. The plastic wrapper made an uncomfortable squeak against my teeth as I tore it open. A blue jay appeared over Jude's left ear, but I couldn't say a word because the cake had just touched my tongue. My pupils must've dilated. My skin must've flushed. I don't think I'd ever tasted something so incredible. Something so not from the forest.

"You know what?" Jude asked.

"Huh?" I replied around a mouthful.

"We should have a regular meeting place. Like a clubhouse."

I swallowed. "What's a clubhouse?"

"It's like a place where you plan stuff and talk. Like from the *Little Rascals.*"

I shook my head, confused.

"They're a group of kids who play and have adventures."

"Where do they live?"

"Well, they don't live anywhere. They're stories from down there. You know, from TV."

"You got a TV?" I hadn't seen one since we moved to the forest.

"We used to. One time my daddy put up a big metal pole he'd scrapped in the woods and rigged up a kinda machine that goes into the sky and picks up the shows. And we watched *Little Rascals* for a while, and *Laverne & Shirley* and *I Love Lucy*, which I bet you'd like because you're sorta like Lucy—"

"Who's Lucy?"

"The woman on the show. I'm trying to tell ya. She talks a lot, just like you."

I ducked my head, my cheeks burning. The Prophet preached the virtue of quietude among women. I'd been quiet for most of my life, but meeting Jude, I felt I could talk freely for the first time.

"Sorry," I mumbled.

"I didn't mean it like that. She's just got a lot of things to say. And she tells them to her friend Ethel. And to Ricky, her husband. He's Cuban and he's in a band and sometimes Lucy does dancing for his shows."

"What's Cuban?"

"It's like a place. Like an island where it's hot all the time."

"It's around here?"

"Naw, it's gotta be like . . . two hundred miles from here."

"Gawl."

"So, anyway, I think we should build our clubhouse out here, halfway between your house and mine."

"They'll find it," I said. By this time, Jude knew *they* were the deacons.

Jude suggested we build it up high in a tree where nobody'd ever think to look. He knew how to lift even planks of wood away from a fallen log, and eventually we whittled together a little camp inside the boughs of the larch. By the time we finished, the larch's fingers were mustard yellow again. The autumn smell of soil and tree breath seeped easily through our meek wooden walls.

On one wall, Jude had tacked a colored photograph showing a brown-skinned woman beside a fair, lanky man with a sharp Adam's apple. She wore a large ivory dress trimmed in violet lace. On the white border beneath the picture, someone had written a caption in pencil.

"What's it say?" I asked.

"'Waylon and Loretta,'" Jude said, "'on their wedding day.'"

"Your parents?" I asked, matching the features in his face to the people in the photo.

He nodded from where he was cutting a window into the east wall with his father's rusty handsaw.

"Your father let you keep this?"

"He won't notice. He doesn't much like to see pictures

of my momma. Says he keeps the best pictures of her inside his head."

He let the saw's handle fall over his wrist. "You know what I wonder sometimes?" Jude asked. "I think there was something my daddy was running away from. That's why he left the city to live up here."

"Like what?"

"I dunno," he said. "I know my grandparents didn't think it was right, him marrying my momma. They couldn't be together unless they ran away. But I wonder why they wouldn't just head to a different town?"

"Yeah," I shrugged.

I wondered it, too. Why would my mother and father leave their families and homes and jobs for the ramblings of a man they barely knew? Why would Jude's parents trek into the woods to live on forest service land with nothing but a camp stove and two Bibles under their arms?

On those quiet fall days, Jude took to playing guitar. Tentatively at first, because at that height we were entirely in nature's territory. Eventually, his strumming grew stronger, and he sang, too, high-pitched and clear in those days, rougher the older he got.

"Every morning, every evening, ain't we got fun?
Not much money, oh, but honey, ain't we got fun?

The rent's unpaid dear, we haven't a bus,
But smiles are made dear, for people like us."

He threw down his guitar and held his hand out to me. I grabbed it, and he wheeled me around the wooden floor in a kind of disjointed dance—neither of us had much practice. Our bodies were feet apart, but his hand felt dry and warm in mine. Beyond the window, the sky was half illuminated with a yolk-colored sunset.

"In the winter, in the summer, don't we have fun?" he sang, slightly out of breath now.
"Times are rough and getting rougher, still we have fun.
There's nothing surer, the rich get rich and the poor get poorer,
In the meantime, in between time, ain't we got fun?"

I was laughing loud enough to shake the trees around, to shake the bones in my own body. Jude swung his legs out the open side of the tree house and started plucking on his guitar again, the backs of his elbows moving up and down as he touched the strings, the sun touching his jaw.

It hadn't occurred to me before to love Jude. I barely understood it as a concept. My only training came from the fairy tales Bertie read me those days by the pond, the princess who recognized, easy as breathing, the moment she loved the peasant boy. The frog who brushed lips with a girl and changed, deep down in his biology. In these stories, the moment of first love was quickly followed by the ringing of wedding bells in the town, and the joy on the bride's and groom's faces at the unquestioned beauty of a minute-old marriage.

Marriage meant something different to me. It was incongruous with my idea of love. But, the quiet, supple way Jude breathed the word "dear," the thimbles of calluses enclosing each of his fingertips, the vibrating pitch in my marrow when his eyes held mine, were almost enough to black out my memories of cold Community marriages and barefoot winter weddings.

"Did you write that?" I asked.

"Naw," he said. "My momma sang it to me."

"You ever write a song?"

"I tried. They weren't no good."

"Wish I could write songs."

"Why cain't you?"

"Never learned how to write," I breathed. "Singing's not allowed anyway."

"Well, you can always sing up here."

"I haven't sung for a long time," I said. "Or played music."

"It's easy. I'll teach you sometime."

He smiled, and from the side, I could make out the

shadowed cleft in his cheek. I wanted to press my fingertip into it, kiss his jaw. The thought was like a kick in the gut. I'd never had such an impulse before. Surely it was forbidden. Surely the Prophet would find out.

Jude never did teach me to play guitar. There was always the unspoken certainty that we'd have forever. There would be time for all the things we wanted to do in our lives. That time could run out, that limbs could disappear from our bodies, was as unfathomable as death.

Chapter 23

My time was coming—most girls were married around seventeen—but somehow I'd come to believe that no man would ever ask me. I was weedy and black-haired and had my father's mannish nose, but more importantly, I'd heard the wives whisper that I was touched in a bad way by the outside. Not like my sister Constance. She was only twelve, but it was obvious she'd be sought after as a wife when she was older.

Everybody loved Constance. She was beautiful, with pale blond hair and a sweet pixie face with a little bow of a mouth that always looked slightly surprised. But it was more than that. She was the first child born into the wilderness. She was entirely Kevinian. She was pure.

Unlike me. The Prophet was the only man who ever regarded me with anything but basic tolerance. He often stared a little too closely, and his fingers could find their way to my waist without anyone noticing. He'd do subtle things, stroke my calf under the table and exclaim, "Such strong legs! You'll make a fine woman someday." The sort of thing that no one could blink at, but which made my stomach go hollow. It was the greatest battle of my childhood, trying to determine whether I was allowed to hate someone so full of God.

I figured it out, in the end.

After the Prophet announced he'd marry me, my father wrapped his arm across my back and steered me away from the courtyard where the others still gaped at me. He marched me up to the maidenhood room, a small bedroom in the attic of our house. I wrapped my hand around the doorjamb.

"Do you really believe God told him to marry me, Father?" I asked.

"The Prophet speaks to God. You know this, child," my father answered in the staccato manner he had adopted soon after he was appointed a deacon.

"How can God want me to marry him when I don't want to?"

"God's reasons are not always clear," he said, his eyes clouding. "But in this case, they are."

"What reasons?"

"The Prophet has seen evidence of the Devil in your eyes."

He didn't lift his eyes as he said this. My hand went slack and dropped to my side.

After he closed the door, I rattled the handle though it did no good. The door of every maidenhood room was fitted with a finger-thick sliding lock on the outside. I'd watched ours bolted on years before. I never realized before that these were the only locks in the whole place.

For a while I lay on the pallet and stared out the small, plastic-covered window, watching the sky grow from pale blue, to navy, to black, thinking about what my father had said.

There was no defending against the Devil's mark. In the early days, the Prophet showed us a yellowing photograph of him and his father. His father had a beer belly and a plaid shirt with the sleeves torn off. The Prophet was a little boy with his knees together like he might wet himself at any moment, giant glasses that made his eyes look bug-like and blurry. He told us how his father leaned a hatchet against the wall in case the children ever misbehaved. And how he always lived in fear of getting the hatchet, and how one day, when the Prophet was grown, he spotted a red flash inside his father's eyes—the Devil's mark—and he understood.

He never told us that he took the hatchet to his father, but I always thought it went without saying.

I stared out that window all night until the noises of dinner and bedtime quieted and I knew everyone in the house was asleep. I didn't think I'd ever get free from that room. The times I snuck out to visit Jude, it was past walls made of thin fabric and through unlocked doors. Jude and I had never planned for something like this.

When I figured it out, I gasped out loud. I sprang up from my pallet and ripped the plastic sheeting from the window, slowly, so the staples popped out one by one. A blast of cold air swept into the room. The window had been built into the roof, and I could only just curl my fingertips over the bottom edge. I pulled myself up and hung there, legs flailing, until I could hoist myself out.

I stood on the roof for a moment, taking in the ugly loop of the Community before me. All of our houses were on the same courtyard which, at that time of year, was just a circle of frozen mud. Anyone could look out their front door and see me perched, birdlike, on the roof, but I paused for a moment. I'm not certain why, still. I think it was with an understanding that I was leaving home for good. I watched my breath rise in front of me, listening to the frozen, creaking music the trees made with their bodies, and filling my lungs fully for what felt like the first time.

I crouched and stretched one leg down the side of the roof, searching for a foothold on the dry shingles. I let go of the roofline and pressed my palms flat, edging down the sheer surface as quietly as I could. I was almost to the roof edge when I lost my footing. I scudded down on my boots and backside and landed hard on my spine, the breath knocked out of me.

The sound of bootsteps on the frozen ground.

I turned over. Barely ten feet away, Deacon Karl stood with a circle of glowing orange between his lips. Cigarettes were banned, so I didn't recognize it at first, not until a drift of ash fell to the frozen ground. Something passed between us, and I knew he understood exactly what I planned to do.

He took one step toward me. Then I ran.

Chapter 24

"What stopped you from running away before?" Dr. Wilson asks. He looks up from his notes.

I lean back against the cinder-block wall behind my bunk, the Post-it on my affirmation wall a yellow blur in my periphery. He doesn't realize what a big, uncomfortable question that is, or maybe he does because he has that crinkled look in his eyes like he knows the answer without asking.

"Fear," I say finally.

"Fear?" he asks.

I shake my head. "No, not fear. The opposite, really. There was a feeling in the Community, like we could never be hurt. Not in the ways that counted. Our veins, our sinews were made of God-stuff. Even with everything that happened, I still felt untouchable. Like bad couldn't really reach me."

"But it was different after the Prophet said he'd marry you."

I nod. "Everything was."

. . .

I sprang up from the ground, my knees crackling, my ribs and back still feeling like they'd only recently collided with the earth, and started sprinting into the woods to the sounds of Deacon Karl huffing after me.

"ESCAPEE!" he shouted. "ESCAPEE!"

I was flying into the forest, but I could already hear the footfalls of deacons punish the hard mud behind me. It sounded like a thousand rushing legs, though I knew it couldn't be more than ten men, and some of them were ancient. But some were spry and young and very capable of outrunning me.

I had the advantage of having taken this path count-less times. The deacons crashed through the trees, but I felt swift and lean and gleeful still, for engineering this escape. I could feel heartbeats in each of my fingertips, blood buzzing inside my body, urging me on.

My feet fumbled over a root when I realized where I was leading them, straight to Jude's house. I lost a step or two while I pieced together a different place I could hide.

I cut to the right and tracked my way to the tree house. If I could scale the larch quickly, they wouldn't spot me. Hopefully they'd keep running around the forest all night, never looking up.

I could hear their voices faintly behind me when the

tree reared up in the distance, indistinguishable from the others, all its characteristic yellow fallen away. When I got close, I launched myself onto a limb and straddled it, upside down.

Their footsteps charged closer. I couldn't risk catching their eyes by scuttling to a higher limb, so I held my breath and hoped they wouldn't look up. The night was moonless and black, and I was high enough to be concealed by branches.

Below, I heard the crunch of running feet over dead, frozen brush. Their footfalls slowed, then stopped.

"She went down the mountain," one of the deacons sputtered. "Toward town, I'm sure of it."

"We're better off waiting till light," another said. "I can't see nothing in this pitch."

"Hang on," a younger voice called.

One set of feet crunched over the frozen undergrowth. I closed my eyes, pressing my face against the cold bark. My arm muscles started to quaver but I didn't dare readjust my hold on the branch.

The footsteps stopped abruptly.

Even then, I thought I was safe. I didn't remember that I'd left my bonnet behind in the maidenhood room. I didn't take into account my braid, hanging in a rope behind me.

I felt my scalp nearly ripped from my head. I crashed out of the tree onto my back on the needle-strewn ground. Abel, a deacon with a mean, pinched face and a patchy blond beard, crouched over me, my braid in his fist. He dropped my hair, picked up his boot slowly, and stepped on my cheek, holding me to the ground.

"You'll get it now, bitch," he spat. "I can't wait to see what Prophet thinks up to punish you."

He leaned over me, putting all his weight on my cheek, and I groaned in pain, fearing my jaw would pop like a chestnut from its socket.

"I hope he lets me choose," he said, his voice sunk into a whisper. "I've got something in mind for you."

I was breathing so hard that little orange orbs had sprung up over my vision, and cold tears fell from my eyes. I saw the boots of the older, slower men finally trundle into the clearing, watched them pause and take in the sight of me, and with them came the understanding that I'd be punished for this. Not only forced to marry the Prophet, but branded or cut or whipped or something else. Some wives who disobeyed their husbands had their heads shaved, only there weren't any razors in the Community so it was done with a knife. A blunt knife, by the look of their scalps afterward.

My father stood on the fringes of the group, not speaking.

"Get her to her feet," Deacon Larry said.

"Let's just take care of her here," Abel said. "The Prophet wouldn't care."

"This woman belongs to the Prophet," Larry said. "We'll leave it to him in his infinite wisdom to select a much more fitting punishment than we ever could."

"Even so amen," a couple of deacons replied.

They hauled me to my feet and frog-marched me through the dark wilderness. When we crashed through the trees, everyone was standing around the courtyard in their nightgowns, the wives holding lanterns, pushing back the night with little pools of light. In those moments, it felt as though this yellow-lit clearing was the only place on Earth, so walled-in were we by darkness.

It was clear from their faces that none of them expected I'd actually make it to freedom. The Prophet stood in the middle, just in front of the fire pit whose dying coals back-lit him with a halo of orange light and smoke. He looked devilish, his eyes angrier than I'd ever seen. I could almost feel heat radiating off him.

"We found her about half a mile north, almost to the property of those filthy Rymanites," Abel said. I looked at his face. They knew of Jude and his family. The idea started my muscles shaking.

"Did they spy you?" he asked.

"No, they must have known better than to show their faces to us."

"Never count on the ability of a Rymanite to think logically. They are devious and unpredictable."

"Don't use that word," I shouted.

The Prophet tilted his head toward me, a smile almost playing over his lips. "I would be worrying about yourself right now, Sister Minnow," he said, deadly quiet. "For it's you who is standing in the shower of God's wrath. It's you who will burn for this."

My breath hitched in my throat and tears began surging from my eyes. I didn't even try to hide them. It was too much, the Prophet standing before me, all gigantic and imposing and furious, and the crowd shifting and excited at the mention of a punishment. I let loose a torrent of slippery unstoppable tears, heavy tears, the kind that feel like they could accomplish something.

The Prophet's smile disappeared. "What do you have to cry about?" he barked. "The blessing of the Prophet is nothing to cry about!"

"I'm crying because I'm sad!" I shouted. "That's usually why people cry, isn't it?"

The Prophet reeled back as though I'd struck him again. I'd never spoken to him—to anyone—that way before.

"God warned me of your wickedness, Minnow," he

said. "I was willing to accept you as a wife because you are so in need of a firm hand to guide you toward the path of righteousness. But God has informed me that a replacement may be acceptable. If you are in some way . . . incapacitated, Constance would serve as a worthy replacement."

Behind me, I heard unconscious gasps leave mouths, enough to tell me I wasn't the only one who knew this was wrong. It went against the whole purpose of marriage as God decreed in his prophecy all those years ago. We married to make children. Constance was twelve, a child herself.

I searched for her face in the crowd, so small, like a pale moon among this sea of white nightgowns and black boots. Her mouth formed a perfect, pink O.

Once, the Prophet taught us that God speaks on a different frequency of hearing. And His voice is there, if we only listen hard enough. That when we pray, that's the pitch our minds speak at, too. In that moment, I heard it for the first time. But it didn't sound like comfort.

It sounded like screaming.

"A punishment is in order," I heard the Prophet say. "A punishment deserved by a girl who has so overstepped the bounds of propriety."

He gestured at the deacons to take me inside his house.

The nearest ones gripped me with their heavy hands before I could even wince. I made my weight go dead so they had to grasp me beneath my armpits and around my waist, their bones like vices. I writhed. I scratched with my fingernails and tried to pull at their faces and the soft spots between their legs, anything to stop them from dragging me up the steps into the Prophet's house. But there were too many of them. I stared out into the crowd and saw my mother, soft tears coursing down her cheeks.

They pulled me inside the Prophet's house and slammed the door. I'd never seen inside his house and, under different circumstances, I would've been interested in the fancy fluted plates and canned food sitting in his open cupboards—all contraband. But I couldn't focus. The room was a crush of men in their rough wool suits and ragged breath and muscles like metal pinning my arms back and, in the middle, the Prophet.

By his side was a hatchet, almost hidden in the black folds of his robes. He raised it and I flinched, but he was only passing it to my father.

"I think this is a job for you, Samuel."

My father's face emptied of blood. He shook his head almost imperceptibly, but the Prophet cocked his head to the side a little, like a question, and my father accepted the hatchet. The Prophet surveyed me for a moment, his head still turned to the side.

"The hands," he said finally.

The deacons came at me in a rush, their eyes black with focus. Some grabbed my arms and the others wrestled me down. They slammed me to the wooden floor and my head knocked back hard. Each one was hanging on to a part of me. My legs, my neck. Someone was holding my hands in his hands. I realized the only person who'd held my hand in recent memory was Jude, and how differently he'd done it. How much more delicately. The idea made me sick, their big meaty hands touching me, their hands that had killed Bertie, that had punished so many girls. If I'd only known what those hands would do, not much later, maybe I would've fought harder. Maybe I would've cut *their* hands off.

My father stood above me, tears falling into his beard. Doing nothing, as always. And now, finally, he had a choice. The first choice he'd had in a dozen years. He held the choice in his hands. He could use the hatchet to hurt his first child, or he could throw it to the ground and stomp out of there and save us all from madness.

I stared up at my father, and for one lucid moment, the light came back to his eyes, and I thought the sight of me lying there, covered in the bodies of ten men, might be enough to shatter the armor that'd built up around his mind, deflecting any sensible thought.

The Prophet saw him waver, too. He clamped his hand heavily against my father's shoulder.

"DO IT!" he bellowed. "DO IT NOW!"

My father raised the hatchet above his head. It wobbled there, breath passing his chapped lips in ragged waves. He jammed his eyes shut as he brought the hatchet down and punched it into my wrists.

Chapter 25

It's hard to figure the worst part of those moments. Maybe it was the ricochet the hatchet sent up my arms, my bones twanging like harp strings. Maybe it was the pain. That's the obvious choice. But, no, I think what hurt the worst was knowing that the hatchet hadn't completely severed the bone, watching it swing down again and again, bloodier each time, the expression on my father's face increasingly frantic, like a boy who's had to shoot his rabid dog, but the dog refusing to die.

There was an eerie, mute moment when there was no pain. It stood slightly offstage, blinded and nervous of the commotion. After a beat, I felt it. The severance. The blood falling away from my wrists with the force of geysers. Every star in the universe bursting over my vision and my jaw careening open and sucking air into my lungs in one long, lurching gasp. I learned later this sudden, explosive pain was the final cutting-through of nerves, the limp bundle of them running like a pale noodle along the length of each arm. My vision turned white. I'm sure I was screaming.

When it was done, the deacons stood and collected around the rim of the room. I lifted my arms from where they'd been pinned behind me and saw my stumps for the first time, pulsing blood with each heartbeat, almost black and shining like something lacquered. I couldn't comprehend what was missing, only that it was something vital and natural and necessary. Something I didn't even know could be taken from me.

The only sound I heard all those long minutes was the *whomp, whomp* of blood in my eardrums, blood pushing out of my body with purpose and sucked into the rough wooden floor.

The deacons flinched away from me and my wild blood, but the Prophet stood still, his eyes fascinated. He stepped forward, unconscious of the blood splashing his robes, and crouched.

"You will be my wife," he whispered. "You *will* be my wife."

I curled on my side away from him, watching my handless arms flail, the blood streaming off like ribbons. One of the Prophet's wives stepped from the shadows and lashed twine around each stump, twisting it tight with sticks. This stemmed the blood, though I knew I had already lost buckets.

I lost consciousness a moment later, but not before catching an eyeful of them in the corner. The hands. The loose fists, curled like snails' shells, in a pool of red.

• • •

I don't glance at my stumps once while I tell this story. Instead, I watch Dr. Wilson, studying his face. I guess, with a story like that, I can't help feeling I've earned the pinch of sympathy, the furrow that forms on people's brows when I tell them. It's a small kind of weapon, this story. I stab someone with it and they hurt, every time. But, the wrinkles fanning the doctor's forehead are flat. His face doesn't once crumple with concern. He has spent the past several minutes rolling the tip of his ballpoint pen back and forth over the red line running the length of his legal pad.

"Isn't that a sad story?" I ask finally.

He looks up, nods. "Sad."

"You don't look sad."

"Should I?" he asks.

"You just said it's a sad story. You should look like you care."

"I might express sadness differently than you. That doesn't mean I don't care."

"I don't buy that," I say.

"What do you want? Tears?"

"Tears would be nice." I nod. "Or at least a frown."

"Like this?" He folds his face up in an exaggerated fake frown.

I grimace. "Nobody frowns like that."

He leans back, rubs his eyes, and links his fingers at the back of his head. "Minnow, as a general rule, you shouldn't try to control other people's faces."

"That's good," I say. "Should I add that to my affirmation wall?"

The bell sounds for afternoon rec time. He flips the rolled-up pages of his notepad back and stands.

"Until next time."

• • •

I decide to spend my rec time in the visitors' lounge. I never get visitors, of course, but I've gone there before with Angel to watch the girls with their families. They're so different. The confident, brash ones lose all their noise when they sit beside bear-sized fathers, and the quiet, strange ones cling to their mothers' necks like rag dolls and cry when they have to let go.

When I walk into the visitors' lounge, a bunch of families are watching a show together on the big box TV because they can't make conversation in this place. It's one of those patriotic talent shows tuned about five times too loud. On-screen, a wheelchair-bound girl with a red crown of hair is going on about her father, who has bone cancer, and her mother, who died in Afghanistan, and her own extremities deformed by a childhood battle with spina bifida. She rolls onstage before the judges, and the beginning notes of "Wind Beneath My Wings" blast from her lungs.

The audience on the TV stands and cheers. In the lounge, some of the mothers cry. Even the hardened juvie girls watch with at least mild interest.

But I can't look. I stand and ask Benny if I can go back to my cell.

"Rec time doesn't end for another half hour."

"I want to go to the library."

"Once you're locked into a room, you can't leave until the end of rec time."

"B-but, that's a dumb rule," I cry. "I can't sit here and watch that show for a single minute more. I don't want to be in this room anymore."

"Why not?" she asks.

"Because—because I'm crazy!" I shout. "Velcro shoes, remember? Let me out!" I duck past her and try to lever the doorknob open, but she has me in a headlock before I can even touch metal. Her thick arm cinches around my neck, and I breathe harder and harder until darkness slams over my brain like a door in my face.

. . .

I come out of it when Benny sits me down hard in one of the office chairs in the assistant warden's office.

"She flipped out at that *American Talent* show," I hear Benny say. "Then she went limp." I still feel slightly out-of-body, so for a moment all I can see are the decades of girls' fingernail scratches scoring the surface of the chair arms. "Had to carry her all the way here," Benny continues. "Not that I mind much, the girl weighs less than my gym bag, but I've got my back to think about."

Mrs. New, the assistant warden, thanks Benny and closes the office door. She walks back to her desk, a small stream of air escaping her throat as she sits. Mrs. New is round and shiny, with beautiful blunt features—red lips and big apple cheeks that make me remember the story of Snow White that Bertie read from her book of fairy tales. Mrs. New always wears skirt suits that reveal her plump, flat-fronted calves and looks healthy in a way no one in the Community ever did.

"So, what happened?" she asks.

"I was in the visitors' lounge."

"And?" she asks. "How do you explain your behavior?"

Mrs. New's dewy eyes sit in her face like raisins pressed into dough. She'd cry if I told her my story, I'm certain of it. She would sob and console. She would care. Unlike Dr. Wilson.

"I don't know," I say. "I just really felt like not being in that room anymore."

"Benny said it had something to do with the show."

"There was this girl on it. And, okay, she was a nice singer, but God, I don't want to hear about her dead mother. And her father who has cancer. I don't get why that has to be my business."

Mrs. New shifts her lips to the side, seeming to consider her next words carefully. "You know she wasn't speaking directly to you. It's a television program."

"I know how TV works," I say through gritted teeth. "I just didn't feel like hearing all that stuff."

"You met with Dr. Wilson today, right?" she asks, looking at a calendar that stretches over the surface of her entire desk. "Did anything happen in your session to distress you?"

I pause. "No."

"What did you discuss?"

"How I lost my hands."

She looks up from the desk suddenly. "And that didn't distress you?"

"Not really," I say. "I'm used to it."

"Was it your decision to tell that story?"

"Well, Dr. Wilson asked about it. But it was weird because he didn't even react. He wanted to know, but he sat there and wrote notes and barely shrugged when I was talking about my father taking the hatchet and all, and that's usually the thing that makes anyone cry. Even the prosecutor at my trial looked like he might throw up. But Dr. Wilson? Nothing."

She sighs. "Well, Minnow, maybe we should consider a counselor reassignment for you."

I lift my head. "What?"

"Dr. Wilson is not a child psychologist. He's used to working with adult offenders. I barely understand how he was assigned as your primary mental health coordinator, but that decision was made about this high above my head." She holds up her small arm as high as it will go. "Perhaps his manner isn't suited for work with juveniles. I think you might be a better match for one of our in-house counselors. Ms. Gottfried works with your friend, Angel." She leans in. "If you were to make a change request, we'd do our best to grant it."

I don't say anything for a moment.

I'm sure someone else would be softer. Would smile like you do at something very delicate, something that might, at any moment, break into a billion pieces. I'm sure they'd tell me how strong I am. How brave. I'm sure I wouldn't have to talk about anything I didn't want to talk about.

I realize something in that moment, my stumps tracing the scratches left on the chair arms. I couldn't give a crap about that girl's sob story on TV because I'm still too consumed with my own. All this time, I thought I was the only one with dead people tied to me like helium balloons. Now, I wonder if Dr. Wilson's lost something, too.

"I'll think about it," I tell Mrs. New.

She looks disappointed. She knows I'm lying.

Chapter 26

Every day, Angel leaves for a couple of hours for school. They won't let me return to reading class until I show "satisfactory interpersonal progress," which Angel says usually requires a week with no reprimands, so I spend the hours staring at the snake-shaped metal supports that keep Angel's mattress in place above me. On good days, I think about Jude, and on bad days I think about Philip Lancaster, but today I think about my hands. I hold my arms out above me and remember the way the hands used to look, the fingers stretching and waving, the way they could form fists with almost no effort. Why didn't I use them when I could have? I punch the metal above me once, and again, and only stop when I see blood. I fall back into the mattress and a sigh gutters from my throat.

I'm not at all better. The last visit with Dr. Wilson has confirmed this. I'm starting to feel like I might never mend. Like the Prophet really ruined me. Maybe you can't recover from that kind of injury. Even after months of healing, it doesn't take much to make me bleed.

• • •

Right after it happened, after my father stopped swinging the hatchet, after I passed out, I woke to a quiet room. I took in my stumps. They were a perfect cross-section, the oblong of bone and the burgundy muscle and the surprising yellow circle of fat. Perfect biology. Perfect fitting-together of cells and marrow and meat. Almost like it was planned that way.

Through the fog, I sensed one of the wives slide the skin of my arms up, like the casing around sausage, and slip heavy stitches through the skin with waxed embroidery thread. The tug of each black, stitched *X* spelled something out in my mind: the Prophet wanted to keep me alive. The wedding would go ahead as planned.

Two of my father's wives, Mabel and Vivienne, edged into the room sometime later, opening the door hesitantly, as though uncertain whether they'd find me alive or dead. I followed Mabel's young face, her forehead pleated, to her hand where she held a wooden cup.

Vivienne made a choking sound and clamped her fingers over her mouth and nose. The blood covering the floor hadn't been cleaned, though it had thickened beneath me and begun to smell like hours-old meat.

I kept my eyes lidded. I wasn't sure I wanted them to know I was alive yet.

Mabel knelt near me, holding out the cup of green liquid, steaming in the chill air.

"The Prophet says drink this," she whispered.

"Well, she won't drink it now," Vivienne chided.

"Fine. Hold her mouth open while I pour."

At that moment, I lifted my head. They jumped back with gasps, their eyes stretched as though I was a reanimated corpse. The idea pulled a laugh from my lungs and threw the laugh into the air where it hung awkwardly, certain there had been some mistake, it couldn't possibly belong in a place like this.

"She's nuts," Vivienne said.

"She's lost so much blood," Mabel said.

"She's always been half-witted. Half crazy."

"It's in her blood."

"Hush, Mabel! Hold her head."

Vivienne pulled my jaws apart with rough, muscular hands. I couldn't taste the liquid. I was too consumed with sensing that pain, that redness, that absence of fingers, that wanting to dig my fingers into a face and pull someone's eyes out.

The liquid, whatever it was, wasn't enough to keep me completely asleep. Again and again, I woke and passed out when the pain crashed down on top of me.

Once, I cracked open my eyes to see the outline of a woman crouching in the shadows. My mother. She wasn't looking at me. In her hands was one of my hands, stiffening and already blue touched. Slowly, she bent the fingers back and stroked the palm, making a face like she was crying. Small noises escaped her mouth.

When I woke again, the hands were gone.

I stared at the corner where they'd been, my eyes growing blurry from tears, and it struck me as utterly pointless, the most pointless thing I'd ever do again. Cry because they were gone, wish they'd never been taken.

At that moment, waves of light spiraled around the room, so bright I had to close my eyes. When I opened them, the lights were dissolving and a boy stood over me. He was tall and wore jeans and a button-fronted shirt with the sleeves rolled up and his head tilted to the side to look at me. I remember little of his face except for two sharp, green eyes.

"Charlie?" I croaked.

Without a sound, he took a step closer. I noticed his shoes made no impression in the blood. They hovered an inch above the ground.

"L-look what they did to me," I cried. Tears came fast down my face again. I held out my stumps. "Look!"

He kneeled near me, staring with his too-green eyes from my stumps to my face. The pupils were intelligent, but in a removed way, like camera lenses. They twitched side to side almost imperceptibly.

"Well, help me!" I shouted. "They'll be back! Help me!"

His features didn't change, expressionless and calm, as though he wasn't really in the room at all, as though this was only a projection of him.

And then he moved, reaching out a hand and placing it near my forehead. From each finger shot a dozen beams of light slanting in every direction. I thought he'd touch me, and with the touch heal me. Give me back what was mine. But he only held his hand there, then stood and slid it back inside his jeans pocket. I stared at him in disbelief. On his hovering feet, he turned and began to walk away.

"Don't go!" I cried. "Come back, please!"

But he kept walking. He opened the front door and let it fall shut behind him. The room grew dark again, and I felt every scrap of hope I had fall through my body like water out a pipe. My arms began to shake.

"I HATE YOU!" I bellowed. "I HAAAAAAATE YOU!"

I screamed my throat raw. Mabel and Vivienne hurried back into the room and shoved the liquid down my throat again. I thrashed for a moment, still trying to scream, but gave in because I knew there was no longer any reason to fight.

• • •

They took me back to my parents' house, to the maidenhood room. All day, I stared at the simple triangle ceiling made of logs that had been dead for so long but somehow still continued to die.

Over the window, someone had nailed a piece of particleboard. *You're never escaping,* the board said. I whispered back, *Like I didn't already know.*

Outside, I could smell the world turning away from autumn, and I pictured the wide leaves of oaks moldering and falling from wooden limbs like hands. My only visitor in those early, blood-hot, handless days was my mother. The sound of the lock sliding on the other side of the door always made me flinch. I lay on my side, arms crisscrossed on the bare floor in front of me.

My mother lifted away the burlap wrapped around my arms. I closed my eyes against the feeling of the raw fabric rubbing raw wounds.

She spread her fingers and held them over my stumps.

"What're you doing?" I slurred.

"Praying," she whispered.

I let out a quiet gust of air, which was really a sob. What did she think? That her faith would grow them back? That white newborn fingers would waggle from my wrists, growing firmer and stronger until they were the toughened hands of a seventeen-year-old girl?

I kept my stumps under her hands until I could feel the warmth from her palms prickle into my open flesh and said, "Okay," and she cleared her throat and blinked and folded her hands in her lap. She held her bottom lip in her mouth, delicately. Tears had dried to her face.

I turned away and waited for her to leave. I'd seen my mother cry too many times for this to mean anything now. I couldn't care about her tears anymore, not when I had so many of my own.

Chapter 27

They call this time of year flu season here, though in the Community the seasons didn't delineate themselves so cleanly, and they've forced all the girls to get poked with a needle to stop us from catching the sickness. The nurses were worried how I'd react but I took it like it meant nothing. I figure my arms have more perspective on pain than to hurt much from a needle.

Angel told me how paranoid they are about disease in jails, about incidents in history when illnesses wiped out entire prison populations in a matter of days, how there's no getting away from it in a place where our bodies are so close together.

People died fairly often in the Community. Wives died in childbirth, and men got small injuries on their hands that could become black and gelatinous in days, and then we always knew what would follow. We were to scrub all cuts in lye and not eat mushy vegetables and be careful around kitchen utensils. Anybody with something worse than a cough was locked in their house or quarantined to the barns on the edge of the woods until they got better or until the smell told us they'd no longer be a problem.

The Prophet, whatever the cost, would not have allowed our spiritual mission to die off from something as insignificant as an outbreak of flu.

• • •

Dr. Wilson visits today, the first time I've seen him since I told him how I lost my hands. I'm still a little bruised by the memory. He sits on his stool and opens his yellow notepad.

"The snow is melting in the mountains," he says.

I look up. "And?"

"The crime scene investigators are finally able to collect evidence. Things may start moving more quickly now."

"What do you mean?"

He opens a file folder and scans a typed piece of paper. "Jude's mother died at home, is that correct?"

"Yes," I say, unable to prevent a wariness from creeping into my voice. "Before I knew Jude."

"What killed her?"

"Stomach cancer, I think."

"What'd she do for the pain? Drink?"

"No. Jude said she never touched a drop of alcohol. She just put up with it."

"That must have been excruciating. Stomach cancer is one of the most painful. Almost too difficult to bear, some say."

"What are you saying?"

He levels his eyes at me. "I don't think Loretta Leland died of stomach cancer."

"How could you know that?"

"Take a look." He opens a packet and pulls out a photo. It shows a burned-out shell of a house, the glass from one window melted and weeping down the logs.

"Recognize the place?" he asks.

"Jude's cabin," I say. "The fire spread that far?"

He nods. "The investigators found the body of a woman, aged between thirty-five and forty, near the Leland family property. She'd been dead for approximately six years. The medical examiner analyzed the remaining tissue and determined that the woman had advanced breast cancer which had metastasized in her stomach. But this woman didn't die of cancer. Do you know what killed her, Minnow?"

My limbs freeze. "How would I?"

He nods like he expected that answer and slides a new photo from the stack. I look at the photo and my mind rejects it almost immediately, like what my stomach did once when I ate a poison berry, but I can't pull my eyes away. In the photo, in a trench of upturned dirt, is a face. Recognizable, even in its horror, even in its decomposition, the gaping orbits, the bare teeth. Jude's mother. The crown of her skull is blasted apart in chunks around her face.

"She died of a gunshot wound to the head," he says. "The bullet wound was so large, it split the skull into five pieces."

He lets the quiet stretch. I take in the big orbits where Jude's mother's eyes had been. I wonder if they were the same warm brown as Jude's, the kind of brown that listens and speaks at the same time. I can't get over how completely her eyes are gone.

"You wouldn't know anything about this, would you?" he asks finally.

"I didn't even know Jude six years ago."

"But I think you may know what happened to her."

I look up at him. "This isn't relevant."

"It's not?" he asks. "This woman was murdered. The Prophet may have been murdered, too. It stands to reason that her killer and his killer might be the same person."

"That'd be so nice for you," I say, my voice rising in pitch. "So nice and neat, wouldn't it? You could go back to

Washington, DC, early. Take your wife out for an expensive dinner in a fancy restaurant and eat till you puke."

"I see I've struck a chord."

"You haven't struck anything."

"I thought you wanted to help me catch a killer."

"I won't help you lay all the blame on Jude."

His eyebrows dart up. "Who said anything about Jude?"

"Stop!" I shout. "Stop talking to me. Leave me alone."

"Minnow, I know this may be difficult for you," he says, "but you suggested this deal. I help you get free, you help me catch the killer."

I squeeze my eyes shut until the bone behind my forehead threatens to break. I breathe heavily and after a moment he says, "Take some breaths," a few times before standing to leave.

He will never get the truth about Jude's mother out of me. Never.

Chapter 28

Being here, I'm only now realizing how much was kept from me in the Community. I've heard the other girls talk and I can tell that they knew much more than me at a much younger age, that when I was learning how quickly a calf becomes a cow and how seeds morph into potatoes just by living in the ground, they were learning how to solve the strange puzzle of their bodies.

In the Community, none of that was talked about. There was no need. Girls and boys never saw beneath their thick garments, and the events after a wedding night were relegated to our imaginations, the dull sounds that penetrated our fabric walls from where my father slept with one of his wives in the night, the sounds we didn't understand but tried to block out anyway.

Today the girls were in a titter because, instead of their normal reading classes, they're to have a special class on sex education. "It's just an ancient video that Mrs. New plays in the cafeteria," Angel said before she left. "Nothing good. Nothing we didn't already learn firsthand years ago."

I nodded, cheeks burning, not wanting to let on how much I'd like to be there anyway. I'm sure if I asked Benny for special permission to go, she'd let me since my suspension is almost up, but I doubt I could get the words out, even to her.

Instead, I sit alone in the cell block, running my eyes across the page of the book in front of me. It has a blue cover, and pages that feel like feathers when I run them over my stumps. This book is beautiful. It is also impossible.

"*Psst.*"

I look up. Miss Bailey stands at the door of my cell.

"Can I come in?" she asks.

"All right," I say. She looks down the skyway and nods to a guard. The door buzzes open.

She adjusts her pink cardigan sweater and sits on the edge of my bed. "You're missing quite the fun downstairs."

"I'm still suspended."

She nods. "What were you reading?" she asks, indicating the book I'd been paging through. A girl's windburned face stares up from the blue cover.

"I asked Angel to get me a book from the library. It's poetry."

"How's it going?"

"Not good."

Miss Bailey nods. "Well, it's one of my favorites. Would you like some help reading that book?"

When I nod, she lifts her tote bag in the air and dumps a pile of books and papers onto the mattress.

"I brought these for you. Hoped you'd say yes." She picks out a big spiral-bound workbook and opens it to page with giant-printed letters. Her finger traverses the page and when it touches a letter, she says it big, with her entire mouth. Her entire face, really. I repeat the sounds.

"MMMM."

"SSSS."

"AAAAAHHH."

"OOOOO."

Eventually, the sounds blend together to make words. *MMMMM-AAAAAHHHH-SSSSS* makes *moss.* And *T-RRRRRR-EEEEEE* makes *tree.* I don't even hide my grin. It's a thrill to rediscover these things in this place, surrounded by so much concrete and metal and recycled air. I read the words and in this cell, the forest blooms to life again, the earthy smell, the way the sun filters through the boughs of pines, the feeling of never being alone.

Chapter 29

"I never been to Disneyland," Angel says. She sits cross-legged on the floor beside my bed, pushing black plastic beads up over the tail ends of her cornrows.

"That one isn't going to work," I say.

"Why?"

"Because, of course, I've never been to Disneyland. I've been to about four different places in my whole life."

Angel and I are playing a game she and her friends from school used to play. If I had been to Disneyland, I would've taken a drink from my water cup. The first person to pee loses. Angel said it works better with something besides water, but this will do.

"Fine," Angel says. "I never . . . met my real dad."

I laugh. "Unfortunately for me," I say, levering my drinking cup from the floor with my stumps and pouring water into my mouth.

"I NEVER KISSED A GIRL," comes a voice from down the skyway.

"You are *not* playing, Rashida," Angel shouts.

"Why, though?" Rashida calls. Her cell is one down from ours. "Tracy's at therapy and Wendy won't talk to me cause I traded her Skittles. I got nobody to play with over here."

Angel grunts. "All right, you can play. But it's Minnow's turn."

"Did anybody drink at mine?" Rashida asks. "Have either of you kissed a girl?"

"Come see for yourself," Angel says.

I hear Rashida throw her plastic water cup at the bars of her cell, and a guard's gruff voice asking her just what exactly she thinks she's doing.

"I never pulled the trigger of a gun," I say.

Angel's smile cocks to the side. She picks up her cup and drinks.

"That reminds me," Angel says. "I've been thinking about genetics."

"How do guns remind you of genetics?" I ask.

"Nobody wants to listen to this boring shit, Angel!" Rashida's voice calls.

"Rashida, why don't you go back to huffing shampoo fumes and shut up!" Angel shouts. "Anyway, genetics. You know how we inherit traits from our ancestors? It's supposed to take thousands of years, but I've seen it happen way quicker. You pick up things you don't even realize. My mom taught me to shoot straight and not give a fuck what anyone thinks. Only things she did, besides how to get meth stink out of clothes. And I never met my dad. He was probably some petty criminal my mom slept with at the shelter in exchange for a cigarette. So I count myself lucky. I got to decide exactly how I was gonna be. Most of these girls have learned from somewhere to apologize for existing. It's written on their genes, I swear. Just listen to them, even if they don't say it, practically everything that comes out of their mouths is the word 'sorry.'"

She looks over at me and I can tell she's thinking I'm one of those girls who apologize for existing. Even if I hadn't lost my hands, I doubt I'd ever be the type to shoot a gun without being scared of the noise.

"It's hard," I say. "Not always knowing what's right."

Angel's face scrunches. "How do you not always know what's right?"

I hunch up my shoulders.

"Give me an example," she says.

"The Prophet always told us stories. They were meant to make us afraid."

"Like what?"

"You really want to know?" I ask.

"Entertain me."

"All right," I say, sifting through memories. "This one time, it was winter and I was fifteen. It was late afternoon, and already black as night, and I stood on the side of a frozen pond, pounding an awl into the ice for water to scrub my family's clothes."

Around the awl, my fingers had already turned blue. This was an all-day endeavor, breaking the ice, hauling the water one leaking bucketful at a time, and repeating the process eight or ten times. Like all of my chores, I was left to complete this on my own.

A clanging noise shattered the quiet. Instinctively, I dropped the awl, pushed myself from the ice, and started running, ignoring the creaking in my knees and my aching blood-emptied fingers.

When I arrived, the courtyard teemed with blue-clad bodies. A cold hand slipped into mine. Constance peered up at me with her giant icy eyes. The Prophet stood at his porch, clanging the bell that hung there, a big ferocious grin playing across his face. "Behold!" he shouted above the clanging. "God's power in action!" He craned his neck up.

High in the blackness, a small light the size of a nail head shot across the dark canvas of sky. A trail of light faded behind it and burned out.

"Shooting stars?" someone in the crowd asked.

Abruptly, the Prophet stopped clanging, and his arm hung in the air where it had rung the bell, so for a moment it looked as though he was reeling back for a punch. "No!" he shouted, walking out into the crowd. "*War!* The Gentiles are attacking. And look! God is stopping them. Those lights are bombs aimed at us, meant to kill us, burning out in the dome of God's protection."

Another light flashed across the sky and some of the children made scared noises and cowered behind their mothers' skirts, but the Prophet told them in a reassuring voice that they were safe, this was proof of God's power and protection and love for us. I looked down into Constance's face. She was nine and her hair was tied in a slippery braid down the side of her head. Her mouth was wide open in wonder, and I could see where the corners of her lips were chapped, her neck hinged as far backward as it could go. Soon, everyone was sighing amazedly, even the adults who had, moments before, called the things in the sky a different name.

Everybody went to bed that night with an ache in their necks and a fullness in their hearts and a certainty that God loved them. That we were doing the right thing. All except me.

"Why not you?" Angel asks.

"I remembered something," I say. "I must have heard

it on TV or in preschool the few times my parents took me, before the Prophet, before the Community." I take a breath. "I remembered those things had a name."

"Meteors," Angel says.

I nod. I remembered the word, and I knew the adults must have, too. And knowing that sowed something uncertain in my mind. I didn't know what it meant—still don't—only that it made me confused. Not doubtful, not yet. Just a feeling like something in me was broken, something that in everybody around me was whole.

Chapter 30

"Philip Lancaster wants to see you," Dr. Wilson says during our next visit.

I look up. I blink twice, hard.

"What are you talking about?"

"I interviewed him," Dr. Wilson says. "He said he'd like to talk to you."

"That's not happening."

"Are you afraid you'd lose control again?"

"No," I say firmly. Because that's not what makes me afraid. I'm afraid of looking him in the eye. It's his eyes, more than anything, that terrify me.

"Do you ever think about that night?" he asks.

"Only sometimes," I say. "Try not to."

"Why?"

"I'd just escaped the Community, just seen Jude die. Walked for hours in the darkness not knowing if I'd see another person again. There's a lot about that night I don't want to remember."

"Don't let it become a part of your mind that you're afraid to touch," he says. "Remembering doesn't have to be a bad thing."

I know he's right. The more I ignore the memory of that night under the bridge, the more space it takes up in my mind till I fear at some point I won't be able to ignore it anymore. Philip Lancaster's eyes will be all I can see.

"It was so cold that night," I say. "I can't believe it really happened sometimes, but then I remember that feeling of cold. Cold enough I worried I'd never thaw out."

It took me hours and hours to find the city from the Community. By then, the ground had been blanketed with pristine snow. I followed the dull glow of light along the horizon and the vague smell that engines make, so different to the brisk, clean air in the high mountains. In the darkness, lit windows of buildings materialized, the faint rattle of a car whizzing past on the freeway.

I followed the river through the night, stopped to rest beneath an old rusting bridge. I learned later that what murders happen in Missoula happen here. Teenagers beat a homeless man to death. Two meth heads have a falling out over a half-empty bottle of cough syrup. Beneath the bridge, there was none of the manicured, easy wilderness I always pictured when I remembered the city, young families plodding in their sneakers down wood-pelleted trails, coffee smells from shops, and the barking of Labradors nearly always audible. This wasn't the place I'd spent years imagining. Beneath the bridge, the water was brown and the bank was made of muddy gravel, and there was a rimless tire threatening to take off into the river, but never quite making it.

"Hey!" a man's voice called over my shoulder. My heart guttered to a stop. I'd been leaning against a rusty leg of the bridge, completely lost in the movements of the river. I hadn't noticed the man behind me.

"Wha's wrong with your hands?" He cocked his head to the side and stared at my stumps. Earlier that night, I'd nudged a pair of maroon gloves over my stumps with my teeth. I glanced down at them. The gloves' fingers were empty and flat and hung off weirdly.

"Nothing," I said. He couldn't have been much older than me, eyebrows thrust up his face, pale breath smoking in the cold. I forced my eyes away. There was only one way out, a steep narrow trail up to the street. It was slippery and precarious in the snow.

I tried brushing by him toward the trail.

"Now stop!" he said. "I jus wanna talk. I don't have anybody to talk to anymore."

There was something wrong with him. For one thing, it was freezing, but all he wore was a light, long underwear–

type shirt and slouchy jeans. But, something more. Something in the way he cast his eyes around, like a spotlight searching for a missing person in the dark.

He reached his arm out and snatched away one of my gloves. He caught sight of my ruby red stump before I pulled it inside my coat sleeve.

"Don't—touch me," I said, deadly quiet.

"Y-you don't have to run away," he said excitedly. "I'm just like you. I'm missing something, too."

I turned my head slightly. "What are you missing?"

"A soul," he whispered.

I reeled back a couple steps. My heart started working again, double time.

"It got lost," he continued. "I'm trying to find it."

"How do you lose your soul?" I asked, curious even as my eyes scanned behind him for an escape route.

"All kindsa ways. But, the number one way that people lose their souls is this." He took a big gulp of breath. "The Devil takes it."

"The Devil," I repeated. When he nodded quickly, I realized that he believed every word he said. My skin began to itch with cold.

I coughed into my elbow. "I need to go."

"Wait," he said. "Will you help me?" His voice was small and pleading.

"With what?"

"Help me find my soul?" he implored. "Please, I just need someone to understand." He grabbed my arm. One of his freezing palms squeezed my stump, and it sent a shiver strong as an electric shock through my gut.

"DON'T TOUCH ME!" I pulled my stump away and stumbled backward a step, slipping where the river had turned the ground to ice and landing hard on my back. Above me, he was silhouetted against falling petals of snow and the scissored black outline of the bridge.

He took a step toward me. I swept with my legs at his ankles, and he collapsed onto the frozen ground. I scrambled to my feet and stared down at him.

His eyes were large and they beamed back at me like a torch. I gasped at the color. Green. Vibrant, bottle-glass green. Godly green.

The decision to kick was entirely my own. I could've run, if I wanted. I didn't want to. I wanted to hurt him. I was wearing the boots from Jude's house. I didn't know there was steel stuffed down in the toes, though I knew it made the boots sink satisfyingly into his stomach. I thought the strength was all my own. Something like pride bloomed inside my chest. I huffed and my blood was hot and it felt good. Power. Purple blotches at the corners of my eyes. Tongue running over my teeth. Not even feeling the cold.

His name is Philip Lancaster. He is the son of an impressive Seattle software designer. He is a student at the University of Montana. He is a paranoid schizophrenic. I kicked out all the molars in the right side of his face. I broke apart his spleen. He was crying when I was done. His blood colored the toes of my shoes.

It took moments for the high to collapse, for the cold to sink into my exposed face. I gazed down at him, my limbs shaking, my muscles so jumpy they felt pulsed with electricity. The blood on my boots stood out like neon.

I wondered, What would Jude think, if he could see me? I doubled over to eject a pint of acid from my stomach.

Chapter 31

"He doesn't blame you as much as you'd think," the doctor tells me.

"Philip?" I ask, flinching at the name.

He nods. "He knows you were scared. He's back on his medication."

I shake my head. The memory of that night is a physical object. When I touch it with the soft fingers of my mind, it feels cold and dark and sharp like metal. I feel at the object blindly, trying to memorize the dimensions, figure out its shape.

Philip has the same object in his mind, I'm sure. The same cutting thing inside us, hurting us in different ways.

"You can't forgive that," I say. "I know because I never could."

"Want to hear what he told me?" the doctor asks. "He said he doesn't always know what's real and what's not. His mind tells him lies. He reminded me of you."

"Why?"

"Philip struggles with what's real, too. Almost like he has his own Prophet. One inside his own head."

"Maybe everybody has one," I say. "How lucky am I that mine's dead?"

The doctor looks at me with a strange expression. We are hovering right on the edge of what he came here for, the smoke-choked moments when the Prophet breathed his last breath.

"Do you ever think about Constance?"

"What's there to think?" I say. "I should've protected her better. That was my job."

"Now that's something you should never do," he says. "Blame yourself. I don't think you can honestly say any of that was your fault."

"This wasn't supposed to be about feelings, remember?" I say. "That's not why you're here."

There's something struggling behind his face, but after a moment's thought, he nods. He flicks through his notes. "What motivates someone to kill?" he asks.

I look up at him. "How should I know?"

"Just take a stab at it." He smiles. "No pun intended."

"It could be a million things."

"Such as?"

I glance at my affirmation wall. "Anger."

"Good. What else?"

"Insanity."

"Yes," he says, nodding. "There's also heat of passion and revenge. There's killing to claim life insurance, there's euthanasia. Do you know what we call these things?"

I shrug.

"Motive," he says. "If you determine the motive, you can sometimes determine the murderer. Why might someone have been motivated to kill the Prophet?"

"Revenge, I guess."

"Very good. He punished countless people. We can add any of them, plus any of their loved ones, to the list of suspects. How about insanity? Was anyone in the Community prone to erratic behavior? Emotional distress?"

"Besides the Prophet himself?"

He nods.

I consider this. "My mother."

"What sort of emotional distress?"

"Just being sort of . . . numb. Dead to the world."

"But she helped you escape."

"That doesn't change the fact that she was absent, in every way, for almost my entire life."

"That sounds remarkably like resentment."

I almost laugh. How do I articulate it to him so he'll understand? Maybe the image of her sitting in the dirt, her eyes locked on a crop of wild buttercups while my father hided my naked back for stealing a rye roll from my sister's plate. Or should I describe the humming sound she made after Vivienne slapped me across my face for refusing to call her mother? It's no use. Nothing could convey what it was like growing up with a ghost.

"Do you know why your mother was this way?" he asks.

I set my jaw. "She was weak."

He nods again and pulls a manila folder out of his bag. He places it open on my knees and reads it aloud.

Missoula County Hospital
Patient: Olivia Bly. DOB: 10/08/72
Admitted: 15 August
Department: Obstetrics
Patient gave birth to a healthy daughter. 8 pounds, 3 ounces.

At 6:30 P.M, patient requested to hold her newborn and had a severe panic attack. Shortness of breath, dilated pupils, inflation of facial capillaries. Attack was unmotivated by any known medical condition. After sedation, blood work showed patient's calcium and magnesium levels were extremely depleted. Patient was put on an intravenous drip to replenish low nutrients. In the morning, patient suffered another attack and was sedated

again. Patient was discharged from obstetrics the follow-
ing day and referred to Dr. Camille Wilcox in psych.
Probable chemical imbalance as a result of giving birth.

I blink at the paper, my eyes taking in individual words that stand out. *Sedation. Birth. Panic.*

"I think you like seeing your mother as weak, Minnow."

"Why would you say that?"

"Because the idea of her being sick, not weak, makes you feel guilty. Makes you realize how unfairly you treated her."

I shake my head, pressing my stumps together in my lap until lines of pain shoot down my arms.

"How many times was your mother pregnant after you were born?"

"Eight times, I think," I whisper to my knees. "A few miscarriages."

I hear the rest as though from a cloud space, miles up. She was drowning, he says. She dealt with it all on her own, he says, her world out of balance every time my father pushed another baby up her.

"Why are you telling me this?"

"It's just more evidence."

"You're lying," I say with certainty. "Tell me the truth."

He purses. "She's a suspect."

A bomb may have gone off. Time may have frozen. I shiver like you do when hearing something that rewrites the entire world. "So, what you've just told me . . . you're building a case against her."

"Not necessarily. She's one of many leads."

"No . . . you're going to tell them I was wrong about her being asleep my entire childhood. You'll tell them she was just sick. Sick but capable of killing."

"I shouldn't have mentioned this," he says, closing the manila folder.

"Who else is there?" I say. "Who else is a suspect?"

"Minnow, please."

"No!" I shout. "I'm angry. I'm angry because this always happens. The wrong person is punished for the wrong crime. And it's people like you who make it happen again and again."

"People like me?" he asks.

"You're a cop," I say.

"You're very certain I'm a bad guy, aren't you?"

"No, I'm certain you're here to help me," I say mockingly.

"That was never a lie," he says.

"I've figured you out, you know? You're a coward. No wonder you jumped at the chance to come here. You're just running away from something."

He scoffs. "You don't know what you're talking about."

"Yes, I do. You're wearing a wedding ring. You have a family. But you left, for months, and leaving made you *happy*, remember? You're just another guy who abandoned his family."

A pale fire shines in his eyes now. "Fine," he says. "Let's go right down the list, if that's what you want." He flips open another file and examines its contents. "Waylon Leland. Had motive, was a drunk, history of violence. He snuck in at night and stabbed the Prophet in the belly with his bowie knife."

"What?" My head shoots up. "That's not—"

"What about Constance, your sister? By all accounts a very maladjusted young girl, physically stunted, puberty delayed. She would've seen what happened to you and wanted to do something to protect you. She would've known she was next. She went into the Prophet's bedroom that night and smashed a lantern over his bed and set him on fire."

I rise from my bunk, looking down on him, the memory of the fire burning in my chest, the heat of it charging my veins.

"Maybe you did it, huh?" I shout. "Maybe you snuck in that night and lit the fire and smothered the Prophet with his own pillow, because you're clearly schizo. Look!

I've struck on it. You're a fraud. You're as crazy as you tell everyone they are."

"Or what about Jude?" he continues as though he hasn't heard me. "Had motive, access, weapons, and let's face facts, wasn't the brightest bulb, was he? It was pretty easy to persuade him to come to the Community with you that night, wasn't it? It couldn't have been difficult to get him to kill the Prophet for you."

"YOU SHUT YOUR GODDAMN MOUTH!"

"You're going to have to stop yelling," he says, disturbingly calm.

"I'M GONNA HAVE TO START YELLING AND NEVER, EVER STOP!" I scream.

He doesn't call for a guard but Officer Prosser comes anyway. The cell door opens, and she grips me by my shoulders and slams me hard to the grated floor. That knocks the wind out of me for a moment. I hear the metal slam of my door closing. After I get my breath back, I fill my lungs and scream again, hurling my arms against the floor.

"Tranq her," I hear the doctor say from outside the cell door.

"She can't exactly damage anything," Officer Prosser says.

"She can damage herself."

"That's higher than my pay grade."

Everyone always assumes it's with hands that people disobey. The Prophet thought so, too. If only he knew, if only everyone knew, my hands were never the source of my disobedience.

Chapter 32

"Minnow, you have to try harder to control these outbursts," Mrs. New says.

I'm in her office again, in the wooden chair opposite her desk. I feel groggy and itchy, but I can't figure out where. Like it's my soul that itches.

"Are you gonna suspend me from reading class?" I ask.

"Your teacher has made the case that you be given leniency," she says. "And I think I agree with her. This isn't the first time you've left a counseling session in distress. I'm going to recommend you begin seeing another counselor."

"No!" I bark.

"Why not?"

"Because it's my choice. You said it was my choice. Well, I choose him."

"Look what happened, Minnow," she says in a measured tone. "Look what you've done to yourself."

I look down at my arms. They're twined with white

bandages. Beneath, the purple of new bruises are visible up to my elbows. The skin around my stumps pulled apart, so in the infirmary, they had to use staples.

"You put staples in me?" I remember asking the nurse after I woke up from sedation.

"It's routine," she said.

"Staples?" I asked. "Let me see them. No, I don't want to. God, this place is nuts." They put something on my tongue that melted away like powder and I went very relaxed. I didn't care as much about the staples anymore.

"I did this to myself," I say to Mrs. New. "Not Dr. Wilson. He was just trying to help." The words still taste bitter in my mouth, but I swallow them because I need to see him again, to get him off the trail of my mother and Constance and Waylon and Jude.

"You could've seriously injured yourself." She shakes her head. "As it is, Dr. Wilson will be taking an indeterminate break from your case while another caseworker evaluates his progress."

"For how long?" I ask, trying to push through the fog the pill covered me in.

"However long it takes."

I don't move. My muscles are locked in loose submission. My bottom lip nestles under my top, and I cry.

• • •

For the rest of the day, I stare at the Post-it on my affirmation wall. *Anger is a kind of murder you commit in your heart.* I've read it so many times, I think I believe it. Today, there was something else in my heartbeat. There was a skirmish. There was a fight.

"Angel, what do you miss the most?"

Angel hangs her head over her bunk. "I miss Pop-Tarts," she says. "And Mountain Dew, and real pizza, and oh, fried chicken. I miss that the most."

"No people?" I ask.

She shakes her head, the tails of her cornrows flicking side to side. "Not a soul," she says. "People like me, we don't look back. Only forward."

"Are you ever gonna tell me how long you're serving?"

"Do you think I'll tell you anything about that with you lying on your bed all mopey and sad-looking? You'd burst into tears."

"Fine," I say. "Be that way."

She disappears back to her bunk. After a moment, I hear her ask, "Are you trying to get me to ask you who you miss?"

"Maybe."

"All right," she says. "Who do you miss?"

"My grandpa," I say.

She slides off of her bed and stands in front of me. "I thought for sure you'd say Jude."

I shake my head. Jude is beyond missing. He's in some other realm where his absence crouches always in the shadows, his hands pressed coldly to my heart.

"He was my father's father," I say. "He's dead now, but I can't help thinking he wouldn't have let any of this happen. If he'd been stronger, if he'd lived, I think he might have saved all of us."

I didn't know my grandparents well. My grandmother was a wrinkled peach of a thing who died when I was too little to think about it, but Grampy was around even after the Prophet showed up. He didn't say much when my father started talking about the new things he'd decided to believe in, but I could tell Grampy didn't like it by the way he'd go silent and hunch his shoulders, all of his muscles bunching up inside the loose skin he lived in.

I was five when he died. We waited for hours in the hospital, and I spent the entire time being fascinated with a sheet cake in the hospital waiting room. My father wouldn't let me eat any. He said it was *touched by the teeth of Gentiles*, or something. So I just stared at the chocolate insides marring the inches of white frosting and only the memory of a message scrawled in green on the top. It was a cake to celebrate someone getting better, being cured, leaving the hospital for good.

Grampy had been in a war years before when, on a foreign street, out of nowhere, he got punched in the thigh by a speeding piece of metal from an exploded car. And here, years later, his leg began to die, the muscle turning to poison and killing him a little with every heartbeat.

In this room, we waited to hear how getting his leg cut off had gone.

I looked at my parents like they'd become new people, suddenly, morphed into misshapen versions of themselves. Things had been changing for a while, ever since the Prophet started stopping by, but this was the first time I'd seen them together outside our house. The fluorescent lights of the waiting room illuminated their strangeness, their apartness. Had my mother's lips always hung so slack? Had my father always had those livid blue veins that stabbed his eyes like pitchforks? My mother had quit her job by now, her swelling stomach stretching her gray shirt. My father's beard was nearly to the center of his chest. It must've been about a month before we'd leave for the woods.

When the surgeon came out, he closed the wooden door behind him and put on a face that was trying to look sincere, but really looked tired.

"I'm so sorry. Donald didn't make it."

He explained how it happened. A bad thing grew out of the blood, formed a ball, and floated through his veins where it became jammed. Everything happened quickly after that.

My father's face was impenetrable. He stared straight ahead, eyes avoiding the surgeon.

"It might not be my business, but do you have a faith?" the doctor asked.

My father lifted his head. "Why?"

"It can help, sometimes, believing in something."

"How do you mean?"

"Well, do you believe people go to a better place when they die? To heaven?"

My father was pulling on his bottom lip. His face was full of extra skin that bagged bluely and made him look tired. "I don't know. I never asked."

"Pardon?" the surgeon asked.

"I don't know if I believe that. I never . . . I haven't thought to ask about heaven."

The surgeon's face wrinkled in confusion. He bowed slightly—"Again, I'm so sorry for your loss,"—and walked back through the wooden door.

They let us see Grampy's body. He looked surprisingly young, no wrinkles, just a big, white, inflated face.

Someone'd tucked a pistachio-colored blanket up under his chin so all you could see was his head. I wanted to reach out my fingers and touch his cheek, but my mother smacked my hand away when I tried.

I don't remember her ever moving that quickly again. She operated in slow motion so much of the time. I think, had she been caught on film, you might've seen the wind ruffle her dress slower than everyone else's, her footsteps always taking an eternity to strike the ground.

Chapter 33

It's claustrophobic here, but not like Jude always said cities would feel. What did he know anyway? He'd never been to one. He insisted the concrete and metal would crush a person, block out the light. But what's suffocating are the people. This feeling that too many sets of lungs are breathing right next to you. Like it's a finite resource, air. It can run out, and we're all breathing a little less well because we choose to live side by side with others. Some days I can barely catch my breath at all.

I haven't seen the sky, the real sky, not the muted one that shines through the milk-colored skylight, since I arrived in juvie. For the first couple of days after they found me, covered in Philip's blood, they had me so full of morphine in that hospital bed that all I could do was stare out the window and try to block out the yellow-tasting chemical smell that never went away. The bed was too soft. Somehow, it made everything ache worse.

A detective visited after I was coming out of the

anesthetic fog of my second surgery. I had tolerated the surgeries numbly, let them move me and poke me and cut me. Before the plastic surgeon had his way with my arms, they spread my legs and stuck a needle in my femoral artery and injected dye to color my blood. On a screen, I watched the veins in my arms flash with yellow as the blood pumped, so much like branches of a tree, but all around the rim of my wrists, the screen was black. Dead.

In surgery, they did something to my stumps, undid the embroidery floss stitches and shaved off some bone and tried to sort out the broken nest of nerves and tendons. The surgeons patched a chunk of muscle and skin from my inner thighs onto each stump with a lacework of fine black sutures.

I woke up feeling unmoored and sick, ceiling lights battering my bruised eyelids. I could still smell smoke in my hair but couldn't remember where it had come from, and I couldn't piece together where Jude was. When the detective came in, I asked him over and over, but he only frowned as though he had no idea who Jude was, and looking back I guess he didn't.

"The place you called the Community has been destroyed," he said. "We believe someone started a fire."

My head snapped back against the pillows and in that

second, all I could see was the Prophet's dying eyes, the heat from the fire pushing redness into his cheeks.

"Is there anybody who'd want your home destroyed?" he asked.

Me, I thought, and shut my eyes hard again.

"What about your mother?" he asked. "Your father? Any of your siblings?"

"I don't know, I don't know, I don't know!" I repeated, more and more loudly each time.

"Do you have any idea how the fire started?" the detective asked.

All at once, the encompassing smell of smoke was too much. I leaned forward and vomited a pile of foamy yellow on the thready hospital blanket. And still the detective kept pushing with his questions, wanting more. Demanding more.

"Every morning, every evening, ain't we got fun?" I heard someone sing. The detective grew silent. The voice was high-pitched and broken with tears, like a sad angel. But I didn't believe in angels anymore.

"Not much money, oh but honey, ain't we got fun?" the voice continued. The detective's face screwed up in confusion. He heard the voice, too.

"The rent's unpaid dear, we haven't a bus, but smiles are made dear, for people like us." My split lip shivered in pain, and I realized I was the one singing. I thought I might lose it right there because the world went white and depthless, like someone had suddenly packed my brain in cotton. They had to sedate me. I decided I didn't want it, so I struggled, and I pissed myself, and they called a big male nurse to come in and press hard on my shoulders till another nurse could stick the needle in the crook of my elbow.

I woke up after hours had passed, late in the evening. They'd changed my hospital gown. The detective was gone.

The male nurse entered my room at the end of his shift. I watched him as he leaned over and plugged something into the wall outlet.

"It's a night-light," he said. "It'll help keep the darkness away."

He flicked a switch, and the light blinked on. It was made of opaque, yellowed plastic in the shape of a rainbow. In the darkness, the light was brighter than any star out the window. It kept me awake every night, though I didn't sleep anyway, just stared at the smeared multicolor half-circle projected on the wall that had probably lit the rooms of thousands of children in the pediatric ward over the past twenty years.

The night before the final day of my trial, I pried open the hospital window and stared out. Even with the glass pushed aside, the night-light blurred out the stars. I sunk to my knees and shuffled to where the night-light was plugged into the wall. Carefully, I closed my mouth over the top of the rainbow, breathing in the hot plastic smell. I shut my eyes from the brightness, the inside of my eyelids turning rosy, and pulled till the light came unstuck from the wall.

The rainbow was hot in my mouth. It tasted like a toy I had when I was little, a plastic palm-sized fish my father got me for my fourth birthday. He told me it was a minnow, though it was larger than a real minnow. Prettier. Brighter eyes.

I carried the night-light to the window and opened my mouth, watching it fall through the green light of traffic signals. The sound it made as it collided with the pavement was almost disappointing. A clatter. Barely an indication it existed at all.

With the light gone, I could see now. Below was a parking lot edged by a clutch of maples and the road that led first to the river, then to houses whose stones must have been stolen from the mountains. Farther out lay those mountains. And beyond them, stars. Whole galaxies of them hanging like a mobile above the pines where I spent my childhood. I had lived beside those trees for twelve years. But, from here, I could make out only a general sense of green. I found I didn't care about them. If I hadn't had my eyes trained on them, they might've only been a starless piece of sky.

Chapter 34

Dr. Wilson hasn't been seen in Cell Block 3 of the female juvenile detention unit in the Missoula Correctional Department's finest yellow-brick, piss-smelling facility for two weeks. I can see now I'd begun to enjoy his visits, the way he's so different from everyone inside, not just because he dresses in real clothes and smells nothing like bleach, but because he is always, always calm. In jail, at any moment, you're never farther than ten feet from someone completely losing their shit. He's left me to deal with this place all on my own. I am certain he is never coming back.

With Dr. Wilson gone, there is no diversion from the everyday tedium of this place. Each day is the same routine, the same hallways, the same meals. The same drumming thoughts. I think about the regular people I saw from my window at the hospital, walking through hip-height snow berms, their faces obscured by scarves, but their eyes bright and unafraid. Always unafraid. I wondered how they could afford such bravery. Didn't they peep out of their real glass windows at the hills circling them like baited wolves and squirm in their houses at night?

How could I ever be unafraid like them?

Beyond this jail is the city I dreamed about. I can sense it, even through these concrete walls. Why, now, is it so much less fascinating than I always imagined? Somewhere, I chant to the inside of my skull, is an old man swinging loaves of bread. And the woman in a coral-colored blouse taking a bus to work. I loved that woman, dreamed of being just like her, getting a job tapping on the keys of some big, gray computer keyboard in an office like the one my mother worked in once. Except computers don't look like they did in my daydreams anymore, and even from far away the gasket sound city buses make terrifies me. The world is nothing like I imagined.

• • •

Angel returns to the cell at the end of the day with new worksheets shoved loose in her binder, which she drops unceremoniously on the floor before grabbing her book and climbing to her bunk. She stops and peers down at me.

"Why do you look like such a mope?" she asks.

"Dr. Wilson's gone," I say. "He hasn't come by for weeks."

"Good girl," she says. "Maybe he's gone for good."

An unexpected pang stabs my chest. "He can't be," I say. "My parole meeting comes up in August, when I turn eighteen. If I'm going to get out, I need him to recommend me."

"You don't seriously think you'll get parole," she says.

I look up at her. "What?"

"I'm just being realistic," she says, and I try to see it through her eyes—I almost killed Philip. What could I ever say to convince the board? To convince anyone?

"Have you been up for parole?" I ask.

"Once."

"What's it like?"

"Boring. They talk for like five hours before they even hear your case, and by the time you get to sit in front of them, they already know everything about you. They ask you a couple questions, and you get this idea that your answers actually matter, but they don't. And then they roundtable, and they tell you parole has been denied."

"What if a staff member stands up for you?"

"Who knows? I've never heard of that happening. The staff has nothing to gain. And none of them gets to know us well enough to come up with compelling evidence. We're just sheep to them. We're just paper to be pushed around."

I think of Miss Bailey and Benny and Dr. Wilson, and want to argue with her, but then I wonder how much I really matter to any of them. How much they actually care.

"What about Benny?" I ask. "You two are close."

"She might do it, if I asked her. But I'll get denied every time. Some cases—yours, mine—it's too black-and-white for them. No amount of good behavior or promises or Bible quotes will erase how they see us."

I nod and rest my head on my knee.

"Minnow," she says solemnly, "please don't convince yourself you stand a chance. You're going to Billings, and next year I'll join you there."

The short-term girls talk about Billings, trying to scare us with stories of rapists and meth-whores who'll stab you for looking at them out of the wrong eye. But the long-term girls whisper about how much better things will be at Billings, finding any reason to avoid thinking about the stories they've heard. They talk about how the uniform is actual clothes—box-shaped burgundy T-shirts and kha-kis, not jumpsuits. They say inmates with good behavior are given a stray dog to care for. They say some of the guards are even men.

"Can't wait," I mutter just as the bell rings for dinner.

• • •

When we arrive in the cafeteria, Mrs. New stands at the front beside a tall, lean woman in a gray suit.

"The warden," I hear hissed around me. The gray-clad woman observes the girls in a removed way, as though watching us from the top of a guard tower with a rifle in her hands. Her short hair is pulled back in a stiff ponytail, blades of dyed blond fanning from her hairline unnaturally. Her skin is powdery and severely pale.

Nobody knows her actual name, the others tell me, and she only shows her face when something really bad's happened.

"Last time the warden was here," Angel mutters once we're seated with our food, "she was telling us outdoor rec time was canceled because some girl hung herself with a tetherball."

"And the time before that," Rashida pipes up, "that girl Roxanne tried to escape by holding on to the underside of one of the buses, and she got smeared all over a speed bump in the parking lot."

"We could see it from science class," another girl says. "Guts everywhere."

The warden steps up to a mounted microphone and clears her throat loudly. The room falls instantly silent.

"Good evening," the warden says in a clipped voice.

"Good evening," we repeat.

"I'm here with some wonderful news. After two years of being closed to new applicants, the Bridge Program has opened several spots and will be accepting applications for admission."

An excited mumbling breaks out among the girls.

The warden clears her throat again. "The competition will be steep," she says. "Every warden in every juvenile facility in Montana is making a similar announcement today. Nevertheless, each of you is encouraged to apply. Mrs. New will distribute applications to the writing teachers."

"What's she talking about?" I ask, turning to Angel.

"It's this program that gives you a place to live and pays for everything after you're released. They let you stay as long as you need to finish college and get a job. That's why spots hardly ever open up."

"Like a group home?" I ask.

"Like a really nice group home where you never have to worry about anything. Like a group home you'd actually want to live in."

A dozen hands dart in the air, and the warden spends about five minutes answering questions. Yes, everything is paid for. Yes, even college. Yes, even food. No, not alcohol, and that's not even remotely funny.

A mousy blond girl with bones like a bird's and a

belly the size of a watermelon raises her hand.

Yes, the warden says, the Bridge Program houses and pays for the girls' dependents, too, if they have any. The blond girl's face breaks open in a smile, her hand widening over her ballooned stomach.

"This is so fucked," Angel whispers.

I turn to look at her. Her face is set in a scowl. "What?" I ask.

"She actually thinks she'll get in," Angel says.

I follow Angel's gaze to the blond girl. Her wide-set eyes are hopeful, and almost every girl in the cafeteria has the same expression. They whisper to one another with cupped hands as the warden answers more questions about entry requirements. And it dawns on me what a horrible trick this actually is, what a cruelty. Most of them won't make the cut.

"I take it you're not applying?" I ask, though I know the answer.

She scoffs. "I stand a better chance at the Nobel Prize."

The warden explains that only girls released or granted parole by their eighteenth birthday will be eligible for the program. Angel will go adult prison after this. For a long time, I'm guessing. And, I'm realizing, probably so will I.

Chapter 35

There are times when I can go full days without thinking about the Community. It's been weeks since I craved nettlecake or the first ripe mushrooms that I could sneak from the pail before anyone noticed, and lately I haven't even spent much time thinking about Jude. This morning, though, he came back in an unexpected rush when I saw a new inmate traveling across the cafeteria linoleum. She held her tray uncertainly, walked around on knees half folded and wavered before she sat down at an empty table. Staining her cheek, big and bright, was the burgundy fist of a bruise. Something went off in my brain like a trigger, and *bang* I wasn't in the cafeteria but right back in the forest, waiting for Jude in the bleeding dusk.

There were days when he would meet me with a bruise purpling the skin around his eye, and he never talked about it. He held his eyes down and barely looked at me. I hadn't met his father, who could quote the Bible and down a bottle of moonshine in the same heartbeat, who came to the wild before Jude was born. Wordlessly, I showed Jude my scars, the red raised skin on the back of my wrists from Vivienne's switch and, years later, the branch-like whip marks that scored my bare back.

"Will you teach me to read, Jude?" I asked one day in our second winter. I sat huddled inside a blanket we left in the tree house for chill afternoons like this. Jude had brought his mother's Bible up to the tree house to show me where she'd written her name in curly pencil when she was twelve, and I held the thick, frayed book in my hands like it was made of precious metal. It had been years since I'd touched a book.

"Teach you to read?" Jude looked up from where he was picking at the strings of his guitar. "What do you wanna learn that for? Don't do me no good."

"I dunno," I said. "Might come in handy. And I could read your Bible."

He stopped strumming. "I'm starting to think I don't really like what's in that book, besides my momma's name. My daddy always talks from it when he's angry, wicked-ness, damnation, sinning. Sometimes I think there ain't no *right* way to live in this world, least not in my daddy's view."

"Then teach me to sing," I said.

"What do you wanna sing?"

"The first song you sang me."

"'Ain't We Got Fun'?"

I nodded. "Your mother taught you it, right?"

"Yeah," he said, strumming. "She was the prettiest singer."

"What happened to her?" I asked, then bit my lip. Jude's brow furrowed a fraction and I knew I'd said the wrong thing. He never talked about her. She was dead, that I knew, but of what Jude never said.

"Here," he said. "Sit next to me." He patted the floorboards near him.

I stood and swung my legs over the side of the tree house and let the large skirt of my dress cascade down.

Every morning, every evening, ain't we got fun? he sang.

I repeated him in a wobbly, high voice.

"Not much money, oh but honey, ain't we got fun? The rent's unpaid dear, we haven't a bus, but smiles are made dear, for people like us."

"Why do they need a bus?" I interrupted. "Most people in town drive cars."

He paused. "Maybe they have a lot of kids."

"Maybe they're Kevinians."

He laughed, and I startled. I'd never made anyone laugh before. The sound echoed out to where the forest sloped away toward the east. The sky was different there. Paler, as though it reflected light from a city. Below, I could see two sets of footprints in the snow, each coming from a different direction.

"Play something," I said.

"All right. You gotta help though. Put your hand there."

I curved my fingers over the guitar's neck and moved my fingers around to make different sounds. It was tight in the opening, and Jude had to prop his left hand behind him, picking at the strings with his right. At one point, Jude rested his left hand lightly on my rib cage. Each of his fingertips touched a different rib. Unconsciously, he pressed down with his fingers, as though he was still playing the guitar.

I'd never been touched by a boy, not like this. Girls were discouraged from even sharing eye contact with the opposite sex. Physical affection was the domain of the Devil. Badness has a way of slipping between skin, easy, like badness does. This, right here, the warmth from his hand penetrating the navy thickness of my dress, my hip grazing his, was enough to damn me for eternity.

It was worth it.

Chapter 36

Someday I'll forget everything about juvie, but I'll never forget the permeating grease smell of the place, recalling the thousands of onions and chicken nuggets that have been fried to death here, or the dull fluorescent glow of the classrooms and the teachers who flinch whenever one of the girls moves too quickly, or the movies on Wednesday afternoons in the cafeteria for those of us who earn the extra rec time. I'm quiet during these movies, the black-and-white ones preferred by the warden, probably because they present such unambiguous models for female behavior. A guard will tuck the first celluloid frame into the projector and hit the lights and just like that every girl in the room isn't in jail anymore. They're inside a dance hall or a Southern mansion or Oz. It's a pleasure, always, to observe these pockmarked girls in orange jumpsuits lit up by the wide, expressive face of Orson Welles as he holds ice to the broken tooth of a girl he aims to marry. I can't get enough of the girls' faces in those moments, their eyes hollowed out by the film's shadows.

My entire life has been an experiment in tolerating the unimaginable. I've even gotten used to juvie, my body regulated to synthetic food made in factories and pressed together by machines in uniform shapes and sizes, gotten used to the constant reminder of what got me here, that green-eyed boy, that frozen winter night. And, after a time, I've even grown used to the missing hands, as much as I can. But I'll never get used to the uncertainty.

After the hands, after I stopped believing in God, or at least stopped believing that I could ever believe in God again, I also stopped praying. I realized my head had been inflated with prayers, and they always looked like:

Please, please,

please, please.

Who else on Earth would I beg to so shamelessly? Please stop the winter, my toes are numb. Please give Mabel an easy birthing. Please take away the terrible smell of Mabel's birthing from the kitchen. Please give me a new pair of boots, my old ones pinch. Please make Jude love me forever and ever.

Even so amen.

Why did it never occur to me that anyone would get tired of hearing that after so many years? Now that I've stopped asking, I can tell I'd been going about it the wrong way all along. The space in my head where prayer used to live is filled with questions now. Some of them I've asked myself my entire life, only now they're not content to go unanswered, instead beating the inside of my skull like an angry drum.

And that's why, after breakfast, when Angel leaves for her counseling session, I don't go back to my cell. I walk down to the classroom corridor and find a yellow door, a piece of paper thumbtacked to the surface. I know I'm in the right place because the only thing on the paper is a large markered cross.

The youth group meets in a blank room with plastic chairs tossed in a misshapen ring around a small multi-colored braided rug. Of the twenty chairs, probably half are occupied.

I only know three of the girls, Rashida, who's sitting near the front next to Tracy, singing a ballad in a high-pitched whiny voice, her arms swinging back and forth at her sides like she's running; and Wendy, who sits by herself with her ankles linked together. Tracy bounces up when she sees me.

"Hi, Minnow!" she says. "It's great to see you again. I'm so glad you decided to visit youth group. Why don't you join us in the circle?"

I sit between an athletic-looking girl with the cuffs of her jumpsuit rolled to the knee and Wendy, who I notice, even though she's sitting still, wheezes a little at the back of her throat. The girl on the other side takes a look at my Velcro shoes and shifts over slightly.

"Minnow," Tracy says, folding her hands in her lap. "Tell us about what brought you to youth group."

"I just wanted to see," I say, my cheeks flushing uncomfortably. "See what it was like."

"That's great," Tracy says. "Why don't we all start by introducing ourselves?"

The girls go around the room, sharing their names and their denominations. Some of them have been religious since birth and others found it in jail.

"Isn't there a pastor?" I ask, when they've gone around the circle.

Tracy shakes her head. "We used to have a pastor, but he was called to do mission work in Burma. He's doing great things there, and I'm certain all those little dying children needed him more than we did. Since then, we lead our own sessions. We read passages of scripture and discuss it, and we talk about the things we're going through."

"How do you know if you're doing it right without a pastor?" I ask.

"Any questions we have, we consult the Bible."

"How—" I start to ask, but stumble on my words.

"How do we know if the Bible's right?" Tracy asks.

"Never mind."

"No, no, it's a valid question. Girls, what can we say to put Minnow's mind at ease?"

Tracy looks pointedly at Rashida who's gnawing on a cuticle. Rashida shrugs and shakes her head.

Next to me, Wendy leans forward and takes a big gulp of breath. "Tell her about your surgery, Taylor."

A small freckled girl with jittery muscles almost jumps out of her seat. "Yeah, yeah," she says. "When I was fourteen, they found a brain tumor in me. I had to have, like, three surgeries to remove it. And during the last one, I felt the presence of God. His grace. And, after that, I knew I'd never have to question Him again."

"You really felt it?" I ask. "How do you know for sure?"

"I just knew," she says, tucking a strand of red hair behind her ear. "It felt like . . . sunlight. Like warmth."

"But . . ." I say, and even as the words come out, I know I should stop them. "Don't you want proof? The light could've been a surgical lamp. The warmth could have been you pissing yourself; that happens during surgery."

Taylor's face falls a fraction. "I guess I choose not to think that way. I'm an optimistic person. Why, do you think I'm lying?"

"No," I say, eyes darting to the side. "But I can't believe in something I don't know for sure."

"Well," Tracy interjects from across the circle, "how do you know anything is real? I mean, Minnow, picture the most real thing you can think of. How do you know it actually happened? How do you know for sure?"

Of course it's Jude I think of. How can I prove he ever even existed? If I had my hands, I'd look at my palm where I had a scar from when he taught me how to whittle a fallen branch into something beautiful like he could. I spent an hour on a whittled sculpture of him but before I was done, the knife slipped over the smooth surface of wood and sliced the meat of my hand, and blood dropped over his wooden face. Jude propped the sculpture on the tree house windowsill. "It's like you're a part of me now," he said. "That seems right."

But the hands are gone, and with them that scar and any proof I ever knew him.

I look back at Tracy. "I guess the answer is you just do," I say finally.

"I think so, too," Tracy says.

She clears her throat and looks over at the others. "Girls," she says to the group, "in honor of our new member, I think we should go around the room and tell one another what made us believers. Wendy, you want to start?"

Tracy turns to Wendy, whose wheezing noise halts for a moment. "I never thought anything about God until Tracy talked to me on my first day here. She said, 'Wendy, you may not believe in God, but God believes in you.'"

The room grows silent. "That's it?" I ask.

Tracy darts me a look. "Thanks, Wendy. That's really helpful. Rashida, want to share your story?"

Rashida's eyes twitch toward the ceiling, as if considering. "I just think it don't make sense not to believe in

God. If I believed and He turned out to be fake, how am I gonna know that after I'm dead? I'll be stuck in the ground with nothing on my mind except there better not be any worms trying to get inside my coffin. But if I didn't believe and He's actually real, well then I just got myself a life sentence in Hades with, like, fire pokers jabbing my ass and having to sit in a Jacuzzi of boiling oil with Hitler and shit, and you are crazy if you think I'll be putting up with that kind of treatment for the rest of time, no sir. This bitch is going to heaven."

Rashida claps her hands and sways in her chair, singing, "This bitch is going to heaven," on a loop.

"Well, compared with Rashida and Taylor, mine is going to sound super-lame," Tracy says. "There was this moment when I was really young. I was just reading the Bible one day at my family's horse ranch. I picked it up just like now." She opens the Bible next to her and bends the cover back to the first page. "And I read the first line. 'In the beginning, God created the heavens and the earth. The earth was without form and void, and darkness was over the face of the deep. And God said "Let there be light."'" Tracy pauses, casting her eyes around the circle emphatically. "'And there was light.'"

She darts an expectant look at me. Beside her, Rashida is still singing "This bitch is going to heaven."

"Yeah?" I ask.

"You don't see?" she asks, and when I don't reply she shakes her head, her bangs whisking across her forehead in frustration. "I just realized, for the first time, how . . . beautiful it is. That everything in the universe was created in that one moment. Everything we are, everything that's ever been and ever will be. Isn't that amazing?"

She's looking at me a little uneasily, as though she knows I can't picture it the exact way she does, can't accept the eye blink of God creating the heavens and the earth and the creatures of the land and sky. And I'm about to tell her so when, in the next moment, I'm thinking of Taylor's story, and Wendy's, and Rashida's.

Maybe the amazing thing is the fact that they can believe, even in here, even when there's no reason they should be able to.

"Yeah, Tracy," I say finally. "I think it is."

Chapter 37

I talked with Jude about everything, but some things didn't really translate. It was the first time I realized that two people could speak the same words and each get very different images coming into their minds. I stopped telling Jude about the Community at a point. He didn't speak that language, and I didn't speak his. We had to invent a new language together, one that didn't have words for everything. When we talked, we navigated around those big ideas that didn't feel right on our tongues. At least for a time.

Once, the summer we turned sixteen, on a night bright with constellations, Jude and I stared at the sky from the tree house, not speaking, thinking our separate thoughts that terrified us. When I glanced at him, an unconscious folded bit of skin had settled between his eyes. He had begun to wear that face more and more. The stars did that to him, but he couldn't look away.

"What are you thinking about when you look up at the sky like that?" I asked.

He shrugged.

"Come on, tell me," I said. "I know you're looking at something up there. Is it the stars? The moon?"

"It don't matter," he said.

Something had changed between us, the language of our childhood no longer fitting our mouths the way it used to. Our bodies had grown. The tree house no longer accommodated us at our full heights, and with every season the walls seemed closer together. We were sixteen and we didn't know how to navigate each other anymore. We no longer ran through the woods together, unconscious and loose-limbed. We were awkward, never touching, always making sure to sit inches apart.

"Jude, what do you suppose the stars are?"

He tilted his head toward me. "What?"

"The stars," I repeated restlessly. "What are they, really? Sometimes the Prophet says they're God's eyes in a giant dark canvas, but other times he says that outer space goes on farther than our minds can picture, and the stars are each a fern-filled heaven waiting for us the moment we die, but he never answers which is which, and you get in trouble when you ask."

"I don't know," he says. "I never learned things like that."

"Neither did I, and that's what drives me crazy. I wanna

know things. I wanna know everything. But it's like asking questions to a tree stump. There's never anyone answering back."

"I can answer anything you need answered."

"But what if you can't?"

"Then it ain't worth knowing."

I crossed my arms and looked away.

"Look," he said, a small huff in the back of his throat, "I can tell you about what kinds of rabbits make that chittering noise you hear sometimes at night, and how many fire ants' blood is enough poison to bring down a squirrel. I can tell you how old this tree is, and how many strokes it'd take to chop it down. So," he asked, "what do you wanna know about?"

"Who put them here?" I ask. "Was it God? Did He do it the same time He placed all those lights up there in the heavens?"

"The stars again?" He shook his head. "Why do you care? What difference does it make to your life?"

"I dunno," I said. "The stars . . . they matter to me."

Moments like this occurred more and more frequently, and I think that was the biggest difference between us. That we could look at the same stars in the same sky, but not have the same questions. Not want the same answers.

One of those days, not long after, we sat beside each

other in our tree house, sunlight filtering through the moss of the larch and casting the entire forest in lime-green light. The air was itchy with a tension that neither of us could articulate.

"What are you thinking about?" I asked awkwardly. "And don't tell me it don't matter."

His face was almost empty, staring off into some other time. His eyes shifted on to mine and stared deep. "My momma."

"You don't talk about her much," I said.

"She said the stars were souls, and every time someone dies, a new star gets put up there in the heavens. I look up there, look and look, but I never see her."

"What was she like?"

"She was wonderful," he said. "On days like this, she'd order me outta the house to do something productive, pick a pail of berries. She'd say 'You're in my way and I have a house to clean!' but I knew she weren't serious because there was a smile in her eyes. And because, by the time I came back with the berries, she'd always have a piecrust ready."

"She sounds like a nice mother."

"She was," Jude croaked. Tears were standing in his eyes now.

"Then she got so sick. She started holding the top of

her belly, where her ribs ended, and she would press down hard until the pain passed. She kept a plastic pail near her bed, and she'd spit out mouthfuls of yellow stuff, saying I'm sorry' every time, like she could help it.

"My daddy was drinking bad by then. He couldn't stand to see her in that kinda pain, but he never cried in front of her. He'd go upstairs to the little attic space there and howl and drink, and downstairs both of us could hear him. I asked him to take her to a hospital but our old truck had broken down and we didn't have no way to get her down the mountain. My daddy told me he and my momma made the choice when they moved here to go without things like hospitals. Over time, it was like we all realized, one by one, that she was gonna die. My momma knew before any of us. And I figured it out last.

"But, my momma wouldn't die. She kept getting worse and worse, and with every turn I'd think this couldn't be life anymore because it looked so much like death. I spent every day working on the truck without knowing how to fix it. I took each part out and cleaned it and saw that everything was plugged in right but the engine would never budge when I turned the key. When I finally fixed it, it was too late. It was just a little silver cap I needed. My momma died cause of one little piece of silver. It makes me so mad sometimes I just wanna take off running and never stop.

"One morning, my daddy came out back to the truck where I was working. He put his hand on my shoulder and said 'Son, it's time for you to do a man's job.' He'd been crying and drinking. I could tell because his face was red and his eyes were red. And before he even explained, I knew what he meant. I started running. I turned around and whipped the wrench at him, but it only bounced offa the ground, and he was already doubled over with his hands on his knees. Crying or puking, I couldn't see.

"I spent two days out in the wild. I never went farther'n the farthest place I'd ever gone. I just couldn't make myself push past it, to the south, where a big stand of aspens grows. I looked out at those aspens, wanting so badly to lie down in the little hollow between 'em and stare at the stars. But I couldn't. I walked the entire night, and by the time I woke up the next morning, I knew. I knew what I'd do."

Jude's entire body was convulsing with sobs. His speech dribbled out of his mouth with the force of an unstoppable river. I didn't know any other way to stop him so I covered his mouth with my hand. He brushed it away.

"I walked back the next day, slow as I could, until I stood in front of the door, and walked in, and picked my daddy's shotgun up from where it was leaning against the wall. My mother saw me, and she closed her eyes and breathed in, then looked up at me and nodded. I plugged two cartridges in, and put the barrels to her head, and—and I pulled the trigger." His face was screwed up tight but somehow tears still seeped out.

"I kilt her, Minnow. I kilt her and she's dead because of me."

This time, I covered his mouth with my mouth, and it worked. He gasped like he'd had an epiphany. He looked at me with his mouth open, his eyes open. In that moment, the tension broke. We both felt it, the rush of it leaving us, and no longer was there tentativeness. There was immediacy and hunger. He reached over and kissed me hard, a first clumsy kiss, a first step in a different direction. And I understood what had been holding us back. We were no longer children with children's bodies and children's thoughts. We wanted more from each other.

Undaunted now, I touched his wet cheeks with my fingertips, brushed them with the back of my hand. His hands tumbled beneath my bonnet and into the dense braided hair, fell to the thick parts of my waist, squeezing me there over the walls of my dress.

For years, we had stood on opposite sides of a divide, calling across because we could never jump the distance.

This was the moment we discovered that, if we both shifted our weight forward, if we abandoned our fear of the drop below, not looking down, we could touch the tips of our fingers together. And though it wasn't much, in that moment, it was enough. We stepped headlong into a new place where we knew there was something other than good daughters and sons inside us. Because for the first time, somebody bothered to tell me why they were in pain. Everybody around me was in pain, I realize now, but none of them ever poured it out of themselves into another person.

Jude taught me what love was: to be willing to hold on to another person's pain. That's it.

Chapter 38

After every reading class, I stay behind in Miss Bailey's classroom. This is normally her lunch period, but she says she doesn't mind giving it up to help me with my reading. We've moved up to real books, slim ones with illustrations, and mostly she just sits in her rocking chair, chewing a sandwich and listening to me fight my way through a story, which for the past week has been about a pig named Wilbur who becomes friends with a spider.

I put down the book, suddenly exhausted.

"What is it?" Miss Bailey asks.

"They used to tell us in my—in my church," I say, remembering how she doesn't want to know anything about our pasts. "They told us that if an animal ever talked, that was a sign it was infected by the Devil."

Miss Bailey uncrosses her legs and sits up straighter. "Really?"

"Every morning, after I woke up, I had to walk behind my house to the barn and look each goat in the eye and ask them 'Are you the Devil upon this Earth?' And if they didn't reply, I could milk them and know that drinking their milk wouldn't give the Devil a foothold in our minds."

She considers this. "Do you suppose Wilbur's possessed by the Devil?"

I look at her face to see if she's making fun of me, but she looks serious.

"No," I say.

"Me neither," she says. "You know, when I was little, my dad told me that if I misbehaved, he'd send me to live with a witch who ate children."

"Really?"

She nods. "I was so afraid of the witch. Feelings are magnified when you're that young, I think, and the fear can stay with you for a long time. I eventually grew out of the fear but even now when I read something with a witch, my mind always traces back to that story. Isn't that weird?"

"How'd you grow out of it?" I ask. "The fear."

She takes a long moment to answer. "I read lots and lots of books about witches."

• • •

The next day, when the bell rings for rec time, I pace downstairs to the jail library.

I roam around the stacks for a while before Ms. Fitzgerald, the twiggy librarian with a mess of caramel curls, asks me if I need anything.

"Can I check out a book?" I ask.

"That's what this place is here for," Ms. Fitzgerald says. "What book?"

I tell her I'm not sure, but I describe the type of thing I'm looking for, the words I've practiced in my head since my session with Miss Bailey.

"Yes, I can probably find you something," she says. I walk behind her around the shelves as she pulls out copies of the Koran and the Book of Mormon and the Bible. She takes me to the science-fiction section and scans the rows before pulling down a few more books, frayed paperbacks, then to the poetry section, and finally into the dusty nonfiction corner that looks like it never gets used.

"There's more than one place to find answers," Ms. Fitzgerald says, unloading the stack into my outstretched arms.

She lets me check them out even though I have more than the permitted three titles in my stack, and I sit at a large wooden library table, sliding my stump over the pages, trying to sound out the difficult words. On one of the very, very thin pages, I read something that stands out.

"Beware of false prophets, which come to you in sheep's clothing, but inwardly they are ravening wolves."

In the back of my mind, it occurs to me that this is something Dr. Wilson might say. And in that moment, he is all I can think about, how he's been gone for weeks, how I think the reason he must've come to Montana was to escape something in Washington, DC, something he lost.

I traverse the packed brown carpet and sit at a computer. Its face is blank and frightening, like the computer from reading class. I raise my arm in the air. Ms. Fitzgerald approaches.

"Yes?" she asks.

"I want to research a death," I say.

"Like a historical death?" she asks.

"No, something more recent."

"All right," she says, drawing out the first syllable. "Whose death?"

"I'm not sure yet. Can you just open up the Internet?"

"Have you ever used a computer before?"

"Why does that matter?"

"You should spend some rec time here," she says. "I can get you computer literate in no time."

"I'm barely even regular literate," I say. "Now can you push the buttons for me?"

She grabs the mouse and opens an Internet box.

"What do you want to search?" she asks.

"I got it," I say, taking a pencil in my mouth, lead-end in. With the eraser, I type all the words I can think of that might confirm my suspicion: "Dr. Wilson" and "Washington, DC" and "death." For good measure, I throw in "wife or son or daughter or maybe parent?" Ms. Fitzgerald fixes my spelling and pushes the search button. About a billion results come up. I scan the page and see results about local news events in Washington, DC: murders, car crashes, home accidents. I make Ms. Fitzgerald click on a bunch of links, but nothing adds up.

"Can I ask why you're searching this?" she asks.

"I just have a feeling about something," I say. "Just a feeling that something happened, and I wanna know what."

"Well, your search terms are too broad. You need a full name or a year at least."

I nod, leaning forward to press the pencil into the delete key.

• • •

When I get back to the cell, I go to set my stack of books on my bunk but trip over something on the ground. Angel's binder. I step around it but see a stapled packet of papers protruding from the top. "The Bridge Program" it reads. With a toe, I push the paper free of the cover.

It's the application that the girls have been working on.

It's turned to the essay questions. "Why do you think you are a deserving candidate for acceptance to the Bridge Program?" I kneel down and budge the letters with my mind until they form words.

I've been through a lot. You only have to Google me to confirm this. And I could make a list of every sad thing that's happened to me as a case for why I deserve something better, but my guess is you've already read plenty of entries like that. I'm not like that, anyway. I try not to dwell too much on the bad that happened to me growing up, in the past. So I'm going to tell you a little about my future. It is beautiful. I write books and get degrees and get married and have babies and go on to do a million other wonderful things that I haven't even thought up yet. I am deserving because even after everything, I'm still hopeful. The people who hurt me couldn't kill my spirit. I'm dreaming still. See me, right now? Dreaming. And, given everything, that's pretty wonderful.

So that's why I'm deserving. Not because I need your help. But because I am going to make it with or without anybody's help.

My knees are indented from the grated metal floor by the time I finish reading. I have to run my eyes over the paper several times to understand, sounding out difficult words like Miss Bailey taught me, watching them sit in the air strangely. It doesn't make sense. Angel told me she wasn't going to apply. She said she stood a better chance of winning the Nobel Prize. I guess she changed her mind. Maybe she figured it couldn't hurt to apply.

I pull my lip inside my mouth and wonder, *Why, then, don't I give it a try?*

Sifting out the answer is like looking directly into a bright light I've been ignoring. It's just that I don't think I could tolerate answering those questions, opening myself up the way some girls do with sneaked-in razor blades and the metal edges of rulers, a thousand small wounds that might end me.

I look up from the essay and flinch so hard, my front teeth nip my lip painfully. Angel stands on the other side of the barred door, watching me. The door buzzes and she walks calmly inside, picking up her binder and throwing it onto her bed. She takes the essay from me and doesn't say a word. She doesn't move to climb to her bunk like she normally does, doesn't reach for a book. She stands there, looming above me.

She nods at the Bible on the top of the stack of books on my bed. "What are you doing with that?"

I swallow. "I checked it out."

"So you've gone and done it," she says. "I don't know why I'm surprised."

"I haven't done anything."

"You obviously have!" she shouts. She holds up her hands, suddenly furious. Her eyes are shiny and she blinks a few times. "I thought you were different, but you're just like the rest of them."

"I'm not."

"Yes, you are." She points to the Post-it on my affirmation wall. "*Anger is a kind of murder you commit in your heart.* See? You're starting already."

"What?" I ask.

"That was Jesus who said that."

I look from the Post-it to her. Her cheeks are framed with palm-size patches of redness.

"Angel, I've read exactly one line of this Bible. And you know what? I liked that line. In fact, maybe I'll read more." I lift the Bible and pantomime reading. "Oh, now *interesting*! This is soooo much better than science. Evolution is wrong! Praise the Lord!"

Angel's face twists into the start of a smile. "No, fuck you, you're not going to make me laugh."

"Just listen to this, Angel. 'Beware of false prophets, which come to you in sheep's clothing, but inwardly they are ravening wolves.' Isn't that interesting? I think it is.

You can think something's interesting without drinking the lemonade."

"Kool-Aid."

"Whatever."

She sits opposite me against the wall. "I guess."

Farther down the skyway, I can hear the faint voices of Rashida and Tracy arguing over a game of Old Maid in their cell. "I went to youth group, too."

Angel looks up. "Are you trying to make me disown you?"

"I'm not ashamed," I say. "It's not as bad as you make it out to be. They're just looking for answers."

"Are you going back there?"

"Maybe," I say. "But probably not."

"Why?"

"They're not looking for the same answers as me."

She nods slowly. "You know why I really hate Tracy? She's just as fucked up as the rest of us, but she hides behind religion, like that somehow erases the fact that she knifed her English teacher's wife."

"She did?" I ask.

Angel nods. "Tracy looks sweet as pie, but behind that face, she's all kinda crazy-ass. She had a crush on her teacher and when she saw him in the school parking lot with his wife one day, she went ape shit. The lady almost died."

"But we've all done stuff, Angel," I say, picturing the pool of blood steaming in the air around Philip Lancaster's body. "I heard this girl Taylor tell a story during youth group. She said she had an epiphany during surgery. That she felt God. And I just think, as long as I live, I'll never feel as sure as her about anything." I rest my chin on my knee. "I know what you say about the Christian girls, but she believed it was true. She was so sure."

"Yeah, I heard that story before. Gets all kindsa mileage with the Jesus Freaks. Personally, I think it's bull. Those blind-but-now-I-see moments, miracles, all those things you see on the news about the Virgin Mary on toast, I don't got time for that shit. There's no easy explanations for nothing in the world."

"Religion's not necessarily easy."

"It is, though, because if there's ever any errors, you can blame it on having faith. 'Oh yeah, according to carbon dating the Earth's older than four thousand years, unlike what the Bible says, but we'll ignore that because we just have *faith*.'"

"Not everyone who's religious talks like that," I say.

"Like what?"

"All nasally."

"Well, they do in my head," Angel says.

"You hear a lot of things in your head, don't you?"

She lets a little grin touch her mouth and runs her long fingernails over the gaps between her cornrows. "If God is real," she says, "he's part of science. But he's never shown up. He's like a deadbeat dad you wait for all day after T-ball practice. He's not in DNA. Not in the Large Hadron Collider. Not in thousands of years of fossils. Not a shadow of him. But if he ever does show up, it'll be science's job to explain him. Until then, we deal with what we've got in front of us."

I look at what's in front of me. A blinding prison jumpsuit. Arms with no hands. Angel.

My head jerks up. "Then teach me."

"What?" she asks.

"Teach me about the universe."

• • •

Angel moves around the cell excitedly, drawing up book lists and websites I need to visit.

"During your next rec time, you'll check out the complete works of Carl Sagan."

"Who's that?"

"Only my personal hero. If he were alive today, and like way younger, I'd walk to his laboratory and get down on one knee and propose marriage right there. I'm serious. You'll understand when you read him. And oh! I can show you his documentaries online. I hope you like turtlenecks."

We're stuck in our cell for the night, but Angel gives me a lecture on the Big Bang, how one moment there was nothing and the next there was an explosion of red-hot radiation that roiled out in every direction and took millions of years to cool, to form stars, to form planets, to form the animals of the earth.

"And everything we are," Angel says at the end, "every organism, everything the universe is, comes down to that one moment. Isn't that amazing?"

"Yeah." I smile. "Amazing."

Chapter 39

The next day, when the bell rings for afternoon classes and I walk to Reading Is Power with the other girls in my class, we wait in a line in the carpeted hall while the previous class packs up and files out of the classroom. They line up against the opposite wall, gripping their binders and talking in low voices. Behind me, Rashida rattles on about a show she was watching during rec time and I nod along, half listening, because I spot Tracy in the other line, face buried in her tiny Book of Psalms.

"Hey," someone whispers from behind her. "Bible girl." I glance down the line and see Krystal, her dark hair up in a tight ponytail and her fingernails newly lacquered in neon teal. Her eyes are locked on Tracy.

"What?" Tracy whispers back.

"Are you?" Krystal asks, holding her fingers up in a circle.

"Am I what?"

Krystal laughs, shoving her hand in her jumpsuit pocket. "What are you doing later?"

"Homework," Tracy says, "then some Bible study."

"Maybe we could get together," Krystal says. "I could help you study that Bible."

"Really?" Tracy asks, her eyes turning bright.

The other girls are watching this exchange curiously, some with trepidation stamped on their faces, but none of them say a word. Inside the classroom, Miss Bailey is talking to a student from the other class.

Krystal sidles up to Tracy and places a hand on her shoulder, and I recall the solid feeling of her hand on my arm in the TV room, how it made my stomach squirm, but Tracy doesn't seem to notice. "You should really come to youth group—"

"Leave her alone," I say, taking a step over the hard carpet.

"What are you doing?" Rashida whispers behind me, and I can't answer her because I don't know what I'm doing, only that I am almost definitely making a terrible mistake.

Krystal turns her head, taking a step toward me. "What did you say?" Her brows are high on her forehead, her face overwhelmed by Crayon yellow circles under her eyes.

"I said, leave her alone. She didn't do anything to you."

"Minnow, it's fine," Tracy says, her fingers absently playing at the tiny cross on her neck. "Nothing's the matter."

"Yeah, Minnow," Krystal says, imitating Tracy's high voice. "We're just having fun." With the pads of her fingers, she pushes me in the chest and I stumble backward. The girls on either side of me shift their weight agitatedly.

"Why don't you go have fun with someone your own size," I say. "Benny, for instance."

Krystal shakes her head. "What are you doing?" she asks. "You keep saying things like that, you keep getting in my way, I'll be forced to deal with you." She glances at my stumps. "And you're not gonna win."

My chest starts to ache with the same adrenaline feeling from the night under the bridge, like my heart has morphed to the size of a small engine, and I'm suddenly running off something more powerful than blood. "If you think I'm gonna stand here and let you—if you think for even a second I'll let you hurt any of them—"

Very slowly, Krystal reaches a hand inside her pocket. She pulls out something long, off-white, and devilish. It hangs from her fist, limp as a dead rabbit.

"Lock sock," I hear the girls whisper. "Lock sock."

I put the words together slowly, the knotted tube sock, the sure outline of a metal combination lock in the bottom. Krystal starts to swirl the lock sock in front of her.

"You don't have your trained gorilla here to fight for you. You better step back," Krystal says.

263

Instead, I take a fumbling step toward her. I think about what Angel would do. I walk the remaining few feet between us.

"Don't mess with me, Krystal. I got Velcro shoes and you know what that means. I'm crazy," I breathe these last words because my lungs are shuddering. "I won't hesitate fucking you up. My charge is assault, not conspiracy to commit like you, pansy ass."

Krystal's face stretches, livid. "I will kill you, hooker," she screams, but beneath it, her voice quavers and in her face, for the first time, I see the unconscious tightness of the skin beneath her eyes. She's afraid, and it almost knocks me backward. The feeling isn't anything like what I imagined.

She launches herself at me, lifting her shoulder and whipping the lock sock like a mace to bring down on my head. I stumble backward, my arms flying over my head.

I can feel Benny's footfalls before I see her as she charges into the hall. She grabs Krystal by the wrists, flipping her easily onto the carpeted ground with a thunk.

Chapter 40

Krystal and I are given three days in solitary confine-ment, soft-walled cells on the lower level with a slat for food and a rimless toilet so there's never any reason to leave. As they march me down, I protest that I'm blame-less but it does no good. The heavy metal door has only one window that the guards can watch me through, but it stays closed most of the time.

The fluorescent ceiling lights give no indication of time passing. Girls go nuts in these cells, in the silence, the aloneness. The pull to replay moments from the past is impossible to resist. I keep thinking on a space of seconds after the verdict was read at my trial: my head bowed, sob-bing, the courtroom disassembling into a teeming mess of jurors departing and journalists talking into voice record-ers and mostly people just trying to get out of the stuffy wood-paneled room. And the part that makes the least sense, Philip Lancaster breaking every court precaution by stepping past the witness barrier and up to my table.

"Hrrrrre," I heard him say in a muffled voice.

He stood above me, his ordinary eyes blinking down.

"Tkk de Klllnxx," he said. Through his lips, I could see the wires that kept his jaws closed. I glanced down to the table where he nudged a box of Kleenex toward me.

I shook my head. "I can't," I said, holding up my stumps.

He nodded and dragged a tissue from the box. He bent over the table and reached his hand toward my tear-stained face. With the tissue, he brushed away the tears. Small strokes, like a painter.

"Bbbttrr?" he asked.

I nodded. "Better."

I made a mistake, I wanted to say. *I wouldn't do it again,* but before I could open my mouth, a police officer was leading me by the shoulder out of the courtroom to a waiting cop car.

I replay the scene again and again, the broken mashed-up face looming over me, the knowledge between the two of us that I'd done it. That act of kindness is still more unfathomable to me than any cruelty.

I sit in the middle of the padded cream-colored floor, rocking on my crossed legs. I can't let this cell make me crazy. If I've learned anything, it's how to be confined. I have to shake Philip out of my head. I have to go someplace else.

266

The only place to go is to Jude, to a night the autumn I turned seventeen, the autumn I lost my hands, before everything changed. By then, there was nothing between us but a mile of dim-lit forest and October cold that numbed our breath when we kissed. I'd told Jude everything by then. I'd told him about my fear of marriage, how I'd once walked in on my father and one of his wives in their cloister, his hair-covered back, the black soles of their feet pushed out the end of the blanket.

I'd told him how scared I was for my sister Constance, the way she commanded every eye in a room even though she was only twelve. How the men already whispered about what a fine wife she'd be, the way nobody'd ever whispered about me.

I'd told him how fiercely I dreamed of meeting God. How I imagined him, a boy our age, walking down a street in a city or plowing a field or going to school. He could look like anything. The only certain things were his name— Charlie—and his brilliant green eyes. Jude just nodded, kissed the bend between my thumb and forefinger.

One night that autumn, I sat on the porch outside the Prophet Hall, leaning back on my elbows. Inside, the Prophet had been preaching for hours and the Community breathed countless lungs' worth of hot breath, until the place was suffocating and stifling and I had to step out. The night air was cool and smelled like browning leaves. Past the walls of trees, stars dotted the sky. My mind searched for a star with a greenish cast, one that might be a window to the place everybody goes when they die.

In the forest in front of me, two stars stared back. It took a moment to realize they were Jude's eyes, reflected off the candlelight from the Prophet Hall.

I ran to the forest's edge. "What are you doing here?"

"I don't know. My daddy's been drinking," he said worriedly.

He explained how his father was tearing through the house like a madman and he had run away, like he always did when his father lost control. I could tell he was afraid, but not for the immediate future. Not for that night. He was afraid for the rest of his life. That it would always be like this, living in that cabin with his father going slowly decrepit from homemade alcohol, getting meaner. I knew because it was the same fear I felt every day. Fear of being stuck in a place forever.

I walked with Jude to our tree house. We held hands and didn't speak. I felt like he must've been able to hear my heartbeat in my palm. When we were inside, I guided his shaking hand to the front of my dress where he fumbled to undo the row of buttons, hundreds of little blue buttons. I stepped out of the dress, and it sat up, stiff, almost like a person, the shape of a good Kevinian girl.

The thought crossed my mind that Jude and I were doing something completely original, something no one had ever done before. It never occurred to me that this was the same thing girls waited under the covers for on their wedding nights, the thing the old men did with their wives to make children. This couldn't be the same. This was as far removed from that world as was possible to get.

The moon was broad and huge above me, cutting a path through the forest as I walked back to the Community. I didn't worry that my buttons were done up crooked, that my hair was unbraided beneath my bonnet, because my body was humming with light, filled with a quaking that stretched to my fingertips. My heart thudded in my chest like it'd suddenly changed form, like it'd become something much sturdier that made a different kind of tick, and I realized this was the first time I ever felt meaningful. Like I might have something big and real and important inside of me that couldn't be killed. If it's possible to have a soul, mine was steel-plated and invincible that night, and I think that's what love does, makes you strong. Makes you think nothing can bring you down.

It's the only kind of lie that I'd be happy to live with.

Chapter 41

The buzz of the unlocking door startles me out of the memory. I jerk up and open my eyes, taking a moment to remember where I am, the cushioned ground, the never-ending fluorescent sky.

In the doorway is the silhouette of a man. For a moment, in my haze, I think it's Jude, but the man takes a few steps into the room in his shined shoes, places a stool on the ground, and I can see it's Dr. Wilson. He smiles as though nothing had ever happened.

"Let's talk about prophecies," he says.

"What the hell?" I ask groggily. "You were gone for weeks."

"So? We didn't have a schedule."

"But I didn't think you were coming back," I say. "Mrs. New said some case manager was deciding if you'd still be my counselor."

"Did she?" he asks, eyes scanning his yellow notepad. "How interesting."

"So you're still my counselor?"

"I'm here, aren't I?"

"What have you been doing all this time?" I ask.

"Research."

"Researching what?"

"What I said. Prophecies."

From his bag, he extracts a book. Its cover is a large piece of purple construction paper folded over a half ream of computer paper and stitched down the side with twine.

"The Book of Prophecies," I whisper, a little leftover reverence in my voice.

He flips through it, revealing paragraphs of the Prophet's even printing. It smells of pine, like everything in the Community did, and a strange feeling fills my stomach. I know the Prophet is dead, but looking at this book, it feels like he could've just stepped into the room.

"Where'd you find this?" I ask.

"It was bagged up with a lot of evidence from the wreckage of the Prophet's house. No one's had time to go through it all, and it's unpleasant work. Just box after box of charred wood mixed with pieces of broken cutlery and twisted chunks of metal. I found this in a steel money box along with about five thousand dollars and some bottle caps from the sixties."

"I never read it," I say. "I couldn't read back then."

"How's your reading now?"

I shrug. "All right."

He holds the book to me. "Want to?"

"I can?"

"No one to stop us."

He flips through the pages. "You'll recognize this one," he says. I take it between my stumps.

Thus Saith the Lord unto My acolyte the Prophet Kevin. It is My Will and commandment that ye set right true Order in My Kingdom. That the marriages of the Sainted male, Mighty and Strong, be plural and many with womankind to bring about the proliferation of My Servants. For I wish My work to continue rapidly and plentifully and without interruption. For this I shall greatly bless thee and multiply the seed of him who enacts My Will, for I am powerful and control all things. So Saith the Lord thy God. Even so Amen.

I stare at it, the revelation that set it up for men to marry multiple wives. It looks so flimsy now.

"You remember it?" he asks.

"Yes." The Prophet read it to us a dozen times, but seeing it written here in his own handwriting—black ballpoint ink, straight-backed letters—is a different country entirely. A different world. I can read it for myself now.

The Prophet wouldn't recognize me anymore.

I hardly recognize the person I was, back when I believed this.

The pages that are covered with prophecies are more flexible and stained slightly from where the Prophet held the book up during sermons. I set it down on the cushioned floor and, on its own, it falls open to an entry near the end.

Thus Saith the Lord unto My acolyte the Prophet Kevin. Thou art unto Marcus, the first man, who did My will by engaging in spirit marriage with many women. It is my Commandment that ye do again this task, with Minnow, daughter of Samuel, for she be in need of spiritual intervention of the kind that marriage provides. Curb her rebellious mind and carry her in your loving arms to the Great Infinity. My Will be done. So Saith the Lord thy God. Even so Amen.

Slowly, I push the book away and slide backward so I'm wedged in a corner between two cushioned walls. I put my head on my knees, muscles slack.

"His name wasn't always the Prophet," I say. "Why do we call him that, still?"

"We could call him by his real name."

"Kevin?" I ask. "How could that be his name, really?"

"I agree, it seems incongruous," he says.

"I don't like to think of him that way, you know?" I say. "Calling him anything other than the Prophet makes all this . . ." I hold up a stump, as though that represents all the harm the Prophet had done to me, which it doesn't. It really doesn't. "It makes all this less meaningful some-how."

"How do you mean?" he asks.

"Sometimes I wish he actually could talk to God. I want this to mean something. I want it to be special for more than that it hurt me."

"It was special," he says. "But not because of him. It was special because of you." And when I shake my head to tell him he's blowing smoke, he continues. "It was special because you survived."

"But why was it on me to survive?" I ask. "Why couldn't my parents have stopped this? They believed him. They didn't have to."

"It would've been difficult, Minnow. People want to believe. It's all any of us wants."

"I want to believe, but not at any cost. Not at the cost of reason. Not at the cost of human life."

"I think they thought they were doing what was right for their families."

I glance at the Book of Prophecies. "I can't believe that."

I stretch out on the padded floor, my back turned to the

doctor. I close my eyes and breathe. Above, the blinking fluorescents cut through my eyelids.

"My father used to gamble," I say, eyes still closed.

"Oh yeah?"

"At the greyhound track in Missoula. Outside, they had these big halogen lamps that moths flocked to. They threw themselves at it, killed themselves over it, because they were confused."

"They thought it was the sun," he says.

My head nods. "I think about those moths. They would fall down dead on the stands, and I'd pick them up and stare at their white bodies, their feathered antennas, their strange soft wings, and wish they'd thought a little bit before they did that. Before they gave it all up for a lie.

"And I think about my parents. They followed the Prophet, but they weren't the ones who got burned. It was us, the children. And the girls in here are mostly the same. Their parents abandoned them, gave them up for drugs. Abused them. And now look at us."

I hear his shoes creak on the padded floor as he stands from his stool. The fluorescent light goes dark, and I can tell he's standing over me.

His voice winds down from high above: "So how do you avoid becoming a moth?"

"You tell me," I say.

"No."

I look up. His face is shadowed against the light. "What?"

"That's how you avoid becoming a moth," he says. "Stop asking others what to believe. Figure it out for yourself."

Chapter 42

When I'm released from solitary, I am so relieved to be back in gen pop that everything is suddenly beautiful: the dirty grouted tiles in the showers, the clinking sound of cell doors opening and closing, the girls with their angry scowls and snaggleteeth. I even manage a small smile when, at lunch, one of the lunch ladies sees me coming and places my customary soup in a stainless steel bowl on the end of the lunch counter.

"That was crazy what happened with Krystal," Rashida says, her mouth full of half-chewed corn dog. "You got that girl good. Oh man, that was a sight to behold."

"Yeah, it was—"

"Why do you get soup when no one else does?" Rashida interrupts, her attention pinging away at blinding speed.

Angel answers for me. "Minnow's nutrition has been seen to by the government. She got a pamphlet from the Association for Americans with Disabilities that explained that jails can't discriminate against inmates with chopped-off hands."

"That means that the lunch ladies make me a different powdered soup mix every day that I can suck through a straw," I say.

"Today looks like Neon Orange Surprise," Angel observes.

"Why's it a surprise?" Rashida asks.

"It tastes like split pea," I answer. "Angel figures it was some kind of mistake with the dye at the soup factory. But it's my favorite."

"I thought your favorite was Puce with Pumpkin?"

"They never give me Puce with Pumpkin anymore."

"Are you guys, like, friends?" Rashida interrupts.

"What's that mean?" I ask.

"Some people been talking, is all."

My cheeks start to turn pink, but Angel rolls her eyes, like she's heard it all before. "Let people talk, Rashida," she says. "I'd hate to deprive anyone of *talk*. Some of these girls might die if they couldn't talk, and I don't want another life sentence."

"You is so fucking weird, Angel," Rashida says. "Don't you care that they're saying you two cross scissors at night?"

"If I liked to cross scissors, I wouldn't care if anybody knew."

Rashida shrugs, as though she's lost interest. "So why'd you get thrown in here, Minnie? Some people say you killed your old man or something."

"I didn't kill anybody," I mutter. Some of the girls talk about their crimes like it's something to hold over the rest of us. The handful of murderers usually don't let anyone forget it, and the girls who committed light drug offenses always try to make it seem like there was fifty years' worth of charges they didn't get caught for.

"I got high and crashed a car," Rashida says. "The judge was really sure I did it, and I asked him how he knew so much when *I* didn't even remember nothing, and then he was like 'Don't roll your eyes at me, young lady!' but then I was like 'That's just what my eyes *do*,' and he was all 'You don't speak to a judge with a raised voice,' and I said 'That's just the way my voice *is!*' and he got really pissed and threw me out. And I was like 'Seriously? You're not my dad!'"

I nod.

"What about you, Angel?" Rashida asks. "I know you killed someone, but I never heard the details."

Angel's chewing on her bottom lip, dipping her spoon

in and out of her pot of tapioca pudding, as though she hasn't been listening.

"So, what did you do?" Rashida asks again.

Angel clamps her hand on her forehead. "Do you ever shut the fuck up, Rashida? Maybe I killed you. You're obviously a ghost come back to haunt me."

Rashida laughs and chews the last part of her corn dog from the wooden stick while Angel mumbles something and props up her book in front of her. To get Rashida to stop talking, Angel fills the rest of the meal with the details of the book she's reading, something about how if you could drive your car straight up, you'd arrive in space in an hour, but there are 60,000 miles of blood vessels in the human body, which would take you longer than a month to drive, which to Angel means something.

The electric tone sounds, signaling lunch is over, and we stand as a unit, each walking slowly in single file to place our dirty dishes on a conveyor belt that feeds back into the kitchen.

Officer Prosser watches us as we exit, arms crossed over the cushion of her chest.

• • •

Some days, I stare out the bars of my cell and wonder at how I managed to exchange one prison for another. But I would take this cell with the constant hoots of girls and the bleary fluorescent lighting and the juddering steps of guards on the skyway at all hours over the maidenhood room any day.

I don't know how long they kept me in the maidenhood room after I lost my hands, a week, maybe more. I slept every moment that I could, but there were always a few wakeful hours when I would stew in the certainty that I would be married to the Prophet before the winter thawed. He would stand above me on a wooden chair, and I would stand below with my head bowed, barefoot in snow. And he would kiss me in front of everyone, his graying beard like brambles against my face.

The only way to distract myself from the thought of my wedding was to close my eyes, listen hard, and paint a picture of what transpired downstairs. In the bedrooms, someone was sweeping, and a toddler was running on small, heavy feet. Wives clinked dishes in soapy water while they talked.

"What did Miss Holy-Holy-Holy have to say for herself?" I heard Donna Jo ask.

"Just a lot of noise," Vivienne replied. "Putting on."

"She did lose her hands," said Mabel weakly. "There was a lot of blood."

"She was clearly in need of a little bloodletting!" Vivienne said. "What with the way she spat in the Prophet's face."

"She didn't."

"Oh, Mabel, not literally, but she did how it counts, with her smart mouth."

"I think she should be grateful," someone said in a small, sweet voice. "She's been given a second chance at righteousness." The pink-walled room of my diaphragm went pinched and strange shaped at the sound of that voice.

"That's true, Constance," Donna Jo said. "We can hope she takes this as a new chance for an obedient life. Many haven't been so lucky."

"Mmm," the wives said in muffled agreement.

My perfect little sister. I hoped she was just playing along. She was good at acting obedient, but then so were we all. At least until obedience became impossible.

I believed the Prophet when he said he would marry Constance if something were to happen to me. I had to think of a way to get us both out.

The thump of boots on the wooden floor below told me my family was on their way to the Prophet Hall. The front door slammed shut, and it was quiet for the first time that day. I lay back and tried to sleep again, tried to ignore the pain that niggled at the tourniquets and radiated up my arms.

The lock slid back on the other side of my door. My

mother stood in the doorway. In her eyes, something burned with the kind of frantic fire that might sputter out at any moment.

She approached, whispering for me to stand and put my arms out. Delicately, she edged a knitted maroon glove over each stump then slid my arms into my navy button-fronted jacket. She helped me place each foot into a pair of leather boots, tying the laces in loose knots. When she was done, she stood and looked at the door.

"Constance—" I started to say, but my mother put a finger in front of her lips again.

"Go," she whispered. "You save yourself."

She shut her eyes tight for a moment, then turned around and walked out.

The door swayed behind her after she left.

For a moment, I could only stare at the open door. A part of me saw it as a violation and wanted to close it, knowing all of the rules it broke. The wind fought through the chinks in the wall and the door began to creak shut again, the gap of darkness that meant freedom growing smaller and smaller. Fast as I could, which wasn't very fast, I pushed my body through the doorway.

Downstairs, the muslin walls wafted in the momentary draft from my mother's exit. It was impossible to tell if someone lurked behind a wall. I slid quietly over the floor toward the kitchen. It still smelled of dinner, a pot on the table skinned with the yellow remains of onion soup, and my stomach walloped with hunger. But stronger than the smell was the breeze coming from the open front door. I stood at the opening, not bothering with food. Not bothering with feeling sorry to leave the home of my childhood. Pushing the image of Constance back, too.

Blood started dripping through the stitches around my stumps soon after I entered the woods, a slow dribble that fell to the undergrowth with audible plops. If anyone was following me closely, they'd easily make out my path, crimson coin shapes glinting with moonlight, leading straight to Jude's house.

Chapter 43

All the women I ever knew had palms like toughened cowhide, inches of built-up callus gloving each hand, fingers rough as a cat's tongue that, when they grabbed my wrist in admonishment, could leave behind raw patches long after they let go.

Those were hands of trowel digging and washboard scraping, but they also were the hands that cupped a baby between them, that slipped slices of boiled potato into a toddler's mouth, that wiped faces clean and patted cheeks in something like love. Their version of love, at least, steel-eyed and always looking for something to improve.

I asked the doctor today where my mother is. He looked up at me like he wasn't sure what to say, but he decided on the truth. She's living in a women's home. She's taking medication and learning how to balance a checkbook and type on a computer, copying articles out of magazines to get her fingers used to making words again.

"You could visit her, you know," the doctor says. "When you get out."

I shake my head because the idea is still too untested, a fragile thin-skinned thing that needs to strengthen before I touch it. "Where are the rest of them?"

"Group homes," he says. "Government housing."

I'm picturing their hands again, only now they're flicking light switches, wrapping around jars of peanut butter, tearing the cardboard top from a package of processed macaroni and cheese. Those hands weren't made for a life outside of the wilderness. They don't make sense here. Now, I wonder if they wish they could take those hands off and put them away, get back the hands they had before.

"Have you given any thought to what you'll do when you're released?" Dr. Wilson asks.

"Not really."

"Did you apply for the Bridge Program?"

I shake my head. "No point. I wouldn't get in, and anyway you only qualify if you're eighteen or younger when released. I'm probably going to Billings, so . . ."

"Sounds like you're giving up."

"Maybe."

"And you're just fine with that."

"What do you want me to say?" I ask. I let my head fall forward to prop it up against my hands, then stop. I'm still forgetting that they're gone. It's been how many months and I'm still forgetting. I stare down at the empty spaces.

"They took my hands," I say. "The police, I mean. They said they'd have them incinerated, do you believe that? Between the Prophet and the law, I'll have nothing left by the end."

"What would it matter if your hands were incinerated?"

"Because . . . because they were part of me. Do you know what it's like to have a piece of your body taken away without your consent?"

He shakes his head.

"Then you don't get to ask that question." I shake my head. "I know it's strange. And kinda gross. But I wish I had them back. They're mine. There'd be a sense of, I don't know, fairness."

He's leans back on his stool, one arm crossing his chest. "Everybody's lost something," he says. "Most of us never get the chance to have it returned."

I know he's right, but a small voice insists, they were *mine*. As much my property as anything ever has been. As long as they're gone, I don't see how I can ever stop being so angry at the world I feel like ripping it to ribbons.

Chapter 44

It's two months until my birthday, two months until they decide if I go free. It's gotten warm, the part of early summer when, if I were still in the Community, I'd be sun-pink at the cheeks and peeling from the bridge of my nose. Here, I stay inside. I've seen those chain-link pens in the yard reserved for exercising, but I don't think I could ever let myself be locked in a cage. Besides the persistent hum of air conditioners, I'd hardly know it was summer at all.

Today, they're driving us up into the foothills to do community service, those of us who aren't considered a flight risk. I had to convince Mrs. New to let me go.

"I've had only good behavior for months," I said.

"You were in solitary for an altercation with Krystal Smith not two weeks ago."

"That was a . . . misunderstanding. I'll be good. You don't have to worry about me."

"Minnow, you know it's more than that. You're . . . understandably weakened. And you've taken no outdoor

288

rec time all year. I don't see why this matters to you."

"The place you're going," I say, "it's not too far from the place I grew up, in the woods. I want to see how it feels, going back. I think—I think it might be important."

She purses her bright lips. "All right. God help me if anything happens. I'm putting it in the books as reward R & R, not as work detail. You're not to do anything strenuous, do you understand?"

In the morning, the broken-up voice of a guard announces over the intercom that we should congregate in the cafeteria for a debriefing before we depart. Rashida stares after me longingly when I leave reading class. The cafeteria tables have been folded into giant A shapes and wheeled to the edges of the room, the linoleum floor shiny where a long mop has just swept.

Angel walks into the cafeteria a moment after me. Somehow, she's been cleared to come, though probably through bribery more than good behavior. I see Tracy enter the room with a couple of other girls. She sees me and gives me a wary smile.

"It's called gleaning," Mrs. New explains from the front of the room. "Basically, you're picking fruit from several acres of wild orchards. Normally private contractors would be hired for this manner of work, but budgets are tight and it remains the state's responsibility to clear the fruit from this area of the Rattlesnake Valley."

"Isn't this child labor?" Angel asks.

"This totally *voluntary* excursion will last most of the day," Mrs. New continues.

Mrs. New explains that, in the next couple of months, black bears will trundle down from the mountains, attracted by the smell of ripening fruit trees. It's a liability, given the number of homes in the area. The bears gorge themselves on fallen apples and plums, and sometimes swipe a Sheltie or Pomeranian on the side, because their guts are vacant. Because they *feel* like it. There's always an element of fickleness in murder, isn't there? That's what I've learned in juvie, among these girls who've committed such monstrous crimes. You get the sense that, on that particular day, there was just nothing better to do. That, had something better been playing on TV or had the softball game been scheduled for Wednesday instead of Saturday, someone might not've had to die. Crime is never preventable because the mind will always grow bored.

In addition to our everyday neon orange jumpsuits, they give us tan hiking boots and a thick leather belt. Angel helps tie my bootlaces and buckle the belt.

"What's this for?" I ask.

"Chaining us to our seats. You never wanna be on a prison bus unless everybody's nice and restrained."

Slowly, we march out of the prison into the blinding sunlight of the parking lot, and I stand on the pavement with my head craned back until the sun warms me all the way through to my bones. Slowly, the girls step onto the yellow bus. Officer Prosser escorts me last.

"Don't suppose there's much point in chaining you up," she says. "Not like you'll do much damage with no hands and a pair of boots."

"A pair of boots is the reason I'm locked up," I say.

From the seat in front of me, Angel chuckles.

"Well, gimpy's got a sass mouth!" Officer Prosser says. "Now sit your ass down."

I settle into the plasticized leather seat and let her chain me to the floor. She tugs hard on my belt after she's fastened the lock.

The girls are entirely quiet as we watch Missoula slide past the windows. The rocking motion of a moving vehicle still makes me a little queasy, and the muscles that cup my eyeballs are strained in minutes, but I can't tear my eyes away. It's all too fascinating, a ring of fallen pine needles beneath every tree and the new bottle-shaped flowers freeing themselves from the earth, the blinding way the sun covers everything in cellophane white.

The bus makes waves of dust along the dirt road bordering the wild orchard. We unload and they run a plastic-coated metal cord through each of our belt loops so we'll have some freedom of movement. Angel is in front of me in line. I'm the last.

"All right, ladies," Officer Prosser says, puffing herself up. "You're here doing a good deed. Pay attention to how it feels because, for some of you, it'll be the first time."

We shuffle forward as a unit through the knee-high grass, a clinking snakelike thing so orange it might offend nature. The fruit hanging from the trees are bell-shaped, yellow-green, and speckled. Pears. They smell like newborn autumn. They hang low enough to touch a mouth to.

Angel and I walk far, the cord tying us to the other girls whizzing through the metal loops at our belts, until we're deep enough into the trees to barely hear the voices of the other girls. The pears are still unripe, none yet fallen to the ground, so Mrs. New instructed us that the best way to glean them was to take a limb of a tree in our hands and shake. Angel approaches a branch and reefs on it. A shower of pears falls. She reaches down and tosses them in a wooden crate nearby.

I kneel on the grass and roll a pear toward me with a stump, up the length of my leg, and hold it to my stomach. I drop it in the crate. Angel's picked twenty by the time I manage one.

I get tired of that pretty quickly so I approach the nearest pear hanging from a bough. I open my mouth and fit my teeth over the buxom curve of it, still slightly hard. It tastes sharp and sweet.

Angel smiles. "You gonna eat your way through all these?"

"If I have to."

I feel the tension around my waist loosen as the guards let out more of the plastic-coated cord so the girls can climb into the trees to reach the higher branches. I walk a few minutes by myself, craning my neck so all I see is the tops of trees, steel-gray mountains, and the sky. I haven't walked through the wild like this since I left the Community. I feel it might not be too late to relearn wilderness, the way shadows bloom like footprints under trees, the way it is never truly silent.

Do I want to? a small voice asks.

The last time I saw the sky like this, it was still swathed in smoke from the fire that devoured the Community. Now, the sky is jewel bright and radiating blue heat, and it's almost enough to make me forget that fire, forget the final moments of the Prophet's life, the room like an oven, smoke falling through the roof in ribbons. Sometimes all I can remember of that night is gray smoke. I try to follow the lines back to that moment, but they get crossed, blurred in all that choking fog.

I've walked so far, the only indication that I'm not all alone out here is the soft voices of the girls through the walls of trees and the silver cord around my waist. I bring my head back down, and my eyes fall to the tree line beyond the meadow. That's where the real wilderness starts, the shadowed pines that absorb none of this sunlight.

A shape at the forest's edge materializes. The silhouette of a person, ragged clothes hanging off bone-sharp limbs. His skin is dark brown, and his pants hang so loose, his suspenders are the only thing holding them up. I stare, and he stares back with big hollowed eyes.

"Jude," I whisper. I glance around to make sure no one hears me. Angel is far behind, buried in the branches of a tree, only visible because her boots are propped up on a low branch. All I can think is I can't let anyone see him. They might catch him and throw him away.

I walk beyond the orchard toward him, but the cord quickly grows taut. Warily, he edges out of the pines and runs from tree to tree until he's not more than ten feet from me.

He sidles to the tree I'm behind, his face stretched in surprise. Bones protrude from his face. He's been starving. His nose was broken and healed in an odd direction, and beneath one of his eyes is a persistent purple sickle of bruise. Over his shoulder is a burlap sack, and I can discern the shapes of pears inside. He must've been raiding the trees before we showed up.

"You're alive?" I whisper, tears springing to my eyes. "I thought they killed you."

His voice comes in an unused croak. "I thought the same of you."

His hands are shuddering, and he presses the pads of his fingers over my cheeks.

"You're really real?" I whisper.

"I don't know anymore," he says. "I've been lost for a long time."

I can't put my hand to his cheek, so I lean in and close my eyes and let my lips traverse the scars on his face, the warm breath sluicing from his nose, the exhale of relief at the touch of skin on his skin. My lips find his open lips and our mouths feel for each other frantically. Jude tastes unwashed and desperate.

"How are you alive?" I whisper.

He hangs his head into the bend of my neck, and I feel him shake his head. "I don't know. I remember them coming at me, and after that nothing but darkness. And then, I don't know what else to call it . . . an angel, a real one with a halo made of orange light and blond hair."

"Blond hair?" I ask. "You're sure?"

"Yeah. She dragged me away. And when I woke, I was

way out in the forest. I could never've gotten there on my own. I woke up 'cause there was fire in air. It was blowing away in the opposite direction, but I could smell the smoke. I got up and started walking and found a cave. That's where I been."

"Are you hurt bad?" I ask.

"Only from not knowing where you were," he says, though I can tell by the sunken-looking bone of his eye, the way he holds his chest inward, that that's not true.

"Why don't you come into the city?" I ask. "You could go to a hospital."

His forehead crinkles. "That place is exactly as evil as I thought. I've seen it, from the hills. You seen the *cars*? You smelled the *air* down there? It's poisonous. You heard their loudness? And seen the colors of their clothes?"

"Like this?" I ask, toeing my jumpsuit with a boot.

"You can't help that." He repositions his legs and winces painfully, his hand wrapping around his middle.

"Jude, you need a doctor," I say.

"I done fine."

"You're hurt."

"It's nothing I cain't handle."

"All right, ladies!" Officer Prosser yells from the area of the bus. "Time to pack it in!"

I dart my eyes behind me, through the tall grass.

Angel is stepping down out of her tree. She looks over her shoulder, and I know she's seen us. She brings her lips inside her mouth and turns to walk back to the road.

"I gotta go," I whisper.

"Go?" Jude asks. "You're coming with me."

"Come with you?" I ask.

"I bet I can pop that lock open with my crowbar."

He yanks on the lock hanging from the belt and pulls me forward a step, rummaging in his burlap sack.

"Jude," I say. "Wait."

"What?"

"I—I don't know if I can go with you."

The words ring out in the still air, and the hurt in his face strikes me right in my chest.

"What d'you mean?" he asks. "I gotta get you outta here."

But I'll miss reading class, I almost say. I shake my head. "I'm in juvie for a reason, Jude. I gotta stick this out. I—I just need a little time."

"I don't unnerstand," he says. "The cave I told you about, it's—Minnow, it's *nice* there. Safe. Good stream not far. We could live there, make a life together."

"A cave?" I ask. "Jude, I don't think I can live in a place like that. And neither should you."

"But, look where you been," he responds. "Wouldn't a cave be better than that?"

"Better than prison?" I ask.

"We could be happy there."

"We'd be all alone."

"We'd be together," he insists.

"That's not enough," I say. And it's not. It's really not.

His face falls. And I finally hear it, the small voice in my mind that I never let speak until now, a voice that asks if you can grow out of people the way you can grow out of tree houses.

"I know it's hard to understand, Jude, but I can't go with you right now. I can't run away from this."

"You just got free of one prison, and you choose another one?"

"It ain't that simple, Jude."

"Minnow Bly!" I can hear Officer Prosser yell from beyond the trees. The cord around my waist tugs. I stumble backward.

I turn to Jude. "I—I gotta go now." Tears brim in my eyes.

"Wait!" he says. "The cave where I'm living, you can find it easy. It's just south of where the big river bends, you remember? Near that heron pond we fished in once. Find me," he says. "Find me," he begs.

I look over my shoulder one last time, then sprint to the bus.

Chapter 45

Incinerated. This is what it feels like to think about Jude. The feeling of my own cells burning out one by one. I imagine the cave where he's sequestered himself, farther in the backwoods than even the Community, practically a lifetime away from another person. The way his nose had knit back together, the haggard way he walked, like he'd been broken and would never heal. So different to how he used to be, but then so is everything. Even the tree house is gone, the tree house that weathered winters of knee-high snow and summers so hot the smell of bodies in the Community was almost too much to bear. Everything Jude and I went through happened in that tree house.

Jude found me there the night I ran away. He stood beside the larch, chopping wood, an ax clutched in his hand. His face was smiling, but it contorted when he saw me, saw what was missing. I didn't realize till Jude caught me that I was falling.

We crumpled to the ground, and I only remember flashes after that—Jude's ax lying discarded in a drift of yellowed pine needles, the sleeves of my dress choked with blood, the blood already on Jude's shirt.

He carried me the rest of the way to his house. In the doorway, his father stood frozen. His skin was pale and flushed heavily at the cheeks, the way I'd learn that his face always looked, as though a lifetime of hard winters and hard alcohol had burst every blood vessel. He looked like a shadow of Jude, like a less alive version with a mess of wiry white beard and a look in his eyes like he couldn't believe what had just crashed into his life.

Jude brushed past him through the open door and laid me down on the couch. I got a good look at my stumps and started shivering. My heart still jerked angrily and my toes had turned a pale yellow, a color the exact opposite of blood.

"What in Sam Hill?" Waylon shouted. His speech was slurred, but I don't think he was drunk. It was just how he talked, like the hinge of his mouth wouldn't close properly. "Who's that?"

"Her name's Minnow."

"She one of them cult people?"

"Yeah, and she's hurt real bad. Oh God, she's hurt real bad."

"Why's she bleedin' so—" He stopped when he saw my stumps, darting a hand to his face. "They did this to her?"

"Shut up, Daddy, and do somethin' useful!" Jude shouted. His hands were squeezing my wrists to try and stop the bleeding.

Waylon scanned the room helplessly and ran out the back door. Jude whimpered a little, his fingers slipping over the blood. "It's gonna be just fine," he whispered, but his throat was shaking so hard, his voice was all but lost.

Waylon barged back inside with a boxy bottle full of clear liquid in his fist. I knew it had to be the moonshine he made, the stuff that had turned his legs to jelly and his mouth to mush.

"No, Daddy! She ain't drinkin' that."

"It's her choice, son," Waylon said. "The drink'll make the pain better."

I shook my head.

"We gotta get those things cleaned," Waylon said. "It'll hurt like a bitch without somethin' to take the edge off."

"I don wannit," I slurred.

"Fine, fine, I hear ya," he said.

Waylon ordered Jude to get a pail and heat some water.

"She gon' be feverin' soon, if she's not already. Thas what'll kill her, if anythin'. Gotta be ready to fight it."

Jude carried in a pot of water from out back and placed

301

it over the fire. After he stoked the embers nice and hot, he kneeled and leaned over me so his face was all I could see. Waylon sunk each wrist into a shallow bucket of moonshine. I tried to hold the scream in because surely they could hear me in the Community, but it tore through my chest on its own.

"I know, I know, I know, I know," Jude chanted. He held my face in his hands, bloodying my cheeks. He was blinking and crying, glancing around frantically as though searching for something to take the pain away.

"Minnow," he said. "You see that light?"

My eyes roved jerkily. The cabin had one glassed window and through it I could see the torsos of pines ringing the house, lit with moonlight.

"That's the forest folk's lanterns," he said. "They're knee-high and they bite, but if you catch one, it has to grant you three wishes."

A fresh wave of pain rolled hotly over me, and I let loose another scream, stifled by my clamped teeth. I knew the pain was unbearable and yet, somehow, I kept continuing to bear it.

Jude spoke again, his voice high and fragile. "I'll go out later and catch a forest folk, Minn. Okay?"

"Okay," I parroted.

"I'll wish your hands back first. Then, I'll wish us away

from this place, to our own little home somewhere no one has ever been. You hear my words?"

I nodded and nodded, but that could've been the tremble that had hijacked my muscles.

"And lastly . . . lastly I'll wish the death of the man who did this to you. I'll do it. I'll make sure he never breathes one more breath in this world, or the next."

• • •

I woke up the next day throwing a mass of acid up from my stomach onto the packed dirt floor. I let it drip from my mouth, because I couldn't lift my leaden arms to wipe my lips. I turned my head slowly back onto the couch cushion. The skin on my arms was white until it reached the stumps where it became swollen with purpleness. A thick ridge of stitches ran across each one.

"You look like death," a voice said.

I turned my head slowly. Waylon was sitting in a chair at the kitchen table. I saw for the first time the inside of the cabin, roughly furnished, every item made by hand. Made by Waylon, I guessed.

"I feel like it," I said.

"He never told me about you," he said. "Not even once."

"I never told my family about him, either."

"Why not? Children shouldn't keep things secret from their parents."

I remembered all the times Jude had come to me with bruises and gashes marking his skin, scarring it. All the times he'd seemed scarred worse on the inside. *Maybe you should ask yourself why Jude felt like he couldn't tell you,* I thought.

Jude walked in the back door with an armful of wood. He walked to the fireplace and stuffed the wood in, stoking it so none of the winter air beyond the walls penetrated the cabin.

Waylon stood and walked out the back door.

Jude sat beside me on the couch. His eyes were dry now and there was something different about them. His jaw had taken on a harder set. Angrier.

"What's wrong, Jude?"

"Nothin'."

"No, really. What?"

He sighed, touched his forefinger to the dark half circle under his eye. "I jus cain't . . . cain't figure it out."

"What?"

"How someone could do this."

"My father's the Prophet's man. I've known that mosta my life."

"Your father did this to you?"

"He was on orders, Jude." I said this with trepidation because in the air between us was the knowledge of what he'd done on someone's orders, what he'd done for faith.

"But, all those people, they musta known you was in there. Bein' . . . bein' hurt."

"Yeah."

"None of 'em did anything. They let it happen. How? *How?*"

Something strong was pouring from his eyes now, scarier than tears.

"They're crazy, Jude. That's all. Crazy people do crazy things."

He opened his mouth then, and his words were so quiet and low I could barely make them out. "I'm gonna kill him."

"The Prophet?"

Jude nodded. "He'll be dead someday anyway, so it cain't be a sin. I want it. I want it on my hands." He held his hands before him, fingers curved. "I want him to look in my eyes and realize all he's done."

This was the second time he'd said this, and I knew now that he meant it. To Jude, violence still held meaning. He truly believed enough of it could make the Prophet realize his errors and repent.

In those moments, I wish I could've articulated how unremarkable brutality is. How common. Till the moment he saw me without hands, Jude hadn't known how capable we all are of violence. But I was so comfortable with it, I didn't hesitate for a second to commit some when I had the chance, when Philip lay prone on the snow-packed earth.

Brutality was done to me. Why not spill a little into the world, too? Just to touch it. Just to know I could.

Chapter 46

After lights-out, Angel and I sit hip-to-hip on my bed near the weak desk lamp soldered to the frame of the bunk, me shouldering my way through a fantasy novel, Angel reading about neuroscience. Every other minute, I let the book fall closed and sigh, casting my eyes out to the darkened hull of the jail. Similar pockets of light shine where other girls are up late reading or writing letters home.

Angel grunts when I sigh again. "You're thinking about Jude."

"Sorry."

"I never had anyone who could do that to me."

"Do what?"

"Interrupt my thoughts when he wasn't even in the room," she says. "Except Carl Sagan, but that doesn't really count."

"I don't know what to do."

"You're stuck in jail. What can you do?"

"When I get out, find him. Walk into the woods and never look back."

She's silent beside me, running her fingers along the edge of the thick tome. "They don't have books in the wilderness," she says.

I nod. Would it mean anything, losing the things that I've gained here, as long as I had Jude? I know a year ago, it wouldn't have even been a question. But now?

"You wanna hear something cool?" she asks.

I shrug.

"I just read that the brain is the fattiest organ. Contains up to sixty percent fat."

"Your brain must be really fat," I say.

"Yo brain's so fat, the last time you got a brain fart, it caused a tsunami in China," she says, guffawing loudly at her own joke.

"Oh yeah," I say. "Well your brain's so fat, it . . . it probably eats extra servings of chicken nuggets."

She squints at me. "You didn't do that right."

The buzz of an unlocking cell door rings out loudly in the sleeping jail. I look up just as Dr. Wilson walks through the opening door of our cell.

"What the hell?" Angel asks.

"Evening, Angel," Dr. Wilson says.

"How do you know my name?" she asks. "Never mind. I bet this one's told you everything about me," she nods her head toward me, "right down to my pissing schedule."

He smiles. "Angel, I'd appreciate it if you could go with this kind guard here. I need to speak with Minnow."

"I'm just sitting here, minding my own business, and a strange man comes in and kicks me out? Of my own *home?*" she shouts. "That's violating my rights. I'm calling my lawyer."

"Get your ass up, Angel," Benny says from outside the cell, "and I'll give you a doughnut from the staff lounge."

Angel considers this. "Fine," she says. "But I'm still consulting my lawyer."

When Angel and Benny depart, Dr. Wilson sets down his stool. I swing my legs off the side of my bunk, waiting for him to reveal what was so urgent.

He presses his lips together. "What motivates someone to kill?" he asks.

"You've asked me this already."

"Consider it review."

"This is why you came here in the middle of the night?"

"We'll get there. Answer the question."

"Insanity."

"And?"

"Anger."

"And?"

"Revenge."

He raises his chin. "Elaborate."

I pause. "Thinking it's the right thing to do. Believing the person deserves it."

He nods. "Many would say the Prophet deserved what he got."

"I'd agree with them," I say.

"Who else would agree with you?"

"No idea. They all seemed pretty in love with him."

"What about your father?"

I hitch up my shoulders. "What about him?"

"We have a new theory. That he may have been involved in the Prophet's death. He may have had motive."

"What motive?" I ask, incredulous.

"Read this for me, will you?"

He passes over a piece of paper lying flat inside an evidence bag. I immediately recognize the slanted handwriting. It's my father's. The paper is stained and creased, each crease a dark line, as though it's been rubbed repeatedly between dirty fingers.

The True and Faithful Narrative of Samuel Ezekiel Hiram Bly

I look up. "My father's prophecy."

"You know of it?" he asks.

"Of course."

He nods. "I need you to confirm its authenticity."

I read it.

And lo, upon the factory floor came the strange and woeful noise of the slamming of machines. The quietest things in that place were the souls, clad in blue jumpsuits and yellowing plastic goggles. Suddenly the place, the noise, began to slow, and stopped completely. Everything froze. Never had I heard the factory in such a state of quietude. A sound like pure light filled the room. The archangel descended from the uncovered ceiling where the clotted mustard-colored insulation clung, the angel being righteous and holy and made of a million pinpricks of light, with a face beautiful like a baby's. The archangel sung me his instructions in a language no human had ever spoken. "You are to follow the Prophet into the woods and never return."

"It's his handwriting," I say. "And it's the same story he told us. This was sort of what ultimately made everyone decide to come to the Community."

"Very good. That's all I needed." He puts the paper back in his bag and rises from the stool.

"Wait!" I say. "How is this motive?"

He sits down again. "It's evidence that your father thought himself a prophet, too."

"You think my father wanted to kill the Prophet to . . . to become the new Prophet?"

"Perhaps."

"But that's ridiculous! My father was loyal. Look at everything he did." I close my eyes, suddenly breathless, picturing the hatchet in my father's loose hand, the Prophet screaming, "DO IT! DO IT NOW!"

"It's a possibility I have to entertain," the doctor says.

"No one would've followed my father. No one."

"Imagine for me that there were some in the Community who were starting to see through the Prophet. Let's say his lies were starting to show. Let's say people were becoming less and less satisfied with his answers."

"What are you talking about?"

"The women who escaped are now raising their own children. Some of them still live as sisters beside their husbands' wives, but they claim their birth children. That's a direct violation of the Prophet's orders, is it not?"

"Yes," I say. "We weren't supposed to know who our real mothers were."

"Those who got out are defying the Prophet's rules

in all kinds of ways. Some have even left altogether. Remember Donna Jo, your father's second wife? She took her children to Los Angeles to live with friends she knew in college. It seems you're not the only lapsed Kevinian anymore, Minnow."

"But if the Prophet were alive," I say, "I don't believe for a second that they wouldn't all go running back to him."

"Some might. But things have changed. For so long he was like a magnet, keeping it all together. But now that he's gone, the cracks are a lot more obvious." He shifts in his seat. "With every religion, there exist certain rules. Every God has to abide these rules, otherwise the entire thing stops working. What was the Kevinian God capable of?"

I shrug. "Anything."

"Anything? He could punish? And reward?"

"Yes," I say.

"Could he intervene in the lives of humans?"

"Yes."

"Did he create the universe?"

"Yes," I say, then pause. "Or, wait. No, he couldn't have. He wasn't born until the seventeen hundreds."

"So, who created the universe, if not God?"

"I don't know," I say. "I never asked."

"You never asked? Nobody ever asked?"

"It didn't occur to me. Don't look at me like that."

"Sorry. It's just interesting."

"What is?"

"He invented a religion. I'm just not sure he did a very good job."

Chapter 47

A few days later, Dr. Wilson's back in my cell, looking haggard, stubbled and hollow-eyed.

"What happened to you?" I ask.

"I went to Deer Lodge for a couple days."

"The prison?"

He nods. "Your father tried to kill himself. I spoke to him two days ago and told him we had reason to believe he was responsible for the Prophet's death. He tried hanging himself that night."

"He's alive?

He nods.

"So, you've got him, then. This proves he's guilty."

"He's not guilty," Dr. Wilson says. "We're not charging him."

"Why?" I sputter.

"We've interviewed all the wives again, some of the older children. They all say he was in the house the entire night."

"They must be lying."

"It's improbable they'd all have the same exact story."

"You can't give up," I say. "I'll testify that I saw him. Maybe I did. Maybe I'm remembering something."

"But you've always attested that you were long gone at that point, Minnow," he says, eyes boring into mine. I look away. "Anyway, I don't even know if your testimony will be usable anymore." He rubs his eyes hard. "A few of them said they saw a figure watching from the trees. Someone who looked a lot like you. Your father was . . . very certain."

I press my eyelids closed. "You think I killed the Prophet?"

"No," he says. "But I think you know who did. And I think it's time that we stop running around in circles."

I feel myself slowly unwind, like yarn from a skein, pooling on the floor. I'm so close to losing it, the control, the grip. Because I think I want to tell him. I think I want to spill it all right now and damn the consequences.

The consequences. Angel said Dr. Wilson would put me away for life if I told him what really happened. But he's different, he's here to help me. He's . . . *he's a cop*, I hear Angel say, as if that's all there is to know about him.

"What motivates someone to kill?" I ask.

He smiles a tired smile. "Haven't we already discussed this?"

"I want to know what you think."

"I think it's control. I think that's why anyone does anything."

"So, who was the most controlling person in the Community?" I ask.

"You tell me."

"The Prophet. You know he was."

"I can't exactly make a case that he'd be a suspect in his own murder."

"Why not? Why aren't we considering suicide?"

"He had no motivation to kill himself."

"He was mentally unbalanced. You've said so yourself."

"He didn't have the kind of mental unbalance that would've resulted in suicide."

All I can think is that Dr. Wilson is going to feel really stupid when he learns the truth. Because he's wrong. The Prophet did kill himself, in a way. He created the weapon of his own demise.

"I almost forgot. I brought you a present." He pulls something out of his bag and places it on my bed. It's a used paperback copy of *Tess of the d'Urbervilles*.

"What is it?"

"I thought you'd've learned by now what books are."

"I *know* it's a book," I say, insulted. "Why did you get it for me?"

"My son loves Thomas Hardy. I thought you'd like it."

"Son?" I ask.

He nods. "Jonah."

"I'll . . . I'll check it out," I say. "If I have time."

After he leaves, I turn the cover of the book. It still has the price sticker from a secondhand bookstore in Missoula, revealing he'd paid a whole two dollars, but I'm still grateful for it in a way I can't quite articulate.

There's plenty in the book I don't understand, and those parts stay behind, bolted to the pages, but there are things I can skim from the surface like fat from a milk pail, and I sort through all the information with something like fingers, fingers inside my mind.

I read one paragraph over and over again.

"I don't know about ghosts," Tess says, "but I do know that our souls can be made to go outside our bodies when we're alive. A very easy way to feel 'em go is to lie on the grass at night and look straight up at some big bright star; and, by fixing your mind upon it, you will soon find that you are hundreds and hundreds o' miles away from your body, which you don't seem to want at all."

I lie on my bed and stare up at the bunk above me, but

the effect isn't at all the same. Even looking out the milky skylight doesn't do it. And, I wonder for the first time, when will I see the stars again? Where can I find some on short notice? I want to know if it would work for me, like it did for Tess. I want to know if there's even anything left inside me that could fly so effortlessly.

Chapter 48

"Hey," Angel whispers after lights-out. "Check it out."

She's crouched beside my bunk, holding a key card between two fingers.

"Did you steal that?" I ask, squinting at her groggily.

"Hardly," she says. "You know I'm in good with the guards."

"What did you do?" I ask warily.

"Christ, I'm not dealing drugs or something. So maybe I worked out a deal with Benny that I wouldn't open up anybody's head for a month, and maybe I made good on the bargain today, and she had to make good on hers or risk me telling Mrs. New she watches soap operas in the back office when she's supposed to be supervising group therapy, but whatever, a good magician never reveals her secrets." I can tell Angel is excited, but not the agitated kind of excitement like after she takes her medication.

I push aside the covers of my bed. "Where are we going?"

She looks over her shoulder at me. "A holy place."

• • •

We tiptoe out of the cell—Angel must have spent some time planning this, because somehow it's unlocked—and walk up a set of stairs that end at a heavy metal door. It's been propped open by a brick.

"We have to be quiet," Angel whispers. "If we wake any of the girls, Benny'll have my balls."

She shoves her bulk into the door, and a warm breeze touches my face.

We stand on the jail roof, a flat surface covered in popcorn-looking concrete that crunches beneath my shoes. Before us, Missoula stretches in a flat grid of lights, bisected by the slick black of the river. Red taillights twine through streets in an infinite swirl.

"It's perfect conditions to see the Perseid meteor showers." She walks across the roof to sit on the edge, her legs dangling over the side. She tilts her head skyward.

I duck instinctively when I see the first light flinging itself across the sky. A dozen more streak past in the first minute and, even though they are less brilliant than out in the forest, the way they have to fight through a gauze of light from the city, they still could almost be missiles crashing toward us.

"Those are meteors," she says. "They're balls of rock that fling across the galaxy. The Earth's atmosphere, it's like this invisible cocoon. Millions of meteors hit the atmosphere every day, but we're protected."

"Why'd you bring me up here?" I ask.

"It's part of your education about the universe."

I shake my head.

"What's wrong?" she asks.

"The Prophet said the Community was covered in a bubble that God made, and these lights were bombs the Gentiles sent toward us."

"So? The people in olden times thought meteors were the tears of God. They needed something to explain it."

"Why?"

"I guess people can't be content without answers, even if they're wrong. We'd rather have a lie than a question that we can never know the answer to."

I nod. "You know one thing the Prophet never answered? That nobody ever wondered about but me? People. What made us. Where we came from."

"But you know that already," Angel says. "From the stars."

"What?"

"Remember the Big Bang? Everything in the universe comes from stars. Before anything else existed, there were just stars. Stars are like ovens," she says. "Inside, they're cooking planets and asteroids, and when they explode, out spews all this, like, space vomit that's been cooking all these years. And solar systems formed, and Earth formed, and algae and eventually oxygen. And small organisms evolved into big animals and after about a billion years we came out, so that's your answer. We come from the stars."

"That's impossible," I say.

"You're only saying that because the idea that you exploded out of a star is scary."

"The Prophet said stars are God's eyes."

She rolls her eyes. "And what did he say the sun was? A really, really big eyeball?"

"Just . . . the sun. He didn't talk about the sun."

"The sun is a star," she says. "And every star is a sun, so far away from us they seem tiny."

In that moment, I feel the Prophet's canvas ceiling lift away from my head, walls flying off me, and a pressure I've never put into words hisses somewhere at the back of my mind as the size of the universe assembles itself in my mind. If I close my eyes, I can see it, the endlessness beyond my ears, and knowing I'm only in a corner of that vastness doesn't make me feel tiny. It is amazing that, though I am small and ungifted and barely educated, even I can appreciate the scale of the universe.

And from this perch in space, for this moment at least, it seems unimportant whether someone made it, or if it made itself.

Chapter 49

The stars bump around in my chest for days and days afterward, light as carbonation against the edge of a glass, and I start waking up in the morning thinking about stars or cities, or nothing: entire seconds spent not remembering to touch the hurt spot where Jude and Philip and Constance live for entire seconds, minutes even.

I have started to think this isn't such a bad thing.

• • •

"Did you like the book?" Dr. Wilson asks when he visits again.

I shrug in agreement. In truth, besides picturing the sky every moment I can, I've done little but read *Tess of the d'Urbervilles* since he gave it to me.

"What did you like about it?"

"Tess isn't a victim," I say. "I mean, she is. For, like, the whole book. But she fights back in the end."

"How does she stop being a victim?"

"She kills the man who abused her."

He nods. "What do you think about that?"

"He deserved it."

"And, by that logic, didn't she also deserve her punishment?"

"No," I reply. "He made her life miserable. He earned the knife in his belly."

"Still murder, though."

"But sometimes murder is justified, and don't look at me that way, that's not a confession or anything. Sometimes circumstances are . . ." I search for the word.

"Extenuating?" he asks.

"Yes, extenuating. And the fact that the law didn't see that makes *it* cold-blooded, not Tess."

"You seem very certain."

"I am."

"And just consider how a few months ago you said you weren't certain of anything. Now you're almost too much the opposite. What do you suppose is responsible for that?"

"If I had to guess, Angel."

"I agree," he says. "I think Angel is becoming a negative influence on you."

"She's a good person."

He laughs. "Is that so?"

"Angel's the best person in here."

"Angel is a convicted murderer."

He says it as though that's all there is to know about her.

"It was self-defense," I say.

"She told you that?" he asks. "She waited in her uncle's bedroom for three hours, a loaded gun in her hand. When he got home, she crouched behind his bedroom door until he was less than a foot from her, and do you know what she did?" he asks. "She shot five bullets into his neck."

I look away, unconsciously pressing my stumps together. "Why are you telling me this?"

"Because you're not like her. You shouldn't aim to be."

"Angel fought back against a man who made her life a nightmare."

"Do you know how many murderers try to excuse their actions by saying they were victimized? It explains their actions, but it can't excuse it," he says. "There is no justifying murder."

He sees things so clearly. But he's never lived in fear. He's never had to dread the choices of big men with their large, dark-haired hands. "I'm just sick of the victim being judged for fighting back."

"It was a victim who killed the Prophet, wasn't it?" he asks. "That's why you won't talk to me. Because you think whoever did it doesn't deserve consequences."

I clamp my lips together. If I answer, the entire story

might fall out of my mouth, and that can't happen, not yet.

"People like you see murder and motive and malice everywhere," I say instead. "Whatever I tell you, you'll take it and twist it and make it sound wrong. Just like they did at my trial. That lawyer made me out like a monster, and I'm not gonna let that happen again. And don't try telling me you wouldn't do it. You're a—"

"Don't say cop."

"Well, you are."

"And you're a convicted felon. Have I ever treated you like one?"

I wince, the image of Philip coming into my head, the understanding that I'll never, as long as I live, not be a criminal.

"You never planned on telling me the truth," he says. "I figured that out the moment we made our deal. But I'd hoped that by now I would've gained your trust. I can see I've fallen short."

He sighs and stands, taking his stool with him.

"But I do trust you," I whisper when he's gone. More than almost anybody, I'm realizing.

But not enough. Not when he still has all the power. Not when I've still got none.

Chapter 50

Constance never left my thoughts when I stayed at Jude's cabin. The wedding preparations were surely going on uninterrupted; the porridge and meat pies already being made; the salves for their wedding night mixed in big stone bowls. If the place my hands used to be was a physical ache, images of what was going to happen to Constance formed a mental one. It would surely be weeks until the wedding, but the idea of their marriage made me want to push up from the couch and start running.

But for the first couple of weeks, I could barely move for the blinding pain and shaking in my limbs that made me sick, and I grew to miss the green liquid they had given me in the Community. Even then, even shivering and burning on Jude's couch, I pictured how I'd sneak back into my family's house, unbolt the door, and whisk Constance out of the maidenhood room to freedom.

I kept all this to myself, and I'm not sure why. There was still that deadness in Jude's eyes, the strange energy that made him never sit still, constantly fetching more firewood until the room was always stifling hot, and the blood-covered couch made the air constantly smell of iron.

"They're gonna follow the smoke, Jude," I whispered. "The deacons."

"Let them," he muttered, putting more logs in the fire.

It was weeks before I could stand and move around a little, haltingly, with my bandaged stumps held stiffly in front of me. Jude gave me a pair of trousers and a button-up shirt that'd belonged to him, and outside, on a fair day when I was strong enough to stand, I watched as he stuffed my old dress through the top of a rusted-out oil drum and set fire to it. I imagined I could smell it, the wool, the blood, the fears that had seeped into the fabric over the course of years, the only thing to show for it a thread of smoke sewn through a white winter sky.

I stayed there through Christmas, a holiday I only vaguely knew about, the baby and the mother and God mixed together in a way that made my head hurt. We ate potatoes and boiled jerky and Twinkies, and they lit special beeswax candles and sang a couple of songs, though nobody's heart was in it. Waylon sat in a straight-back chair to the side of the couch, eating from his dented metal plate with slow concentration. Jude and I stacked together on the couch, close to the fire. The house smelled like pine needles and skin.

"What do you do for Christmas?" Waylon asked out of nowhere.

"We don't have Christmas," I said after a moment. "But, in spring we celebrate the story of Chad and the Golden Bear. Chad is one of our heroes. He killed a bear who was terrorizing America and wove a crown from the fur."

"That sounds ridiculous," Waylon said.

"So does Christmas to Minnow," Jude interrupted.

"Christmas ain't ridiculous," Waylon said.

"Would you shut up, Daddy?"

"It's my duty to spell out wrong when I see it."

Jude slammed his plate down on his knees. "Don't you dare, Daddy," Jude said. "Nobody wants to hear it."

Waylon looked like he'd been struck. He opened his mouth to respond but Jude spoke first.

"I can tell you're getting ready to tell Minnow she's a sinner, tell her she's damned, and get your Bible to thump at her, but I won't let you."

"You kept this girl secret all this time, doing who knows what in those woods, for *years*. Fornicating out of wedlock, for all I know. Ya'll are sinners!" Waylon bellowed.

"Who hasn't sinned, Daddy?" Jude said, shouting now.

"You made me a sinner. You made me violate the most important commandment when I was too young to know better. You're the worst sinner of anybody here. And I won't sit by and listen to you tell me we're damned because you'll be damned before us, you old drunk!"

Waylon breathed in through his nose loudly. Jude's limbs tensed, as though ready to spring up at any moment. In the fireplace, a log fell over and sent a spray of embers up the chimney. I watched a spark land on the couch and burn straight through to the stuffing.

"I—I know I done wrong by you," Waylon muttered.

"Darn right you have," Jude said.

"I know you deserved a better daddy than the one you got."

Jude crossed his arms.

In his lap, Waylon kneaded his reedy fingers. "I didn't know how to be a daddy, truth is. You don't know this but your momma had a baby before you was born. Jezebel. She came out perfect, but she had something twisted and hard in her belly. We couldn't afford no doctor, so we tried to take care of her at home. When we took her to the emergency room, it was too late. They wheeled her away in one of those little gurneys for babies, with them clear plastic sides. She was paining, but she stretched out her hand to us, to your momma really, all her fingers reaching for her. She weren't never baptized in church. They let us see her one last time, and your momma sprinkled water from the tap on her even though she'd already died by then. I didn't tell her it wouldn't do no good. I thought, if anyone could bless a child's soul to heaven, it was your momma."

Jude swallowed hard, his jaw clenched.

"We buried Jezebel in the poor cemetery, and nobody came to the funeral but your momma and me. There were lots of people who said we were deserving of it for letting her go without baptism, for not being married." He shook his head. "It weren't about the Bible, what they were saying. It weren't about God neither."

Waylon wiped his sleeve over his face, sniffed hard twice. He stood from his chair and opened the back door. A chilly gust blew into the room as he left.

"Off drinking," Jude said to my unasked question. "He'll never quit. He needs that stuff to keep from coming unglued. Trust me, he's better with it than he is without."

"What are you gonna do?" I asked, and he knew I was really asking him if he was going to stay here forever.

Jude shrugged. "Someone has to stay with him. He'd die if there weren't no one here to take care of him."

"What if you were free to do whatever you wanted?"

I asked. "What if you could leave the mountain? What if you could start over in the city? Live in a real house?"

"Ain't never gonna happen," he said in a voice colder than I'd ever heard.

"Why?"

"My momma and daddy wouldn't have moved out here if it was such a good life in town. It's poison down there. I know that's why momma got sick. The dirty sprawl, the factories blacking out the sky, the people stealing your own breath because they can. Here's the only place you can be safe from that. I figgered it all out."

"What?"

"Why people move to the wilderness. Remember we used to wonder about that, why they leave everythin' behind? It's not to run away, like I thought. And it ain't got nothing to do with God," he said. His eyes were stretched open like large windows. "It's hope."

"Hope?"

"Hope for somethin' better. A better future. My momma used to talk about it. People have been expanding into the west"—he spread his fingers wide—"longer than memory. They were called pioneers. Pioneers. Ain't that a good word?"

"I guess," I shrugged. "So?"

"So, what if we did it, too? Made a life for ourselves out

here? What if we made a new civilization, just us two?"

"What's wrong with the civilization down there?" I gestured toward the direction of the town.

"It ain't ours. We lived our whole lives in these woods. You think it would be easy to start over there? You think they'd let us? They'd take us to homes, orphanages. They got laws about that. They'll lock us up because we don't make no sense to them."

"What do you wanna do, Jude? Run and hide?"

"I'm only talking about you and me, living." He smiled, and for a moment he looked like the boy I met in the night all those years ago. But there was something sharp underneath, too, something that never used to be there.

"This isn't the first time, Jude," I said, realizing it even as I said the words.

"The first time what?"

"That you've made me feel like you'd bottle me up in one of your father's moonshine jars if you could."

"What's wrong with that?" he asked. "I cain't see you getting hurt again. I cain't see it."

"This just sounds too much like . . . like the Prophet."

"Don't say that! I ain't nothing like him. I don't even think God's real anymore."

Jude's face was still.

"Don't you?" I asked.

"No. I haven't for a long time."

"How do you know?"

"Just do." He shrugged. "You know what my daddy used to say when I'd cross him? 'I brought you into this world and I can take you out just as easy.' And ain't that just like God? Like you're at some old man's mercy, someone who don't even have his own life together?" Jude swallowed hard. "He told me my momma was up in heaven but I know better now. I knew it, that moment. The moment I kilt her. Inside her head, where my daddy told me the soul lives, there weren't no soul. Jus . . . jus gray sponge, jus mess." He set his jaw.

The air had turned black and heavy with Jude's words. My lips could barely find air to breathe, but Jude seemed relieved. He sat back on his haunches and picked up his guitar. He strummed it absently.

"I'm never gonna learn to play now," I whispered, and at once, the image of Constance came into my mind. I had to save her. I felt it in the thrum of my entire body, and even though I still walked crooked and my stumps felt like fire, I knew the time had come to rescue her.

"Jude, I been thinking—" I started.

"You won't need hands," he said at the same time. I closed my mouth to watch him fiddle with the strings. "Not when you got me to play you songs. I never forgot what you told me. I been starting to make my own, just simple ones. I wanna keep writing you songs forever."

He picked the strings faster and faster until a quick harmony grew. He started singing.

"Once I had my own fine girl
Smile so wide and eyes like pearls
Filled my heart with peaceful sound
Said ain't nothing gonna bring us down.
Ain't nothing gonna bring us down.

"If evil comes with his evil plan
To touch our hearts to the muddy ground
Take us away and see us drowned
Tell him ain't nothing gonna bring us down.
Ain't nothing gonna bring us down.

"When I get out this far-eyed wood
Love you true like I said I would
I'll build a house with my own two hands
Tell you ain't nothing gonna bring us down.
Ain't nothing gonna bring us down.

"When we're old as the desert sand
I'll sing my songs and sow my land
Pick daisies and make you a crown

Say ain't nothing gonna bring us down
Ain't nothing gonna bring us down."

The song petered out and he put down his guitar.

"You like your song?" he asked.

I nodded, though a knot had formed in my chest that I couldn't name.

"I been thinking," I said again. "Thinking about going back to the Community."

He looked up from his guitar strings. "What?"

"I've gotta get my sister, Jude. It's been nagging me since I came here. The Prophet said if I ran away, he'd marry her instead. And I know he wasn't bluffing. He announced it in front of everyone."

"But, Minnow, they'll kill you if you go back there. You know it."

"She's only a kid, younger than us the first time we met. Can you imagine letting a little girl get married off and doing nothing to stop it?"

"What makes you think she ain't already married?"

"She might be. But, the courtship is usually longer, sometimes a month or two."

"If they catch you, they won't let you leave."

"Then I won't let them catch me. I've snuck out a thousand times, and I never once was caught."

"Yeah, 'cept that one time. When they cut your hands off."

"Well, they can't cut them off twice."

He shook his head slowly, eyes clenched. "I don't unnerstand it, Minnow."

No, you don't understand, I thought. I was realizing how much he didn't understand about me. He didn't understand why I couldn't let the Prophet touch my sister. He didn't understand the desire to leave the wilderness that grew every day. He didn't understand why singing me a song wasn't ever going to replace me never being able to play music myself.

"At least I'll be with you," he said. "I'll protect you."

"No," I said. "Stay here and I'll meet you when we get back."

"I'm not letting you go in there alone. And I meant what I said. If I get the chance to kill that old man who hurt you, I'll take it," he insisted. "I'm going with you."

In the end, I agreed. Maybe if he saw what it looked like when people build up secluded lives for themselves in the wild, the stink of bodies living close together, tiny wooden rooms where they lock away what might hurt them, Jude would understand why the last thing I wanted was to live the rest of my life alone in the forest, whether he was there or not.

Chapter 51

All week, my mind flits on a loop between Jude's broken-up face in the pear orchard and Wilson's words the last time I saw him. *You never planned on telling me the truth.* Like one of the warden's old movies, they pass over my mind, frame by frame. Except for reading class, I don't move from my bed, lying on my side with my back to the Post-it on my affirmation wall, only getting up to relieve the periodic pang in my bladder. Angel sits above me, humming, not asking any questions. When she adjusts her body weight, the bed frame creaks.

"Special delivery." Benny stands on the skyway, holding a white envelope in her hands.

"For me?" I ask, rising from the bed slowly.

"That's what it says." She shows me where my name is written in blue ink across the front.

"Can you open it for me?"

"Already did," she says. She turns the envelope over, and I see a finger's been run beneath the seal. I take it between my stumps and walk back to my bed. I tug the paper out with my teeth and spread it on my lap.

> *Dear Miss Bly,*
>
> *We are pleased to inform you that you are a finalist for admission to the Bridge Program. Over one thousand young women from juvenile detention centers across Montana applied, and only five spots will be granted this year. Several representatives from the program will be present at your parole meeting at which time a decision will be made regarding your acceptance into the program. Earning parole is one of the requirements of the program, so your admission will be contingent on your satisfactory exit from detention.*

I scan the letter again, uncertain whether I've really learned to read after all. The black-printed words on the page don't add up. I notice Angel has stopped humming.

"How?" I ask aloud.

Angel steps down from her bunk and scans the letter.

"I didn't apply," I say. "I never completed an application."

She shrugs, her pale eyes not meeting mine. I remember, then, the application that I found on the floor in her handwriting. *"So that's why I'm deserving. Not because I need your help. But because I am going to make it with or without anybody's help."*

My mouth drops open. "You did this," I breathe.

"I don't know what you're talking about—"

"You did this," I repeat. "You applied for me."

She crosses her arms, her eyebrows thrust together.

"Why?" I ask.

"Why?" She shrugs. "Why not? Because I was bored. Because you weren't going to. Because there's nothing good in this place except the possibility of you getting out and making it."

She sits heavily on the floor, her back to the cinder-block wall. Her hand covers her forehead.

"Why won't you tell me how long you're in for?" I ask.

"It's too depressing."

"I can handle depressing."

"You'll just cry."

"I won't," I say. "Or, I'll try not to."

She sighs. "You know, after I did my uncle in, I got sent to a holding cell at the police station. The pastor from my uncle's church came to visit. Did you know they can give you religious counsel whether you want it or not? He

341

started lecturing me about how I needed to repent, how I'd done a sin only Jesus was capable of forgiving. He was so specific. What hell smells like and what it feels like to have all your skin burned off, and how you never breathe the same when God leaves your body for good. All I could say was, 'You're about ten years too late.'"

She scoffs. "He acted like he didn't know what I was talking about so I explained to him what my uncle did to me. I used details, too. Anatomical details. I made him squirm, watched his face fill up with heat and his temples go all slick with sweat. He stood up to leave and I told him I had the right to religious counsel, didn't I? I said 'Listen. I have a confession,' real quiet so he had to come back into the room. I told him how I'd crouched in the dark, and when my uncle opened the bedroom door, I held the gun to his Adam's apple and pulled the trigger. The blood came spurting out of his throat and covered me, head to toe. And it felt good, because I knew it was the last time my uncle would ever touch me again.

"Well, the pastor's face gets all disgusted at this, but I could tell it wasn't disgust at what my uncle did, no. He was disgusted by me."

She's quiet for a long time. She squints like she's thinking hard.

"You wanna know how long my sentence is? It's forty

years," she says. "Forty years. And assholes like my uncle never get caught. The entire system is so fucked."

Her brow folds and a tear slides beside her nose. I've never seen her cry. She covers her face with her hands. "Fuck!" she shouts.

The word reverberates around the cinder-block walls. For no reason, I shout it, too. "Fuck!"

She looks up, surprised.

"Fuck!" she shouts again, staring at me.

"Fuck!" I shout.

She lets her head fall back and closes her eyes. "FUUUUCK!" she screams.

"A MILLION TIMES FUCK!" I scream with her.

"What on God's sacred green Earth is going on?" Benny calls from the skyway. She approaches the bars, her arms crossed.

"Nothing," Angel and I say in unison.

"Didn't sound like nothing. Sounded like I should give you both solitary for a week."

"We were doing group therapy," I say.

"Yeah, it's on doctor's orders," Angel agrees. "You can't punish us for that. It's against the law."

"We could sue," I say, nodding.

"I better just let you off with a warning, then," Benny says. "But if I hear another piece of profanity leave either of your mouths, I'll get up in your molars with a bar of Irish Spring, you hear me?"

"Yes, ma'am," we chant back.

Benny recedes back to her post.

I smile at Angel.

"Fuck," I whisper.

"Fuck," she whispers back, a smile creeping onto her face. And, inside that smile is the knowledge that some things are just too sad, too screwed up. Sometimes there's nothing for it but shouting "Fuck" with your best friend at the top of your lungs.

Chapter 52

In the morning, a moth flies into my cell, a floating gray piece of barely anything, rising and falling with irregular wing beats. It finds the flat rectangular fluorescent light set into the ceiling and immediately starts banging itself against the beveled plastic.

I stand and crawl up onto Angel's bunk, waving my arm toward the moth to knock it away. "What the hell are you doing?" she asks.

"Help me," I tell her, my eyes still trained on the crooked gray body. "Capture it. Set it free."

"Why?"

"It's going to kill itself up against that light," I say. "That's what they do. They think it's the sun."

Angel looks at me in that clench-eyed way that tells me she knows we're brushing against something important, something from the past. She puts her book away and leans out toward the middle of the room, palms curved in cupped shapes. She swings once, then again, and the moth is inside her closed hands.

She leans back onto the bed, bending her fingers to make a crack so I can see its beating wings, held together by scales and veins. Angel carefully swings off the bunk. At the bars, she lowers her hands, then throws them in the air so the moth can fly out of the cell.

"It's gone," Angel says. "It's free now."

But I shake my head. "It'll only do it again, somewhere else."

"You can't prevent that," she says. "You know that, right? It's not your job. It never was."

And it's then that I know she can tell what's just fallen into the fingers of my mind: the rememberings I've kept back for months, those frozen moments pushed to the dark corners of my mind. The night Jude and I went back to the Community. The night when everything, all of it, came tumbling down.

• • •

That night, the entire world was frozen, including the air, which seemed to hold all things suspended. I looked to my left, where Jude stood, his breath a milky curtain before him. All around, the rigid trees groaned with human-like voices, their insides frozen in the position they'd held themselves before winter hit. I imagined how it might've gone, one night in November, they were sleeping and suddenly their entire bodies became stuck like steel. I felt like I'd been in that position all my life, frozen. And, now, suddenly, I could pick my head up and face the winter sky and glimpse the tops of trees and move my body in any motion I chose.

We knew we'd arrived at the Community by the tiny squares of dull orange light that materialized through the trees, windows of houses where I knew nobody was home. I could smell the purple smoke. They'd be in the Prophet Hall, and he'd be silly with the smoke, face inflamed, eyes tense and bright.

We circled to the back of my house. In their coops, chickens cooed at us just like they always did at someone they thought might feed them. Jude turned the handle of the back door. We passed bedrooms, the empty kitchen, and climbed the small rickety stairs to the maidenhood room. Jude pushed aside the sliding lock and the door creaked open. Inside, it was dark, but I could make out a small body lying on a pallet. She lay over the covers, her back a slim white sickle in the darkness.

"Constance," I whispered.

She flipped around, her blond braid tucked between her

neck and shoulder. Her lips parted almost imperceptibly.

"You're back," she whispered.

"Yes," I said, taking a step into the room.

"To marry the Prophet?"

"No," I said, in disgust. "No."

"Then why?"

"To rescue you. To take you with me. To tell you about what it's really like out there."

"We know all that."

"No, you don't. You only know his lies."

"He doesn't lie."

The room was freezing but I noticed Constance's cheeks were flushed. Sweat dappled her forehead. Something about her was different. Something about her had changed.

"Minnow," Jude said, his voice low. "Look at—"

"Who's he?" Constance interrupted, eyes darting to Jude for the first time.

"He came with me to save you from this place. That's what I want you to know. There's life outside, Constance. There are people, chances to be happy. Jude and I are going away from all this . . . this madness. And I want you to be there with us."

"What are you talking about?" she asked. "I'm getting married."

"But you don't have to. You can escape."

Constance's lips turned up at the edges. "But, I don't want to escape. I want to marry him."

"Minnow," Jude repeated again, his voice adamant. He tugged vehemently on my shirt sleeve.

His eyes were hard on Constance, but not her face. I followed his gaze to Constance's lap. There, folded like rotting meat, were two crumpled, purple stumps.

The air turned cold. Each cell in my body bucked.

"Your hands," I breathed. "Your hands!"

I knelt beside her bed where her legs were slung to the side. All she wore was a nightgown, the sleeves barely brushing the thin place her hands used to grow from.

I pictured the scene, Constance wrestled to the ground by those men, her body so much smaller than mine, so much more like a bird than a girl. Did our father cut hers off, too? I hoped she looked him in the eye, like I did. I hoped the look on her face killed him.

"Minnow, don't look so stricken." The way she said it made me look into her fever-blushed face. "You never were very quick, were you? I asked to have them cut off."

The entire scene went out of focus. Blurred, then came back again even sharper till I could spot, even from here, the crooked half circle of *X*s stitched around her stumps, hear the fevered hitch at the back of her throat when she breathed.

"After you left, the Prophet repeated God's message," she said. "That I was to be his new wife, not you. And I knew I had to do something to be worthy. To prove my devotion."

I stared at her. This girl with blue, blue eyes. This girl who I saw as a baby still, the steam that rolled off her little red body on the winter morning she was born. The tuft of damp blond hair. Her hands that gripped at nothing.

"Do you—do you have any idea what you've given up?" I cried.

"It's nothing when you've got a higher calling."

I gaped at her, raw panic rising in my throat. "You're crazy!" I bellowed, my voice breaking, tears forming at the corners of my eyes. "You're a lunatic!"

"Me, a lunatic?" she scoffed. "You're the one who broke the rules—knowingly. You understand what happens to girls who fraternize out of wedlock." She shook her head. "And with a *Rymanite*. You're sick. You've damned yourself for good." Her eyes were wide open. She was afraid. Of *me*. She lived in a house of horrors, and she was afraid of me?

"You can lie to me," she said. "You can lie to yourself. But you can't lie to God. He sees straight through you."

"Shut up!" I screamed. I struck her across the face, and she wheeled back, her arms crossed in front of her, barely able to move, too sapped from fever. Her stumps were new, so when she swung to hit me and her stump connected with my cheekbone, she crumpled in pain. I swiped her with my elbow and her head flung back. When Jude wrestled me off of her, I saw that blood trickled down her cheek.

"Minnow, we have to get out of here," Jude said. "*Now.* Someone probably heard."

"She's coming with us," I panted.

"What?" he demanded. "But she doesn't want to."

"It doesn't matter. She's—brainwashed. I can't let the Prophet have her."

"But, she wants to marry him."

"She's twelve!"

"Fine," he barked. "Fine, but how do you suggest we convince her?"

I looked down at her, a steely look of defiance wound over her features. "We don't," I said. "She's not going to come willingly. We're taking her with us."

Chapter 53

"You're back," I say when I see Dr. Wilson in the doorway. I thought he might have disappeared again.

"For now," he says. "I'm going away for a day or two."

"My hearing is coming up," I say. "My birthday's at the end of the week."

He nods.

"So, are you going to make it?"

He doesn't respond. "What are you reading?" he asks instead. I look down at the library book in my lap and move my arm so he can see the title over a backdrop of a whorled galaxy. *"Cosmos,"* I say.

"Any good?" he asks.

"Yes," I say. "I'm learning things."

"Teach me something," he says.

"Teach you?"

"Sure," he says. "Teach me the best thing you know. The best fact in the universe."

At first, I don't answer. An unconscious prickle of heat

has been filling my cheeks, and I can't figure out why until I realize that no one has ever asked me to teach them something. I never could. I didn't know anything before.

"Most of the energy on Earth comes from the sun," I explain. "We all run on sun power. And did you also know that everything on Earth, including people, is made of particles of a star that exploded? We're stars who run off stars."

"Wow," he says. "That really is the best fact in the universe."

"You know what I can't stop thinking about? Jude never knew any of this. He's alive out there, I can't tell you how, but I figured it out, and he wants me to find him in the mountains. But I keep thinking that, even if I did find him and told him everything I've learned, he wouldn't understand it in the same way I do now. I don't know how that can be."

"Nobody's got the same mind. Nobody perceives the same."

I nod. "The Prophet said stars were God's eyes and all that time I knew he was wrong, but I believed him. How is that possible? Belief shouldn't be compatible with lies, but is."

"Did you know any of this stuff six months ago?" he asks,

and when I shake my head he says, "If another Prophet came, you'd be ready. You have weapons."

I hold up my hands, but he shakes his head. "I'm not talking about those kinds of weapons."

"I know some facts about stars, but that doesn't even begin to answer everything. There's still too much I don't know."

"You know what I heard the other day?" he asks. "I was listening to the radio in the car and I had to pull over, just to listen. They said scientists think there might be other universes, maybe an infinite amount of universes. Maybe a new universe forms every second. And these universes might have different versions of ourselves, making different choices and leading totally different lives. Problem is, nobody knows if any of those theories are true, but that doesn't discourage the scientists. The way they see it, if we keep looking, one day we're bound to find out. We have to be happy to keep searching and not knowing all the time."

"You're talking about God."

"No," he says. "I'm talking about anything you can't see."

I shake my head. "That's not what Angel thinks."

"I know what Angel thinks. I'm talking about what you think. It's my opinion that you shouldn't deny your mind the chance to stretch, to go places, simply because you don't have evidence. I think it's high time you figure out what you think."

• • •

That night, with the dark of the jail unchinked by even a single pinprick of light, I lie on my thin mattress and consider this. I'm realizing that I'm the only person I never asked my questions to. I never thought I could count on my own answers.

I think about the universe, and the earth, and the stars, and I ask myself a question.

Is Charlie there?

No.

But is something there?

Maybe.

Maybe.

• • •

In the morning, Benny drops an envelope off at my cell. Inside is an official notice that my parole meeting is on the 15th. My eighteenth birthday. Three days from now. I have prepared myself for it, how I'll look over my shoulder at the meeting room door, hoping Dr. Wilson will show. But he won't. Waiting with held breath for their decision to fall, which will crash over me like a chest of broken china. *Denied*, they will say in their voices of metal. I'll be shackled by some brusque guard who will drive me to Billings and dump me in a group cell block of muscled women with face tattoos and rotten teeth. And suddenly every good thought this place managed to inflate inside me will be punctured, because that cell door will clang shut behind me and nothing will be my choice again. The future is locked in place.

I'll have to say good-bye to Angel, whose work getting me into the Bridge Program will have been for nothing, and Benny and Miss Bailey and Rashida and Tracy, and everyone at juvie I'll miss when I'm gone. I wonder if Dr. Wilson will say good-bye. I wonder if I'm useless to him now that he knows I will never give him the truth he wanted.

And I wonder if I've really lived out my life. If, even when I'm eventually free, a year or two or five from now, I'll still be trapped, just like my parents were in their trailer park lives, in the drudge of everyday, the weeds in the backyard that never died, the rusted-out truck that broke down every morning. The only thing that blurred that to the periphery was the Prophet, who cast a new kind of clean light on their lives with every step he took closer to them.

And I almost understand now how you can be so trapped you'll throw the whole world away just to get free.

But I didn't understand it then, the last time I saw the

Community, before the fire ate it all and ruined everything. That night, there was no room for anything but one thought: get Constance. Save her.

. . .

Jude lifted Constance in his arms. She was bucking and fighting, her screams cutting through the empty house. We ran down the stairs and Jude wrenched the back door open with his free hand. Standing in the doorway was my father. I only saw his face for a moment because Jude kicked the door closed and shouted, "Run!"

We tried the front door, but it was no good. They were all there, filing out of the Prophet Hall and into the courtyard. From their fists hung lanterns. In their eyes burned hatred.

The men came at us quickly. Jude set Constance on the ground and put his hands in the air. This means surrender, in the real world, but we weren't in the real world. We were in some nightmare world where there's no such thing as justice.

The deacons dragged Jude to the center of the courtyard, his boots scraping against the frozen ground. I ran for him, but someone ripped me away and held my stumps with iron grips. I lost all my breath, saw the scene through a gauze of white pain.

My eyes scanned the courtyard, taking in their ruddy

scowling faces, and I realized I never could have rescued them. I thought all I'd have to do was tell Constance she could be free, that soon the rest of them would follow us off the mountain. But the offer of freedom doesn't mean anything to people who already think they're free.

The Prophet marched out of the crowd with a kerosene lantern held high. He brought the lantern near Jude's face where he struggled on the ground, then glanced at me, and it was clear in his steel-tipped smirk that he understood.

He walked over to Constance. "What has occurred, wife-to-be?"

"Minnow came back with that boy to steal me away. They live in sin together in the woods."

A great gasp went up. The Prophet straightened, holding his arms out to the sides. Even though he wasn't standing in the Prophet Hall, I recognized these motions. He was preparing a sermon. He was thinking through a punishment.

He raged on about fornication and sin and damnation and fraternizing with Rymanites, but his face was calm. He looked happy. Overjoyed. This was his moment to smite someone, really and truly. On the ground, Jude jerked beneath the grips of the deacons.

Finally, the Prophet ended his diatribe, and it became

so quiet in the courtyard, I could hear the trees creaking. The Prophet savored it. He stretched out the silence, looked at me, then at his deacons.

"Kill the Rymanite."

I watched the words fall from the Prophet's grizzled lips. I hear those words in my mind still. They are a chant. A hymn. I thumb the words in my mind like prayer beads. That was the moment I realized there would be a cost for all of this. A cost for believing. A cost for thinking there was a way to escape.

The deacons stood and there was a silent moment when Jude might've tried to make a break for it. He levered himself up on an elbow but, in the next moment, Deacon Jeremiah swung back and landed a fist into Jude's face and he flattened back to the ground, a curved crimson wound cupping his eye bone. I traced the trajectory of each pair of heavy boots and tightened fists, the rush of blood that flew from Jude's mouth with the first few kicks to the face, the molar that sailed gracelessly through the air and became lost in the mud, planted like a sunflower seed. His cheek puffed up and bruised with blood, and broke apart like an abscess after a cruelly aimed kick from Deacon Timothy. The deacons each took a turn, their fists and boots and knees and elbows hammering Jude down long past the time he'd stopped moving. I screamed, just to avoid hearing the sound of their fists sinking into Jude's body.

I didn't pray when my hands were cut off—it was much too fast and my mind could only process the basic information of the moment. Now, though, I screamed at God—at Charlie—at anyone—to make it stop.

"Samuel!" the Prophet shouted. My father had been standing to the side with his wives. "Are you a deacon or not?"

My father's mouth was clenched. He swallowed with difficulty, then marched toward where Jude lay. He swung his leg back for a kick and I shut my eyes, screaming still, because Jude had stopped screaming. He'd stopped making any noise at all.

The women started to look uncomfortable and covered their children's eyes with large hands. The rabid energy in the crowd gradually bled away as Jude began to look less like a boy and more like something butchered. The deacons panted, their kicks growing feebler and feebler. In the clearing, it became so quiet practically the only thing you could hear was my sobs.

And then my father, of all people, uttered, "That's enough," barely loud enough to hear. The deacons looked from him to the Prophet, their faces shiny with sweat and flecked with blood. The Prophet nodded and the men stepped away. It felt awkward then, those men covered in gore standing in a loose circle, shifting their weight from foot to foot. The outsider's body on the ground was like a spotlight on every ludicrous aspect of the entire place. The men who'd been holding me let their grip go slack, and I ran to Jude. I knelt beside him.

His eyes roved around, unfocused. It was hard for him to wipe the fear off of his face. He tried to smile but the teeth were broken in his mouth, protruding in different directions. He tried to talk but it came out like a gargle. He swallowed some of the blood and said—and said—

"Every morning, every evening, ain't we got fun?"

His voice echoed around the clearing. Tears fell from the bridge of my nose and cleared a path through the blood on his cheek. "Not much money, oh but honey, ain't we got fun?" he continued.

"The rent's unpaid dear, we haven't a bus," I began, but Jude had stopped singing. He was struggling to breathe.

"But smiles are made dear, for people like us," I sobbed.

His eyes slid shut, and I heard the Prophet pronounce, "The Rymanite is dead," and my father's impossibly strong arms pulled me from the ground.

"No!" I screamed, jerking against my father's grip, but he didn't let go.

The ground was so frozen, the blood just pooled on

the surface and rolled over to where they were standing, touching the hems of their dresses and pants. They backed away from it, like death was catching.

And I beat against my father's arms the way I should've years and years before, because all I wanted was to keep looking into Jude's face, but by then the tears were obscuring my vision, and the white-hot rage was coloring my periphery, and so I contented myself with sobbing his name over and over so if he lived, he'd know I was still there.

The last thing I remember, before they dragged me away, was looking into the woods and catching sight of Waylon, his face a half-moon behind the trunk of a tree. He must have followed us. His mouth was open in a silent scream, fingers gripping his face like claws.

His eyes latched onto mine. I opened my mouth and screamed.

"RUUUUUUUUUUUUUUUUN!"

Chapter 54

I wake up the day of my parole hearing, and around me the world is acting as if everything is normal. It's not. It's my last day in juvie. The last day I'll drink powdered soup in this cafeteria, the last time I'll observe this procession of girls in orange, the last time I'll see Angel for who knows how long, the last day I'll go to reading class. I sit beside Rashida on our upturned buckets around Miss Bailey's rocking chair as she opens up *The Giver* and begins to spell out the story of a boy who learns to see the world as much more than he'd ever imagined.

Jude is waiting for me, right now. While Miss Bailey reads, I bring to mind the directions he gave me to the cave where he's living: south of the bend in the big river, near the heron pond where we fished once. The place he wants us to spend the rest of our years, the cave in the wild where he thinks we'd be safe.

A knock comes from the classroom door. Benny peeks

her head inside the room. "Miss Bailey, Minnow is needed upstairs."

"Can't it wait until after class?" Miss Bailey asks.

"No, it's important. Official . . . prison business."

She sighs. "Fine. Go ahead."

I stand and walk with Benny out of the classroom. She's acting strange, glancing around corners before she enters hallways, and her pace is much quicker than usual. I have to hop to keep up with her.

"Where are we going?" I ask.

"Shh," she hisses. "Can't you tell we're doing something covert?"

When we arrive at my cell, the door is open and Angel stands beside my bed, her hands clasped in front of her.

"Happy birthday!" she says, gesturing toward the bunk.

"What's going on?" I ask.

"We pulled some strings," Angel says. "I told you I run this place. Go ahead. Open your presents."

On my bed, there is a small collection of items. One of them, unwrapped, is a book with a picture of space on the cover. "I got you your own copy of *Cosmos*," Angel says. "You'll need your own wherever you're heading next. Benny helped me order it."

I stroke the book and look up at her. "Thank you," I whisper.

"And Benny got you a Spanish doubloon."

Inside the folds of Benny's hand is a rough-edged gold coin. I take it between my stumps. "What is it?"

"It's just a replica," Benny says. "Back in pirate times, if you lost a limb, the captain would pay you. A missing hand got you thirty doubloons. Not a replacement, more of an acknowledgment of something lost. It was the sense of justice, more than anything. Figured you deserved a little compensation."

I smile at her, a warm feeling rushing up from my stomach.

"Thanks, Benny," I say, slipping the coin onto the copy of *Cosmos*.

The last gift on my mattress is a shoebox. The lid has already been removed and placed to the side. Inside, I can see only a mound of crumpled gold tissue paper.

Lightly, I dig through the jumble of paper till my stumps touch something cold. I push the paper aside and see them. Two hands made of silver. My mind can't make sense of them, but my heart is drumming hard against my ribs, like it recognizes them. Even in the artificial light, they gleam. The fingers are thinner than real fingers, leaner, like knobby twigs.

"That doctor of yours is pretty full-service," Angel says. "House calls, obstruction of justice, the whole nine."

"What are these?" I ask.

"You don't recognize your own hands?" Angel asks. "I told Dr. Wilson he should've had them flipping the bird, that way every time you look at them you can be giving the Prophet a big fuck you."

I pick up my left hand. Inside me, something heavy and dense falls into place, a feeling of rightness I haven't known in months.

"Dr. Wilson did this?" I ask.

She nods. "He had to break into an evidence locker. Violated about ten laws in the process."

"Why would he do that?"

She shrugs. "He's a weird guy. Said it was worth it because now you're even. Now you've got something on him."

The metal fingers are cool against my stumps, these fingers that once grew from my body, these fingers that began as chains of cells in my mother's womb, and for seventeen years they existed as part of me, until they became something else, really just an idea. But to me, like this, they are perfect, like all along they were meant to be coated in silver, not flesh.

Chapter 55

After one of the wives threw a sheet over Jude's body and the blood on the ground stopped steaming in the freezing air, the deacons led me to the edge of the Community near a giant pine whose boughs extended over my head like a rafters. I scanned the tree line and saw Waylon had gone. My chest felt a little lighter. I hoped he'd pack up, get in the truck, drive down the forest service road and never look back. And, an angry part of me thought, I hoped he'd understand now what a mistake it was coming to the woods to begin with.

The Community made low noises behind me, but I couldn't look at them, the dull congregation in their dull, decade-old clothes, eyes so full of the Prophet they were almost popping out of their sockets, so I craned my neck to the sky. It was almost night. Dark clouds covered the pale blue in a holey blanket. To the east was the moon, almost full. My whole body was quaking, but I couldn't take my eyes off that moon. Even as the Prophet approached me, shouting in a screeching voice that reached down into my soul and grabbed the necks of the angels that lived there, I could hardly care about anything but the almost-oval of moon hanging over the forest I'd known almost my entire life, clouds sliding across like doves.

The Prophet grabbed my chin hard and pointed it at his face.

"Are you listening to me?" he screamed.

He'd never hurt me himself before. The feeling of his hand around my face shook me awake. I looked boldly into his face and noticed his eyes were covered in a thin white film. He used to wear glasses, before the Lord fixed his sight.

"No," I said. "I won't ever listen to you again."

Over his shoulder, I could see the color of blood seeping through the sheet they'd covered Jude in.

He threw me to the ground hard, but I stretched out on my back and put my arms behind my head, staring up at the moon again. The women looked uncertainly at one another. I was acting odd for someone about to be punished, but it could almost be happening to someone else, any other girl in any other society where girls are manhandled and bruised easy as pears.

When the men tugged the boots from my feet, I didn't move. When they tied the rope around my ankles in a thick noose, and when they winched me up into the tree, hanging upside down, I didn't move. I let my arms fall beside me in a graceful arc. The rope twisted, and for a moment I faced the forest, the dark bodies of hibernating pines crowded together. It looked almost black in there. I wondered how I'd ever convinced myself I might see the paleness of angels in that forest, if I looked hard enough.

Behind me, the Prophet's heavy footfalls crunched over the ground.

"With this water, we cleanse you of the sin of fornication and disobedience," he shouted.

Water hit me like a pane of glass. I gasped. The force of it made the rope spin till I faced the Prophet, an empty bucket in his hands. Behind him stretched a line of people, each holding a bucket of cold pond water in their curled white fingers. I couldn't see all their faces because most of them held their heads down, ladies' faces guarded by bonnets, but I was certain they were all there, all the people I'd shared my childhood with.

The Prophet jerked his head, and the next person in line, a deacon, marched up and doused me, and in his water was a triangle of ice from the surface of the pond. It hit my forehead and I was sure, from the sudden bloom of warmth along my hairline, that I was bleeding.

The Prophet waved his palm in a circle. "With this

water, we cleanse you of the sin of fornication and disobedience."

One by one, they threw their water till I was soaked and shivering with a vehemence that could've broken bones.

My father's wives came in a group and threw their water all at once. They turned around without a glance. My siblings came after, the smaller ones with their arms quaking from the weight of the bucket, lifting it onto their thin shoulders and tossing it with all their might. My oldest brother, Jedediah, threw his water directly on my face and I had to lean up, body doubled, coughing, trying to blow the water from my nose. I didn't see Constance. They must've taken her back to the maidenhood room.

I heard a little boy whimper that he was cold. I heard water slide from my dowel-straight hair and collect on the ground. And I heard the Prophet's repetitious chanting as though from miles underwater. Every minute, I felt myself dip almost out of consciousness until the next bucketful landed and I'd come rushing back.

Eventually, the water stopped. Over the groan of the rope, I could make out the smack of boot falls as the Community receded into their houses. The Prophet, too. Beneath me, the water was forming a thick pile of ice. My hair was hard with it.

I realized, then, that they were going to leave me here.

To freeze to death. Without thought, I accepted it as one does a hand of cards. I relaxed and tried to ignore the burning in my legs, the bright blush in my cheeks from heat that didn't make sense. Jude was dead. There was nothing left. No future to imagine. I wanted to sleep, just to sleep.

Like a meteor, into my mind came the memory of Constance locked up in the maidenhood room, her whole body burning with infection, her mind burning with lies she'd been fed since our mother pushed her out into the world. More than anything, it was my duty to keep her safe. And she'd never be, not with the Prophet still around. I would die and he would marry her and this place would go on for years, tucked tightly inside this forest, inside its own twisted, violent logic.

I knew it would be a choice. To let myself disappear or to straighten my limbs, wake the cells from their dying sleep, and try to get out of this.

I started swinging. Mostly to see if I could. I budged my body back and forth, my frozen hair barely moving. After a moment, I was swinging fast, and I bent up, doubling myself in half. I tried to wrap my arms around my legs, but I slipped and fell back, my body rocking, the rope tightening around my ankles. The tree groaned loudly and I held my breath, praying no one would leave their houses to check on the noise. When no one came, I swung myself again and managed to wrap my arms around my legs.

The tail end of the rope was looped through the middle of the noose. If I could tease it out, the noose might loosen. I bent my knees and gripped my legs with my elbows, my back bent as far as it could. I lifted my mouth to the rope. With a massive hoist, I latched my teeth around the bottom loop. I yanked at it, tugging with my whole head. It was frozen, and the tucked-in piece wouldn't budge. When my teeth were aching and my body felt like it might break in half like a frozen blade of grass, the rope began to slip free. I tugged it away from the noose and the rope unwound lazily, then went slack, and I fell to the ground in a heap.

I held my stomach and breathed against the hardened mud and ice. My bottom lip had broken against the ground and I tasted salt. Slowly, I eased myself up from the ground, thrusting my shivering, bloodless feet back into my boots.

The courtyard was quiet, and I saw for the first time that Jude's body was no longer there, the only evidence of him a few crimson puddles and a wadded up sheet, stiff with frozen blood. I stared at it for a long moment. I was uncontrollably angry, but it was a quiet kind of anger, the kind that doesn't even simmer, doesn't make a noise. Real anger, the deadly kind.

This was the moment I'd been hurtling toward my

whole life, and I knew what I'd do. The Prophet lived by himself. His wives slept behind his house in a couple of ramshackle cottages. He must have enjoyed his privacy, because most never saw the inside of his home.

I climbed his porch steps, careful not to let the old wood creak. I took the Prophet's round door handle between my wrists and pulled in opposite directions, leaning against the door with my elbow. The handle clinked. The door drifted open.

I stepped lightly over the threshold. A low fire burned in the hearth, illuminating the front room enough to make out a massive dark stain on the wooden floor. My blood. My eyes drifted to the fireplace. Over the mantle, beneath the silver scroll of salvation thumbtacked to the log wall, were a set of white finger bones, held together with loops of golden wire. They rested on the heavy wooden mantle delicately, like ornaments.

It was almost a privilege, the sight of them, fingertips slanted like they could've been playing the piano. Not many people get to see their bones outside their body. I grabbed the hands between my stumps and placed them in the pockets of my loose trousers, wrist end first.

Behind me, a squeak. I turned. From where I was standing, I saw straight into the only other room, the Prophet's bedroom. He was sitting up in his unmade bed. I could tell he'd just woken up by the dark half circles under his eyes, puffy with sleep.

He saw me. His eyes stretched wide.

My boots were almost silent on the cold floor. His breath started leaving him heavily, eking from his ribs with a loud, almost-afraid sound. In the heat of the house, water began to drip from my thawing clothes.

I sounded like a cloudburst. I felt like thunder.

"You thought I was dead, didn't you?" I asked, my voice low.

His breath came louder, like he'd just run a great distance, his fingers grabbing the sheets on his bed with bloodless knuckles. I wondered at this. Did he fear me? The idea was electrifying.

"I've figured you out, you know that?" I said. "The way you lied to us. The way you converted us—"

"I didn't convert anyone. God converted you."

"You're sick," I spat. "You're a killer."

"When the children of God become disobedient—" he sputtered. "And idolatrous and wicked—they suffer at the hands of God."

"The hands of God," I scoffed. "God isn't the reason Jude is dead. You are."

"I act for God," he sputtered. His breathing grew more beleaguered.

"Did you act for God when you cut off my hands?"

His fingers pulled at the neck of his robes like the touch of the collar on his skin was choking him. This wasn't fear, I realized. This was something else, something beyond me. He wedged his stiff fingers beneath his mattress. In his hand he held a curious object. Part plastic, part metal. I couldn't figure it out, until he raised it to his lips and squeezed.

He squeezed again and again but it obviously wasn't doing what he wanted because he groaned, a high whining sound, and threw the object to the ground. In the next moment, he was keeling off the bed, hitting the floor knees-first with a bone-shaking smack. He curled to the ground, his chest jerking upward, calamitously.

A dial turned in my mind, slowly. "You said God cured your asthma," I breathed. "You . . . you . . ." I processed this like my entire world was being translated to a different language. "You lied," I whispered.

His fingers reached toward a dry pine dresser on the opposite side of the room. I walked over and kicked open the bottom drawer. Inside, five more inhalers rolled like wayward spinning tops.

"Please," he gasped, his forehead pressed to the floor.

"Why should I?"

"You can—come back—to God. He is—forgiving. He will—bestow hands—on you—anew."

His rib cage buckled under his heaving gasps, fingers stretched toward the dresser.

I stood a long moment, listening to the sickening sound of his throat slapping together.

"I'm sorry," I said finally.

He turned his head toward me, creases of fear cut into the beardless places on his face. I recalled the photo he'd shown us of him as a five-year-old boy with thick eyeglasses, hiding behind the moon-colored creases of his father's jeans. The man who made him fear hatchets. The fear that bred fear that bred fear. On this night, I would end the cycle. I would kill it forever.

"I'm sorry. I can't reach it," I said. "I haven't got hands."

He let out a groan from deep in his throat. I stared down at him, the pale lump of him, the tar-colored beard of him. The spasms grew slower. His eyes began to slide shut.

I might've stood there longer if not for the smell of fire. The room had grown hot, but I didn't notice at first. The heat radiated from the roof, off the thick thatch and pine shingles. The roof groaned loudly, then snapped. A mass of thatch in the main room fell to the floor in a fiery mess. In seconds, the house filled with smoke. I ran from the bedroom, past the aluminum foil on which the gibberish words of God had been scrawled. It was melting, curling away from the yellow thumbtacks that fastened it over the mantle.

I grabbed the door handle between my forearms and tried to twist, but my shaking arms were clumsy and sweating. I heaved against the door as the smoke drove into my eyes, into my mouth, into the delicate pink passages behind my face.

Finally, the door handle turned and I crashed out of the house, down the front steps, onto the cold mud of the courtyard, gasping for clean breath.

Before me, the Community was a circle of flame. Nearly every house was burning from its roof, streams of embers and back-lit smoke wending through the black sky. And in the middle of it all was Waylon.

Chapter 56

In the beginning, I wasn't sure who I was protecting, myself or Waylon. It's still foggy who did the killing that day. But a couple things have parted that fog. One of them is the return of something I lost long ago—not the hands, but what they meant. A kind of power I never knew I had while they were attached to me. The power to do what I know is right. The power to free myself, finally.

An hour before my parole meeting, Dr. Wilson comes in like he always does, unannounced, except this time he doesn't ask me how I am, or what's happening, or what motivates someone to kill. He doesn't say a word. He just looks at my face as if to say, *What else is there to talk about?* And I understand. There's nothing else to say. Nothing but the final thing.

I look down to where the silver hands rest in their box beside me on the bed.

"I wanted to thank you for . . . what you did," I say.

He nods.

"You could get in big trouble for this, couldn't you?"

He shrugs. "What are you going to do with them?"

"I haven't thought about it."

"People who get limbs amputated sometimes bury them, have them cremated."

I shake my head. "The Prophet had them on his mantelpiece. Like a trophy," I say. "I don't want to hide them away. I want to see them every day, like he did. They're my trophy now."

He nods wordlessly.

"Are you going to be at my hearing?" I ask to break the silence.

"Remind me of our deal again."

"I help you find the killer, you recommend my release."

"That was it."

"So?" I ask, undeterred. "Are you gonna be there?"

He smiles. And waits. He waits and waits and waits.

In the beginning, I didn't trust him. But he's proven good on his very first promise, to help me. And he's proven something else. They're not all the same. They don't all want to hurt. They don't all want to lie. So maybe he deserves a little trust. A little truth.

I lay the pieces out one by one, the inhalers, the

Prophet's lungs straining in the smoke-strewn air, the moonshine bottles and the blue flame they made, the way the hollow houses fell easy, like nothing was really holding them up.

. . .

Waylon stood at the edge of where Jude had lain, and at his feet was a wooden box filled with bottles of moonshine. He stuffed a cloth down the neck of a bottle, lit the cloth with fire, and threw it to the roof of a house where it exploded in a sheet of sharp-tongued flames. From his throat came rusty noises, like a truck engine refusing to start.

"Get out of here," I shouted. "They'll see you."

Waylon fell to his knees beside the puddle of blood, taking in the empty space that Jude had occupied before someone had dragged him away. His eyes squeezed shut in a sob. "He's d-dead?" he asked, even though the answer was, even as we spoke, soaking into the knees of his trousers. "He's dead?"

"You need to leave," I croaked. "They'll kill you, too."

He stared at me for a long moment, blankly, as though looking at a wall, or the sky.

"Waylon?" I asked.

"Look at what we are," he said, his voice raw. "We ran away to the wilderness 'cause we thought the outside weren't civilized. But the wild don't change who we really are. It makes it worse."

In his lap, his hands tore at each other, gripping the rolled sleeves of his shirt.

"Look what it turned us into. *Savages*." He was yelling over the roar of the flames. Flakes of ash drifted through the air.

"You need to leave. Now!" I shouted.

He shook his head, eyes mad with tears.

The noise of the fire vibrated my eardrums. "If you want to live, Waylon, get out of here! For Jude. Make this worth something."

Without a word, he started nodding, mouth stretched in a deep frown, then stood and shuffled toward the woods, arms wrapped around his moonshine box.

I ran to the tree line and crouched in the dark of the forest, watching my home smolder. At first I thought everyone would burn in their sleep because none of them had emerged from their houses, until I heard a shout, then screams. Slowly, white shapes streamed from the houses, first only a handful, then a flood of men and women in long nightgowns and little nightcaps, children dragged along like lost white flags in a windstorm.

I braced an arm against a tree and watched my family pour from the front door of our house, littlest children in the arms of their mothers—their real mothers. Constance still hadn't stumbled out with the rest of them, stuck up there in that attic room, the door likely latched. A moment later, my father reeled out of the front door, his face shell-shocked and covered in soot, with Constance behind him. She coughed into the crook of her handless arm.

My mother stood with some of the small children, her eyes bright and conscious. She hunched over the baby in her arms, her newest, a girl with double streaks of smoke beneath her nostrils.

"Where's the Prophet?" Constance asked. Her voice cut through the churning sound of the flames.

People looked around, aware that nobody had thought of him before that moment, too caught up in pressing their children as close as possible to their bodies. They lifted their heads, taking in the trappings of their Kevinianness burning around them. They couldn't have known that the body of Kevin burned then, too. Their entire religion up in smoke within the span of moments.

"WHERE IS HE?" Constance screamed.

She ran around the crowd, staring into soot-streaked faces, frenzy in her eyes. Surely she was thinking of the sacrifice she'd made for him. If he was dead, it all meant nothing.

Her pink, sockless feet slapped over the frozen ground, running toward the Prophet's house.

"Constance, stop!" my father screamed.

She pushed through the door of his smoldering house.

Everyone loved Constance. This was true up to the moment of her death. When she stepped over the crumbling threshold of the Prophet's house, the fire fell in love with her. So much so that it devoured the delicate blond threads of her hair in screeching, smoking kisses, instantly filled her cheeks with pink and red. It loved her so much that, in an instant, the entire house collapsed around her in a hug.

I think I screamed, though no one heard me because in that moment the entire world screamed, the physical screaming of faithful people, the screaming of fire as it demolished the hard labor of a decade, the screaming of trees as their sap boiled inside them, the screaming of tiny mammals woken from the peace of hibernation to find their bodies aflame.

Hours later, after I'd climbed down the mountain, the sky blushed with sunlight. Snowflakes started falling like white moths, and the stars winked out one by one, without a sound.

Chapter 57

"We found Constance's remains at the crime scene," Dr. Wilson says.

I nod.

"Can I say something?" he asks, pushing his glasses up his nose.

"You don't need my permission."

"I just want you to know, you're allowed to feel badly about this."

I pick up my head. "What?"

"You've been through something terrible. And maybe I haven't done my duty in assuring you that you have no reason to feel guilty. None of it was your fault. Losing your hands, your childhood, Constance dying—"

"Of course Constance dy—" I swallow a throatful of bile. "Of course her being gone is my fault."

"I can see why you might feel that way. But it's not logical. It's grief making you see things unclearly. Do you realize that, as long as I've known you, these many months, you've never actually acknowledged that she is dead?"

"Why is that important?"

"So you can accept it. So you can move on."

"Move on?" I ask, the blood rising in my face, my veins stretching with it. "You don't know what the hell you're talking about. You're so out of touch, you know that? As if you can relate to a single thing I say. You with your expensive clothes. With your tie clip."

"My tie clip?" he asks laughingly.

"Nobody who wears a tie clip could possibly understand."

"And why not?" He smiles like the whole thing is a joke, and that makes me angrier.

"You don't get it. If you did, you wouldn't tell me to *move on*. Hey, why don't *you* move on? Get yourself back to DC and live your nice life in your fancy house with shiny things that make you feel good inside. And go out with your wife and eat expensive food, and give your son a car because that's what good fathers do. And give up on me and give up on the Prophet because he's deader than dirt, and so will we all be someday."

"You're very intuitive, Minnow. You got so very much right in that last statement. All but one thing. I don't have a son anymore."

I shake my head. "Yes, you do," I say. "He likes Thomas Hardy. His name's Jonah."

"I did have a son named Jonah," he agrees. "And now I don't have a son named Jonah. And that is that."

The air vibrates numbly, the way it did in the forest the moment before a lightning strike.

"I said that to myself a lot at first, after it happened. Like an affirmation. I had a son named Jonah. And now I don't have a son named Jonah. And that is that."

"What happened?"

"I bought my son a car for his sixteenth birthday. You even got that part right. How did you guess? Carol—that's my wife—didn't want him to have it. He'd barely passed his driving test and anyone could've seen he wasn't ready. But I bought it for him anyway, because it was his birthday and because I could. And because my father didn't for me. And that night he wrapped the car around the trunk of a tree."

The room grows perfectly quiet. I look away.

"So how do you deal with it?" I ask.

He shrugs. "God, I can't answer that. You don't. Or, time heals. Or, you get used to it. I don't know."

"Time doesn't heal," I say.

"You're damn right it doesn't." He rubs his forehead. "You know, I studied in Paris when I was about your age."

I glance at him. "Yeah?"

He reaches into his back pocket and pulls out his wallet. "I've been carrying this picture in my wallet since my son died. It's my identification photo my school in Paris took on the first day."

He holds out the photo between two fingers. The doctor in the photo is much younger than the one in front of me, with a head of bushy, overgrown hair and a collared, striped shirt. He's standing on a sidewalk with a curve-sided yellow stone building behind him. I flip the photo over. On the back, written in the doctor's careful cursive, are the words, "Darwin Neil Wilson."

"Your name's Darwin?"

He shrugs. "I go by my middle name now."

I pass the photo back to him. "So what's Paris got to do with anything?"

"What do you know about Parisians?"

I pause. "They smoke a lot."

"Yeah, they do. Back then, they allowed smoking in bars. When you walked in, you'd see everything through a blanket of blue smoke. I'd be at a bar stool, alone, and I'd look around and hear all these foreign voices layered over one another and see these people moving around in foreign clothes with foreign faces. And then I'd realize that, actually, I was the foreign one. I was the one who didn't belong. There's something about grief that makes you feel like that, like a foreigner. When I lost my son, I became a citizen of a country I never knew existed. And all of the people I ran into on a daily basis were speaking a different language, only they didn't know it. Because I was the one who'd changed. I'd sit around the office and soak in the sounds and realize that I would never be like them again. And you know the strangest part?"

"What?"

"That idea made me happy. I started carrying this picture around, just to remember the feeling. It felt good to be different. It made me feel closer to my son. Closer to my guilt. The trouble is, though, when you lift your head back up and look around, everything's different. Things have been moved, people have walked out."

He flicks the photograph back and forth between his fingers.

"The grief world isn't closer to where the dead live," the doctor says. "You only trick yourself into believing that. If you stand up and move around and look at the living world, and start participating again, you're closer to them anyway."

He lets the picture fall into the water-filled bowl of the stainless steel toilet beside him. The young Darwin looks up from the shadows of the trough of water. Wilson curls his fingers around the handle and flushes.

I watch the photo spin around and around until it disappears down the drain. I rest my chin on my breastbone. "Constance is dead."

"And that is that."

Chapter 58

"What will happen to Waylon?" I ask.

Dr. Wilson shrugs. "We've been looking for him for months. He's been a suspect since the beginning."

I straighten up. "Why didn't you tell me?"

"I was waiting for you."

"Will you promise me something?" I ask. "If the police ever find Jude, promise you'll help him."

"Help him return to the wild?"

"It's the life he wants," I say. "He ought to have the choice. Everybody should."

"So will you be joining him?" he asks. "If you get parole."

"I'm still deciding."

He moves his jaw back and forth. "I hear you got into the Bridge Program."

"How'd you know about that?"

He smiles. "You're not the only one who talks to Angel."

I nod, chewing my lip. "Will Waylon go to jail?"

"Who knows if we'll ever even catch him," he says. "He hid for twenty years without detection."

And it seems as though he's saying it'd be okay if Waylon never was found. It'd be okay if the case got cold and went to bed.

He looks up suddenly and casts his eyes around the ceiling. "Do you hear that?" he asks.

"What?"

"Thunder. I think it's raining."

I can hear it now, plinking on the metal roof.

"Storms are so quiet here," I say. "Thunder was deafening in the Community. Loud as cannon blasts. Sometimes, I'd wake in the night and think the war must've started."

"What war?"

"Between us and the unbelievers. That's what the Prophet said. A war was coming. The Gentiles were out there with their nuclear weapons and automatic rifles, but we had the greatest weapon of all, God. The war never came, though. Good thing, too."

"Why?"

"God doesn't stand up well in the face of a gunshot. Or a hatchet. God can't protect you against very much at all."

"Is that how God works?"

"That's what the Prophet told us."

"But what do you think?" he asks. And he looks at me with an expression that tells me the question means something. And so does the answer.

"I don't know," I say finally. "I don't know, but I'm gonna find out."

Chapter 59

Ask anybody and they'll tell you I got sent here because of a boy. Because I kicked his face in, and sat down on the hard snow beside the result, and didn't cry.

That it was a boy who planted the seeds of rebellion in my mind, who helped turn my own thoughts into weapons. The boy I loved and didn't understand simultaneously.

Or maybe it was the Prophet who got me here with his rules and edicts, his mystic justice that threaded through every pore until I was a walking prayer shawl, and the prayers were all his.

Or my father who sold me away on that first day beside the fist-tight apple tree when I was five, when he told me to listen to the Prophet and do whatever he said.

It wasn't any of them, you know.

"It was in the stars," is an expression Miss Bailey taught me the other day, and by that she means that it was fated this way.

What if it was in the stars for me to be here? That I was hurtling toward this inevitability for my entire life, because now that I'm about to leave it, everything about this place seems entirely meant to be.

. . .

Benny visits as Dr. Wilson is leaving, an oversize brown paper sack under her arm. She rolls down the top of the sack and pulls out the outfit I wore to court, six months ago, the skirt and blouse and belt.

She lifts out the last item carefully, like she's holding an ancient relic. Jude's shirt. I wore it every day for a month after he died. It's stained with coin-sized blotches of blood and decomposed down to threads, but the shoulder seams are there. I could wear it. It would still fit.

"Keep?" she asks.

Slowly, I pick the shirt up between my stumps. I hold it out to her. "Not anymore."

. . .

There is a place in Missoula where goldfinches swoop yellow and plentiful as sunflowers. It is beyond this cell. Soon, I will find it. The day will be spring, I'll make sure of that, when the trees are perfect with new green that stuns the eyes, and robins stuffed in branches, and mice flying down little mice trails that only they can see. I'll be out meandering through streets and, without meaning to, happen across a park in the center of the city. I'll sit among the people and the noises of basketballs smacking concrete and children screaming in a way that means joy.

And I'll walk through a stand of white trees that'll be rediscovering themselves, feeling they are maybe more than white, maybe they are something like green. And they'll push green from their fingers as if to prove it to themselves. The air will smell equally of gasoline dust and greenness like it does in the city.

There will be a feeling that anything is possible this springtime. There will be a feeling that I am more than a girl in a wool dress not of her choosing. There will be an atmosphere of decision making that day. The power to understand myself, finally. To believe or not believe, to know which it is.

I will crane my neck to the sky, the kind of odd evening sky that allows for sunlight and stars at the same time. I'll find a star and hang on to it with my eyes. The periphery of greenery will swish away as my vision rises and rises and rises to greet that star. I will feel my body left behind.

When I tear my eyes away and shake my head, my brain

will become bleary with the suddenness of my soul sailing through the atmosphere, back into the spacious cavern of my skull. For a moment, my head will feel heavy with it. How much heavier than I'd ever imagined. How much sturdier.

Acknowledgments

I never realized just how many people shape a book. This book would not exist without the dedicated efforts of many professionals, friends, and family members. I'm especially grateful to the amazing team at Dial who worked so passionately to get this book made. My editors, Stacey Friedberg and Nancy Conescu, deserve the highest acclaim for their tireless work on this book. From our first phone call, it was clear you believed in Minnow and understood her like you'd known her forever.

I'm also eternally grateful to my enthusiastic and hilarious agent, Jennifer Laughran, who saw the potential in this book and believed in it before almost anybody. You're the reason Minnow is meeting the world.

I owe a huge debt of gratitude to everyone at the MFA program at Eastern Washington University, particularly my poetry cohort and my poetry professors, Christopher Howell, Jonathan Johnson, and Melissa Kwasny.

Thanks to the educators and students at Mercer Middle School in Seattle and Libby Center in Spokane for being so over-the-moon about this book, especially the wonderful Kristin, Larry, Priscilla, Susannah, Maggie, and Alex for the Minnow party, complete with goldfish crackers. Thanks to the Chetty family for your support and the awesome cake, to Fran Bahr for the good chats and great feedback, and to the incredible Christa Desir who read multiple versions and has been my staunch ally through this entire process.

Finally, thanks to my entire family for your whole-hearted support for my dreams. Especially thanks to my mom, Annie Oakes, who has been the most enthusiastic cheerleader that anyone could ask for. You have inspired me and shown me it's never a waste of time to dream big and stare at the computer screen for hours on end.